(OF COURSE IT'S A FANTASY . . . ISN'T IT?)

Alexander the Great teams up with Julius Caesar and Achilles to re-fight the Trojan War—with Machiavelli as their intelligence officer and Cleopatra in charge of R&R . . . Yuri Andropov learns to Love the Bomb with the aid of The Blond Bombshell (she is the Devil's *very* private secretary) . . . Che Guevara Ups the Revolution with the help of Isaac Newton, Hemingway, and Confucius . . . And no less a bard than Homer records their adventures for posterity: of *course* it's a fantasy. It has to be, if you don't believe in Hell.

But award-winning authors Gregory Benford, C. J. Cherryh, Janet Morris, and David Drake, co-creators of this multi-volume epic, insist that *Heroes in Hell* is something more: that if you accept the single postulate that Hell exists, your imagination will soar, taking you to a realm more magical and strangely satisfying than you would have believed possible . . .

WELCOME TO HELL

D1042886

science fiction

HEROES IN HELL

A Baen Books Original

In Canada distributed by PaperJacks Ltd.,
330 Steelcase Road, Markham, Ontario

First printing, March 1986

ISBN: 0-671-65555-8

Cover art by David Mattingly

Printed in Canada

Distributed by
SIMON & SCHUSTER
TRADE PUBLISHING GROUP
1230 Avenue of the Americas
New York, N.Y. 10020

CONTENTS

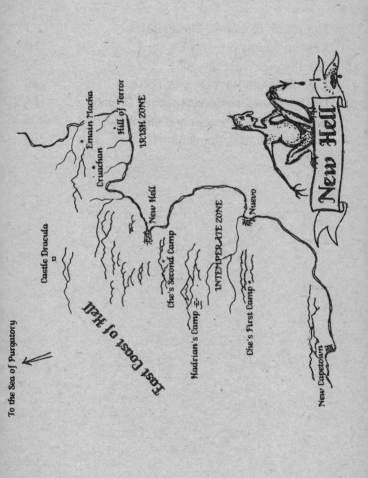

To the Sea of Purgatory

Castle Dracula

East Coast of Hell

Emain Macha
Hill of Terror
Cruachan
IRISH ZONE

New Hell

Che's Second Camp

Hadrian's Camp

INTEMPERATE ZONE

Nuevo

Che's First Camp

New Capetown

New Hell

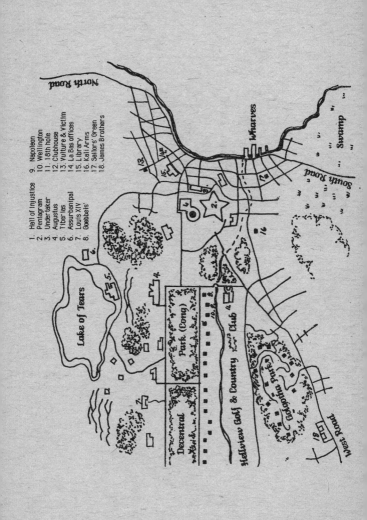

North Road

Lake of Tears

1. Hall of Injustice
2. Pentagram
3. Undertaker
4. Augustus
5. Tiberius
6. Assurbanipal
7. Louis XIV
8. Goebbels'

9. Napoleon
10. Wellington
11. 18th hole
12. Clubhouse
13. Vulture & Victim
14. La Bas offices
15. Library
16. Kali Arms
17. Sailors' Green
18. James Brothers

Wharves

Swamp

South Road

Decentral Park (Cong.)

Hellview Golf & Country Club

Gehenna Park

West Road

SON OF THE MORNING

Chris Morris

An apology for the Devil: It must be remembered that we have heard only one side of the case. God has written all the books.
—Samuel Butler

The Devil's long black claw tapped the computer keypad in his office on the top floor of the Hall of Injustice.

The screen before him shivered, blinked, and then the flame-colored letters of his database appeared: *guevara, e. (che)*, 666.6666.66666.666666.

But when he typed in the first string of sixes, the whole system went down—his screen flared international-distress-orange, black letters appeared transiently (SYSTEM ERROR), then his terminal went blank.

Infuriated, muttering curses which turned the dull red sky outside into an infernally bubbling storm, Lucifer slammed a fist into the display monitor before him just as something sank its sharp pointed teeth into his right calf.

The pain lancing up his leg from oft-chewed muscles turned his curses into an inarticulate howl of rage.

Outside, the storm subsided, lightning ceased, and thunder diminished to a steady thrum like the sound issuing from the throat of the furry, winged creature that had its teeth sunk firmly into his leg.

"Quit it, you fat little bastard," the Devil who was Lord of Hell cajoled between gritted teeth which could have bitten his pet's neck in half in an instant.

Instead, he reached down and stroked its fur. A batlike, fanged head came up as jaws that were a miniature of his own relaxed.

Two pairs of wings rustled—his great black pinions; its smaller, clawed replicas.

"Here. Come, up." The Devil patted his lap and the creature sprang into it.

The pet—and perennial dispenser of little agonies—he had dubbed Michael, in honor of a certain archangel who had been in contention with him over a mortal named Moses, long ago as sinners measured time.

He put up with Michael's bad habit of munching on his legs as he put up with everything else— Hell's sprawling, chaotic inefficiency (putting Howard Hughes in charge of Public Works had made matters worse, not better), the Undertaker's fetid breath and foul jokes, the Welcome Woman's spates of geriatric rut, and the general tendency of things to muck up wherever human souls were involved. Which they were, everywhere.

But Satan wasn't about to put up with a revolution. This Guevara, some Cuban cowboy in jeans with a scruffy beard and an inordinate appetite for suffering, wasn't playing by Hell's rules—he was, after a fashion, *succeeding* in uniting the dissidents and exporting revolution throughout the Underworld.

And, although humans tailor-made Hell by their expectations and their ridiculously stubborn hopes and dreams, creating their own tortures, in the case of Guevara something had gone disastrously wrong. The guerrilla was *enjoying* himself. His life on earth had been so torturous that he hardly knew the difference here. He believed in hopeless battles and drew inspiration from every setback.

And now, informants whispered, he was about to take the initiative.

Something would have to be done.

The Devil sighed and scratched his familiar's ruff of matted black fur and the creature drooled contentedly—an acid spittle that ate its way through cloth and skin in instants, so that the Devil's thigh began to suppurate.

He pushed at his pet but it sank its claws into his knee and drooled more—the usual attention-getting ploy.

Absently, Lucifer picked it up; its claws came away with a sound like tearing Velcro.

He slapped it against his shoulder and it hung there as he strode to the window (glassless and bereft of geometry, a leering, gaping maw of Hughes's design that might never be finished and surely would not open and close if it were—the angles were all wrong) and let the hellish wind blow around him, sulfurous and dank.

Below, New Hell stretched, twisted and convoluted, putrefied by the human dross that thronged it.

Why wasn't he taking action in the matter of Guevara? Why did he find it so fascinating? What was the attraction he found in this added disorder? Like an itch that couldn't be scratched, the matter was always with him lately, the solution just out of reach.

People weren't supposed to *enjoy* their sojourns. *He* wasn't supposed to enjoy the flouting of his Will, Guevara's mockery of his Supreme Commander and all the Fallen Angels who tromped in black boots or thundered on horseback or sped on motorcycles or flew in choppers or transatmospheric weapons-platforms to terrorize the populace.

That, if truth be known, was the rub: *he*, Satan, Old Nick, Mephistopheles, etc., etc., was supposed to do the terrorizing. It had never happened, in all the centuries of his stewardship, that a mortal had successfully challenged his Infernal Mandate of Misery.

But it was happening now. And it was, if nothing else, interesting.

Nevertheless, he had a job to do, one he had never wanted—his own torture, punishment for a mistake made among the supernal host long ago. He had thought he could do it better ... he had dared question the omnipotence of the Supreme Being and his fey Host. And his hubris had gotten him here, Prince of Darkness in a counterrealm of eternal reeducation.

So perhaps it made good sense that a soul like the guerrilla-philosopher's interested him. This Guevara, who had refused to adjust to Hell's rules and twisted all the negatives of existence into positives, was making Satan unhappy . . . discontented, though the Devil had not cared whether he himself was happy or sad for eons.

Had the Supreme Being, whom he thought of as Biggie, decreed this additional punishment for Lucifer? Was Guevara an agent of Heavenly purpose? Could a mere human soul bring hopes to fruition and give reason to suffering? If it came about that this was the case, what would happen to the Devil then? Would he be disenfranchised? Would Hell—or control of it—be lost? Could so miserable a realm *be* lost? And would it matter if it were?

In a silence broken only by the slurping sounds Michael made gnawing on Satan's shoulder, he admitted that it would. That, miserable as his Kingdom was, he liked it. Liked it just the way it was.

And, admitting that, he decided to decree an end to joy among the bushes, to sacrifice for purpose, to blood shed in a Cause. There were to be no Causes in Hell beyond the First Cause that brought sinners here and the Last Cause which he himself embodied.

Therefore, he changed from his great and winged dark form (upon which no man could look and keep his bowls closed) into a human form, executive in aspect, square-jawed, clear-eyed, silver-haired, and pinstripe-suited.

Michael stiffened in his arms, then relaxed, folding its wings down to let them melt into its fur, aping a feline aspect to suit its master's less daunting image.

But cat claws were still sharp, cat scratches septic, and cat bites bound to fester.

He cast the "cat" from his arms and turned, spreading them wide, disdaining the intercom which connected him to his dumb-but-willing secretary, Marilyn, in the outer office.

"Marilyn!" he bellowed. "Get me Niccolo Machiavelli and Hadrian, the Supreme Commander."

Those two ought to be fulcrum enough to lever the revolutionary loose from his fanatical sense of self.

But he entertained discomfiting doubt as the secretary came teetering in on red shoes whose heels were six inches high and as sharp as razors.

Her breasts preceded her and Satan squeezed his eyes shut. The penitents here often could not consummate the sexual act. But he could.

"Sir?" she breathed, her painted mouth a fetching red O. "Could you spell those names . . . slowly?"

He spelled them very slowly, watching her breathe in her snug sweater and white skirt that was so tight. . . .

Hell being what it was, she was the only secretary he'd been able to get; Marilyn Monroe being what she was, they didn't get much work done.

Michael, sensing an interruption of work in the making, headed for Marilyn's silk-stockinged calves, ears flattened and cat fangs bared, its tail bushed to twice its normal size.

"Oooh, oooh, no," Marilyn mewled, and began retreating toward the door.

"And . . . Andropov," he added, in disgust, as he swooped in to interdict Michael's assault. The cat was flailing wildly as he hefted all thirty pounds of it into midair by the scruff of its neck. "A-N-D-R-O-P-O-V. He's new, so look under RECENT LISTINGS. Then come back. Wear lace."

The frown on Marilyn's face turned into a pout as she backed through the door and shut it.

But she'd do as she was ordered. And that took half the fun out of it. But only half.

He'd have traded Marilyn for Susan B. Anthony to know what it was about the Guevara case that made him so uneasy.

Yuri Andropov had known it was all a mistake—he was no *zek*, no prisoner. He was also no believer in afterlives.

So it had been some kind of psyop: some clever trick by Romanov or Gorbachev—his protégé, no less—to take advantage of his failing kidneys, to hasten the day when a younger man would succeed Andropov as Chairman, Secretary, and President of the Soviet Union.

When he had waked in the gulag, with a guard-medic bending over him older than anyone alive in the Politburo, he had not been so sure. He had thought of God—of what it would have meant if there really was a god. Silly, like thinking about what it would have meant if Marx weren't a Jew or Stalin was really alive somewhere.

There had been an elevator ride, then an elaborate play meant to disorient him—supported by drugs, no doubt, since no women, not even Soviet women from the Organs, had tongues which licked from their twats. There had been an apparatchik disguised as Hitler, that was who he had seen, papering walls in the subbasement of a building as big as the new KGB headquarters outside Moscow (perhaps it was that very basement). How they had managed the rubbery-skinned, fanged, and winged demon about the size of a Borzoi, he couldn't fathom. Hypnotic suggestion; psychotropic drugs.

Now he would get to the bottom of this, he thought, glancing askance at the oddly uniformed guards holding him by either elbow. Big, Slavic boys with three-pronged tridents on their uniform collars.

As soon as they took his gag off, he would complain loudly. He would tell whomever he was seeing how foully he had been treated, and especially about being put in the same cell with foreigners.

He stumbled, and almost dropped the box he was carrying in his trembling hands. Everywhere, he must carry the box. It was attached to his navel like some sort of portable dialysis machine, which at first he'd thought it was. But his kidneys, through some miracle of State science, were functioning—at least there was no bag attached to the box which must be emptied, no other machine to which he was attached and through which his blood was siphoned for cleaning.

There was only this box, two feet by two feet, and a tube going into his navel, a tube just long enough to let him stand erect with the box on the ground. He never remembered micturating, though he must, or defecating. In fact he had not, to his knowledge, performed "bodily functions"—including eating—since he had come here. Again, part of a campaign to break his spirit, he was sure. He had orchestrated too many such not to know the signs.

The guards jerked him roughly sideways as they turned a corner.

Startled and weak, he instinctively put out a hand to keep his balance—and the box crashed to the floor.

"Allaho Allam!" swore the guard on his left, and more in Arabic.

"Fuckin' A!" said the guard on his right, and dropped to one knee so that Andropov could see his pink scalp under his pale brush-cut. "You want to take it easy with your nuke, old guy? You'll blow us all to—" The frown on the face of the guard (an *American* guard, or at least someone wanted him to think so) turned to a rueful grin. The blond shrugged, ". . . blow us all back to Square One—the elevator, the Undertaker, and all." The guard lifted the box and handed it to Andropov. "Got it okay, fella? Hold on tight. Nobody wants to glow in the dark."

Andropov shouted into his gag: "Nuke? What imperialist trick is this?" in Russian, but the blond had him by the elbow once more and was now talking to the other guard on Andropov's left: "Wonder what these guys with the backpack nukes—and box nukes—are supposed to do with 'em? Protect their personal airspaces?"

The other guard just called once more upon Allah,

who obviously wasn't listening, in what Andropov thought was a Lebanese dialect.

Then they turned down a corridor that had missing panels, open to the night, and far below and away Andropov could see lights of a city, and farther pastoral fires, which could not have been Moscow or any city in the USSR—the elevation of the tower through which Andropov was being marched was simply too great.

The height, now that he was aware of it, was dizzying.

The box—the *nuke*—in his hands began to slip.

The American guard scowled at him, muttered, "Don't drop it again, okay, Ivan?" and reached out to pound with the side of his "prosecutor," a specialized nightstick, on the door that said in deep-carved letters: "THE BOSS."

Definitely America, then. The box he was holding was suddenly a horror. Obviously, it was meant to detonate, eventually, and take Andropov with it. Perhaps by radio; perhaps on a timer; perhaps one of these times when he dropped it. No doubt it would give him warning. Perhaps, if he chose to tell all the inner, most secret workings of the Politburo or the KGB to his American interrogators, the countdown would be aborted.

How had this happened? If ever he had a chance to exact retribution for this from Gorbachev, it would be neither slow nor halting.

And then the door opened and a vision of America incarnate stood there: JFK's infamous slut, Marilyn Monroe. Andropov had seen many American movies—*know thine enemy*—and the woman

in the obscene red sweater and white skirt that
was, he noticed as she turned to usher them in,
rumpled and stained yellow where she sat, could
be none other. The walk gave testimony to her
identity.

Even at his age, it was hypnotic: back and forth,
back and forth, swayed the famous hips. . . .

Then they disappeared behind her desk and she
turned: "Thank you, gentlemen," she said in that
ridiculous, decadent voice. "Just take him in. I'll
be waiting for you both out here."

And "in" he was taken, through a door which ill
fit its frame, where an American waited—not Ken-
nedy (though deaths, Andropov knew, could be
feigned and he had been expecting the American
warmonger to be behind the door his whore tended),
but someone who introduced himself as "Lucifer.
Call me Lucifer."

The big, white-haired man held out his hand
and Andropov, nuke clutched in slippery palms,
muttered into his gag an epithet which the big
man, somehow, seemed to understand.

Then—while the two men hesitated, the captor's
hand outstretched in a gesture of friendship Andropov couldn't, with his nuke clutched to his paunch,
return—a huge cat jumped, from nowhere, square
onto the box.

The thirty-pound cat landed with a thud. The
box fell from Andropov's slick grip and crashed
down on his *zek*'s shoes.

The whole world spun and annihilation threatened.

Pink and red dots peppered his vision and the
floor rushed up to meet his face.

The next thing the former Secretary knew, he was sitting in a chair with Marilyn Monroe's breasts nearly suffocating him as she wiped his forehead with a damp cloth, his unexploded nuke tucked under his feet like a footstool.

His gag had been removed. He sat up straight, brushing his nose against Marilyn's cleavage as he pushed her firmly away. "I demand the rights of a prisoner of war as set forth by the Geneva Convention. I demand—" He was speaking loudly, clearly, in English.

Marilyn Monroe, on impossibly high heels, had teetered backward. Now she fell, giving him a splay-legged glimpse of her wanton charms.

"Nothing! You demand not one thing—there's no Geneva Convention in Hell," the big man interrupted, sitting on the corner of his desk.

In one hand he held a small, boxlike device and Andropov had a sinking feeling that he knew what it was.

But no one would push the button with his own person in jeopardy.

Andropov sat back. Marilyn scrambled to her feet, fingered a run in her stockings, pouted, and then, with a "Hrmph, nasty old goat," went to answer a knock at the door.

In came a dark, quick man with sharp features and darting eyes full of intellect.

The silver-haired American said, "Marilyn, leave us," and the floozie swished away.

The newcomer—a Mediterranean type: an Italian, a Florentine, or a Jew from his features—muttered, "My pleasure, sir," and executed a cultured, if minimal, bow. "How may I serve?"

There was ice in the veins of the newcomer—no man who had survived in KGB as long as had Andropov could miss the signs. This was an operator, perhaps his interrogator-to-be.

Andropov tapped his heels on the nuke between his legs, wondering if a good thump would set it off—one wanted to control one's own destiny at times like these. Then he wondered what would happen if he ripped the connecting cord from his belly.

He fingered it, got a good grip, and then listened once more to the English being spoken around him: "Niccolo, this is Yuri Andropov, a newcomer to our ... shores. One who has a certain amount in common with you, and in whose company I charge you to work, henceforth, on the matter of Che Guevara's insurgency."

The name Guevara was familiar. But Guevara was dead. Americans mixing in the affairs of young nations struggling for freedom was nothing new. . . . But Guevara was *dead!* Andropov's stomach began to sour.

Still, he said nothing—he didn't want to give aid and comfort to the enemy, and the Americans were his heart's enemy, had been for a lifetime.

When the man named Niccolo spoke again, Andropov detected a slight accent—Italian. A Fascist, then. Andropov pulled at his lip with the hand which wasn't clenched on the umbilical cord binding him to the nuke in the box under his feet.

"What of Hadrian, sir?" the Fascist purred. "One doesn't want to overstep, not when Hadrian's the Supreme Commander of the Fallen Angels, whose task it is to keep order in the ... domain."

"Don't play coy with me, Machiavelli," said the American.

Then Andropov's head snapped around and he stared at the man he had thought a Fascist. Almost, his resolve cracked. Hadrian, a dead Roman emperor, a builder who had constructed a Temple of Jupiter on the site of the Jews' Great Temple in Jerusalem—it could have been some other Hadrian the white-haired executive had meant.

But it could not be some "other" Niccolo Machiavelli. Andropov, now, remembered the face from studies, the form from descriptions, the kinship he had felt when the dark man came in.

He met those eyes and saw in them the beginnings of his discipline, the fount from which the wisdom he heeded had sprung. *"The Prince?"* he muttered.

"Him, not me," Machiavelli demurred with a flick of his chin in the direction of the American.

And then Andropov's spy's mind began working, putting together all the pieces, all the clues, all the bits of data. *Lucifer.*

But it was too much for him to bear.

The Devil was an American.

Sick in his heart at the final revelation that the Prince of Darkness, the second-greatest power in a universal order he had dared to disbelieve, was an American—with all the consequences for his Motherland this revelation implied—Andropov yanked the umbilical out of his navel and the nuke went off under his feet.

*   *   *

"Marilyn!" the Devil bellowed. "Get your ass *in* here!"

Here, in the wake of the nuclear blast, was a shambles, despite the fact that he'd been ready for it. Several more of his office's panels had crumbled, windows had blown out, his desk was up-ended, and Michael was hanging from a ceiling-mounted light fixture, the creature's cat-guise forgotten, growling and gnashing its teeth while its tail lashed and, directly below, Niccolo Machiavelli held both arms above his head to protect him from the acid spittle Michael was drooling.

Machiavelli had been shielded to some extent by the localizing effect of the force-field generator Satan had been holding pointed at Andropov. But not completely: Niccolo's hair was singed, his face blistered and bleeding, and his eyes blinked much faster than they should.

At the sound of Lucifer's voice, Machiavelli's head turned. "Sir? It will be more difficult to serve you blind."

"Good point," the Devil allowed grudgingly, and moved among the softly glowing rubble to touch Machiavelli once on each eye with a long black claw.

Then Michael dropped from the light fixture onto its master's left pinion, delaying Satan's transfer back into pin-striped form, so that Machiavelli went paler than radiation could account for, glimpsing the Devil unadorned. "But don't push it, Machiavelli—your luck, I mean. We were talking about Guevara and his dissidents. . . ."

Familiar on his shoulder, the Devil sat down amid the pleasantly warm wreckage and rested his chin on his fist, fondly watching the soul with whom he shared a common name.

"If I may ask, sir," said Machiavelli in a weak voice (his blisters were beginning to bleed), "what was that?"

"That?" The Devil motioned behind, to where the remains of Yuri Andropov smoked and stirred. "The Premier of the Union of Soviet Socialist Republics, a totalitarian state—"

"The explosion," Machiavelli's eyes roved round the room.

"A nuke. A personal nuke, actually—very small, very containable. For those who purveyed them in life, only, so don't get any ideas about using them on your enemies. You'll recover on your own, without a trip to the Undertaker, never fear. I need you to gather intelligence, on your own recognizance, until Andropov is"—Michael began gnawing on his shoulder—"reconstituted."

"On my own? Better than nothing, I suppose," Niccolo Machiavelli said with the lassitude of a man in excruciating pain.

The Devil bared his teeth, ignoring the grating of fang on bone that sent jolts of agony up his neck from his shoulder as Michael began to purr. "Anything is, Niccolo, anything is."

Then Marilyn opened the door, wrinkled her nose at the destruction, and hesitated pointedly on the threshold, so that the Devil had to heal up Machiavelli completely and telekinetically transfer Andropov's remains to the Undertaker's mausoleum and generally clean up the mess before she'd consent to take one step into his office.

But it was worth it: she'd remembered to wear lace.

NEWTON SLEEP

Gregory Benford

*May God us keep
From single vision
And Newton Sleep.*

—William Blake

1

The demon was a nerd.

It chewed raptly on a huge wad of yellow gum, obviously relishing the gooey smack of it, jaw muscles bunching. The white open-collar shirt, bulging belly that hung over a plastic belt, too-tight brown slacks, six pens in the shirt pocket (several marked STYX BANK in glowing red), mousy brown hair sloppily combed and parted exactly down the center of its skull, bottle-thick lenses in transparent frame glasses—all said *overaged blimpoid undergraduate* to Gregory Markham.

The thing looked like a subnormal student in Physics 3A, a certain candidate for the cut at the end of the first quarter. Grinning, it blew a bubble. The filmy orange sphere popped but the demon caught it with a sudden lashing of its black tongue, popped the wad back between its molars and smacked it with delight.

"I . . . I don't follow," Markham began.

"You'll catch on." The demon's eyes widened with friendly interest and it said enthusiastically, "How you like these new elevators?"

"Ah . . . well, they're . . ." *Absolutely ordinary*, Markham thought. Gray steel, no carpeting, only one button on the console: THERE.

"Just got them installed. Howard Hughes did the work. Terrific!" the demon snapped its gum again as punctuation.

"And we're going . . ."

"To Hell, yeah." The demon glanced at its watch. "Right on time, too."

"What happens when I get there?"

"That's not my job. Boy, I'll tell you, these elevators are *great*. Before the Hughes contract came in—late, sure, but under the bid—we had to lead you guys up the Socophilian Stairs."

"Up?"

"Yeah, that stuff about Hell being below is just rumor, y'know. Anyway, those stairs—what a pain! Cold granite all the way, no handrails, corners worn off so you'd slip and bust your ass."

"The pits."

The pun seemed lost on the nerd. "No foolin'. Goin' back down was the worst. Any blood at all on those worn-down steps and *whang* you'd roll down, ass over entrails. And likely smack into a party of lepers or saints on the way up."

"Saints?"

"Sure, we get a lot of 'em."

"But I thought—"

"That's *their* opinion, of course. Y'know—*my sainted mother*, all that. Man, it's incredible, what people think of themselves. You talk about de*lu*sions."

"Is . . . is that why I'm—"

"Don't ask me, man. I'm just a go-fer."

The elevator stopped with a labored *chunka chunka*. "Ah, great. I sure don't miss them stairs."

The sliding door was dinged and smeared with something brown. *New to the demon, maybe,* Markham thought, *but I know recycled junk when I see it.* He wondered what turned brown when it dried.

The door slid open with a hiss. An absolutely featureless floor of azure stone stretched limitlessly in all directions. *Lovely.*

"C'mon, move it. I gotta go back down."

Markham stepped out. *I wonder*—

The floor was not in fact stone. It wasn't anything except the illusion of substance which comes when you look at the utterly empty sky. Markham stepped and fell straight down, suddenly feeling warm air rush past.

Falling. This was the way it had been the last instant, when the plane went into the patchwork of wintry trees, the wings snapping off barren black branches as they came in too low, too fast—

He screamed. The vicious shrieking wind blew his tie into his mouth and he spat it out, all the time tumbling, arms flailing. He had never gone sky-diving, had a repressed fear of heights, but had once gone to one of those vertical wind tunnels that supposedly simulated the experience. It had been at a meeting of the American Physical

Society in Las Vegas, and he had been cajoled into it by colleagues.

So— Spread your legs ... arms out ... turn— there. He stopped rolling and hung steady, face down.

Ocean. He was above a vast glinting steel-blue sea. A green land mass lay some distance away but he was going to hit the water. Not that it made a difference. He remembered that after falling only a few hundred feet, striking water was the same as pancaking into concrete.

How can this be Hell? Falling forever?

Through his panic he tried to think. He had felt little when the plane went in, just an instant when the bulkhead crumpled and trees and steel and the head of the man in front of him came spraying back, a single flash-instant of concussion—

The air howled and he could see whitecaps lacing the sea. He had reached terminal velocity now and the hard blue surface burgeoned with detail, the sweep of hidden currents crinkling the water.

Coming up fast now—

Markham had time to scream once more.

2

It looked like a bank president. Three-piece suit, touch of gray at the temples, the sagging jowls suntanned and well shaved. The demon clearly thought it was doing a job beneath its station.

"But how come I was just shoved out like that? That guy said—"

"I can't keep track of every customer," the demon said. "You're probably remembering something from the Other Side."

"The hell I am!"

"These fantasies will pass," the demon said stiffly. He impatiently tapped one polished black shoetip on the elevator floor, shot his cuffs, and clandestinely tried to catch his reflection in the cloudy steel walls.

"But damn it—"

Chunka chunka. Again the door hissed aside. Beyond it lay another blue featureless expanse. The blue was darker, with a deep blue-green mottling that recalled ocean depths.

"I'm not stepping out there."

"Come, come." The demon made a smile which was broad and showed perfectly regular white teeth, but the corners of the smile did not turn up. Markham had seen a similar smile once when a Merrill Lynch broker had tried to sell him a limited partnership in natural gas.

"*You* go out there."

A sigh. "Very well." The bank president demon stepped with assurance onto the shiny surface. It stood with hands behind its back, the smile twisted into a condescending smirk.

Markham took a tentative step. His foot held so he brought the other forward—

And fell.

This time the bottom-dropped-out sensation lasted only a few seconds as the demon dwindled above, grinning with satisfaction. With a bone-cracking jolt Markham hit the water.

He gasped, sputtered, began to dog-paddle. His glasses had fallen off but he could see there was no land nearby. He cursed once, then choked as a wave seemed to leap deliberately into his nostrils and throat.

The water was mild, salty. Markham stripped off all his clothes. He began to swim steadily, trying to keep to a straight line. Only a sullen red glow lit the clouds above; it was impossible to navigate by it. He kept going, changing regularly from breaststroke to sidestroke to backstroke. Summers, when he wasn't in Europe, he swam every day in the ocean near his home in San Juan Capistrano. He could probably last a good hour this way, longer if he just floated.

He was right. His Seiko kept ticking away. He set the timer and at the very end—exhausted, purple beeswarm dots dancing in his eyes, legs and arms numb, chest aching, mouth puckered with the taste of salt—noted that he had lasted two hours, 13 minutes.

As he watched the digital dial it abruptly changed to 666.

Then he drowned.

3

Markham sagged against the gray steel. The demon was a woman.

This time he could not force his throat to work, to voice any protest. *Hell is this elevator*, he thought, fogged with fatigue. *It's that simple. Infinite death, infinitely prolonged.*

He had always been terrified of heights and he had died in an airplane crash. They had played on that. Then they had added the ocean, knowing somehow that while he loved the sea's raw power he had also feared it, felt vaguely uneasy with the green depths. He had overcome that by taking up scuba diving. Still, those deep anxieties had come out in the long struggle to reach shore. He could feel the effects, how close he was to hysteria.

The woman gave him an empty stewardess smile. Then she slowly reached down and lifted the hem of her red dress. Tantalizingly, with the same fixed glossy smile, she lifted it to show exquisitely formed, creamy thighs. She wore black stockings fastened with a red garter belt. Markham licked his lips. *So they know I like that. So what?*

The cotton dress slid easily over her head. She wore nothing else. She simply stood, smiling and silent. Then she winked and languorously blew him a kiss. It was exactly like a hologram Markham had seen years ago, and about as erotic. She was overweight and her skin had an odd sickly cast. *Like a corpse floating underwater*, he thought. *Or the underbelly of some deep ocean fish, the kind with bulging eyes and a contorted, purple mouth.*

She licked her lips and made obvious, grotesque sucking motions. Her breasts trembled like jelly and he saw that she had something tattooed on each. He squinted. The right breast said WELCOME, the left one WOMAN. They had been seared in, like the deep brown burns on a cowhide brand.

He stepped back. She cupped the breasts and held them out to him, her mouth still making the liquid, gluttonous sucking slurps. *This*, he thought wildly, *might already be Hell.*

Chunka chunka. This time there was a sandy

beach stretching away in a broad curve. An ocean nuzzled at the shore in sets of rolling breakers. *Exactly the same blue as that water I . . .*

He backed away from the door. The woman stepped toward him, offering her breasts, reaching down to finger her black pubic bush. Her left breast oozed pearly pap.

Clearly, Hell lay beyond the elevator door. So it was either her or . . .

Nobody was getting him through that door, Markham knew that much. If he could distract the woman, figure out how to close the elevator—

He forced a grin. Her eyes widened with anticipation. He tentatively reached out toward her waist—and a black tongue licked quickly out from her pubic cleft, a slick oily thing like a whip. It encircled his hand, drew it toward her. He pulled back as he caught the moist, sulfurous, rotting scent the tongue gave off. It clamped itself about his wrist, squeezing with convulsive power.

He gasped. "No!"

She caught him in an expert judo grab, one hand at his shirt collar, the other clamped into the small of his back.

Anger filled her jet-black eyes. Her spiked high heel bit into his right foot. She roughly rubbed herself against him in a parody of erotic frenzy.

He started to wrench away from her rank foulness and that gave her the momentum she needed to complete the throw. "Perhaps I can be of assistance," she said in a flat, impersonal stewardess voice, and threw him out the door.

He landed—*crunch!*—on the sand.

He rolled. Spat out grit. Sat up.

The elevator was gone.

"Hey, fella! Got a board?"

A tanned young man stood fifty yards away, holding a white fiberglass surfboard. Blond, blue-eyed, lean, and muscular.

It seemed an absurd question to ask of a man in rumpled brown slacks, a camel jacket, and a button-down blue shirt. "Ah . . . no."

"Too bad. Some good ones breakin' out there today."

Markham eyed the waves curling into foam about a hundred meters offshore. It *was* a good surfing spot. *So much for the old fire and brimstone.*

"What *is* today?"

Genuine puzzlement flitted across the blandly friendly face. "Why . . . today. It's always today."

One could scarcely argue with that. "I . . . Look, what's going on? I—"

"Hey man, they're breakin'. Get outta those things and try some body surfin'."

"You go ahead. I want to . . . sunbathe for a while."

"Okay, just come out when you're ready."

"What's your name?"

"Donny."

"I'm Greg. Greg Markham."

"Brook's my last name. Good surfin' here, Greg."

"It's safe out there?"

"Sure. Sharks don't come in till night."

The man trotted into the surf. Markham was trembling, his mind churning. He sat down. He remembered a place like this on St. Thomas, where he had vacationed. At night the sharks had come in close to the beach, hunting along the edge of the

Gulf Stream. From the balcony of their cabin he could hear the splashing of the fish the sharks hunted and if you went down to the beach you could see the phosphorescent wakes they made in the water. At night the sharks feared nothing and everything else fled. In the day they stayed out away from the clear white sand. Maybe it was because you could see their shadows rippling over the floury sand and get away.

He remembered that and noticed a dull glow at high noon, diffuse and red through the milky, blue-veined clouds. A midwinter sun, if he had still been in California.

Thinking about that calmed him. There was some continuity between his . . . *My life? But I still feel alive.* His life before, and . . . this. Hell.

He had died in an air crash. That much he remembered clearly. Then someone with a harsh, foul breath leering at him, hovering over his stripped and battered body, under raw piercing orange lamps. All he could remember was that awful, green-lipped face.

His body was knotted with tension, his nerves spinning jittery along a tightrope. He had died, essentially, by falling. Then that fear had repeated in the long plummet from at least a mile up, into the sea. And the bank president demon had followed that with a real drowning.

They had his number, all right. Those were two of his greatest fears. He had been a swimmer all his life but had never overcome the feeling that eventually the ocean he loved so much would claim him.

Stop thinking about it. And don't even imagine any other deaths. They can probably read your mind.

Think back further. Regain some of your own identity. That was all you had to protect yourself.

He had always retreated from the world into his delicious realm of mathematical physics. That was his profession and his dearest love. Concentration on an intricate problem could loft you into an insulated, fine-grained perspective. There were many things you could see fully only from a distance. Since childhood he had sought that sensation of slipping free, smoothly remote from the compromised churn of the raw world.

He had used his oblique humor to distance people, yes, keep them safely away from the center where he lived. It even kept away his wife, Jan, sometimes. He saw that now with a sudden pang of guilt. Was that what had sent him here?

He had used the lucid language of mathematics to overcome the battering of experience, to replace everyday life's pain and harshness and wretched dreariness with—no, not with certainty, but with an ignorance you could live with, endure. Deep ignorance, but still a kind that knew its limits.

Markham stretched out on the sand, feeling his muscles surrender to their aches.

Limits. The limits were crucial. Galileo's blocks gliding across marble Italian foyers, their slick slide obeying inertia's steady hand—they were cartoons of the world, really. Aristotle knew in his gut the awful fact that friction ruled, all things groaned to a stop. *That* was the world of man.

The wonderful childlike game of infinite planes and smooth, perfect bodies, reality unwrinkled, cast a web of consoling order, infinite trajectories and infinitesimal instants, harmonic truths. From that cartoon realm it was always necessary to slip back, cloaking exhilarating flights of imagination in a respectable deductive style. But that did not mean, when the papers appeared in the learned journals, disguised by abstracts and references and ornate, distancing Germanic mannerisms—that did not mean you forgot being in that other place, the beautiful world where Mind met Matter, the paradise you never mentioned.

So I died scribbling mathematics on a transatlantic flight, he thought wryly. *Okay. That's who I am. Professor of Physics, 52 years old, caught in Hell, unarmed and unprepared and definitely unwise.*

He sat up, brushed away clinging sand. *Odd thoughts. Not memories of Jan or friends or a world forever lost. Instead, I recalled my work. What does that mean?*

Maybe that defined most deeply just who he was. *Okay, then. That's how it damned well is.* He smiled mirthlessly at the pun.

His fear had ebbed. Nerves still jangled, muscles were stiff from spasm, but the ocean had begun to work its old magic on him.

Right, then. The first thing to do was figure out how this place worked. Reduce it to a problem.

He studied the dull ruddy glow that hung in the exact center of the sky's bowl. The sun? But it hadn't moved.

It's always today, Donny had said.

Maybe that dull glow never moved. If it was the sun, then this place was tide-locked, one face forever baked by that wan reddish radiance.

Slight offshore wind. Tall coconut palms that looked bent inshore by a trade wind.

He would've expected Hell to have a little more pizzazz. Out beyond the breaking waves he saw gliding shadows. They flitted smoothly, never coming close to Donny.

He got up and walked to an overhang of rock at the end of the crescent beach. Donny caught a wave and stood rock solid on his board as he swept in. The man waved and Markham squinted. Somehow Donny's lifted arm looked black, scaly, like a reptile's sinewy leg and claw. Then Donny turned expertly out of the white, hissing foam and paddled out for the next wave.

Markham sat on the prickly volcanic rock and dangled his legs over the drop. Below, waves battered the sheer stone face with explosions of brilliant white froth. *If this is Hell, I think I can stand it.*

He had never believed any of that kid stuff, anyway. Even if you burned forever, any mind would be driven into erasing madness after a while. They simply couldn't keep you on the edge of excruciating pain and torment forever. Elementary features of any neurological system dictated that it would saturate, overload. Protracted agony would blow away consciousness itself. There would be no *you* to suffer, because the system of memories, relations, habits, and patterns that was you would dissolve before such a battering, searing, consuming onslaught.

So it made no sense, all that childish babble the moist-eyed ministers had prattled from their pulpits. He had once listened to it, had even been an acolyte in the Episcopal church, but the usual adolescent skepticism had ripened into a scornful contempt for such delusions.

Though there is *a Hell,* he reminded himself. *It's just not the one anybody envisioned. The Christian idea simply wouldn't have worked. To really make you suffer, they'd have to give you a break. Let the mind recuperate. Relax the spasms, cool the fevered firings of neurons. Then return that dread-drenched mind to its own personal rack, tighten the screws again, begin afresh. . . .*

He preferred to think of matters this way. *Reduce the world to a series of mechanisms—subtle, but understandable bit by bit—and then deal with each mechanism in turn. It was comforting, it worked, and in the end—*

His name is Donny Brook, Donnybrook. A free-for-all fight.

From somewhere in the air around him came a low, evil snicker.

He looked down in time to see the thing come leaping up from the water. It was sleek and silvery and not a shark. It had a yawning mouth with teeth that circled the entire huge maw, spikes of glinting razor sharpness. Out of the crashing breakers it came in a stupendous leap, straight up in the air, arrow perfect and relentless. He saw the blazing little red eyes, not like those of a fish at all, filled with hate and raw rage—saw it all very clearly just before the thing reached the top of its arc and the round mouth closed around his feet.

The sudden huge pain stopped his scream, froze every muscle in a spasm of rekindled fear. The thing shook him with a convulsive jerk, raked him from the rock ledge, pulled him down into a long excruciating fall as it gulped in midair and then gulped again in its feeding frenzy, the lancing fire shooting up through him in agonizingly long yet infinitesimal instants before he hit the cool watery clasp. The great throat worked and he slid in, his face a rictus, the sour dank stench of the gullet the last thing he knew.

4

He sat on the floor of the elevator this time.

He was a mass of bruises and aches and lightning flashes of memory would come to him, take him back to that endless pinned agony.

He forced himself to breathe, to think of something else.

They had known of his fear of the depths, of something slick and fast and all appetite coming after him. But they had played it subtly this time. Coaxed him out with Donny Brook—and when that didn't work, had sprung the trap just as he noticed the pun.

The Welcome Woman squatted over him, trying to arouse some flagging interest. He did not have the strength to push her away. Her breasts brushed his face and he caught the sickly dank toad smell from her.

He had now an analytical understanding of this endless conveyor belt carrying him forward to his deaths. He would be forever terrified and forever taken, seized casually and put to the point. So that was to be it.

Or perhaps not. Each time had been a surprise. Maybe even this conclusion was wrong, was another way to set him up for another surprise.

Or maybe it was all a colossal infinite jest.

Sure. Or maybe this is Heaven and you're just in a bad mood.

He could go on being terrified at the moment of death, brooding about it long beforehand, letting it crowd everything else from his mind.

Or he could cling to something else. But what?

His former life . . . *the* life . . . was now vague, diffuse. It slipped away eellike when he tried to grasp it, remember his wife or their children, his friends, his small triumphs and defeats. Gone, or at least fast fading.

All that remained was his precarious sense of self.

He allowed the Welcome Woman to drag him to the elevator door and tumble him out onto a carpet of dry grass.

Getting up was too much effort. He saw trees, a somber sky . . . and slept.

He woke to find the empty vacant staring sky and the same scrawny trees. Mimosas, pine, eucalyptus.

He got up painfully, inspected the healing wounds in his legs and abdomen. Purple swellings oozed a clear pus. He would have to be careful of them.

Carefully, limping, he began to walk.

A long time later he staggered along a sandy roadway. He had seen several people pass but had stayed back in the pines, watching. His stomach emptied itself if he stopped to rest and think. Nothing but green bile came up, but his system insisted on going into its clenching spasm whenever he began to reflect on what had happened.

A thumping in the distance grew rapidly louder.

Markham leaned against a fragrant eucalyptus tree and gazed blearily down the road. Three Roman chariots came charging through the rutted sand, horses struggling and sweating, their eyes wild and fever-hot as the drivers lashed them.

Markham roused himself from his sick stupor when the first chariot braked abruptly. A tall man wearing olive fatigues held up a commanding hand, stopping all three chariots. "Anyone been through here, my man?"

"Ah . . . somebody on horseback . . . I didn't see . . ."

"What did he look like?"

"I . . . Beard, blue jeans."

Two men, obviously guards, leaped from the other chariots and drew revolvers. Markham wanted to blurt out questions to them, but this didn't seem the best of times. The tall man waved a fleshy arm ahead. "Going this way?"

"Yeah. Hey, what's going on? I just—"

A guard stepped forward and clipped Markham neatly on the chin, sending him reeling. "You will speak politely to the Supreme Commander."

Markham got to his knees. The blow had not hurt him—*How can anything, after what I've been through?*—but instead sent a hot jet of anger through him. "Who are you clowns, actors from—"

The boot caught him in the shoulder and this time it definitely did hurt. Markham struggled up slowly.

"The Commander Hadrian will order you dispatched if you sass 'im," a guard muttered softly. "Stay down if you know what's good for you."

Hadrian? Familar, somehow. A poet? Markham's

head buzzed. *No, a general. Took Britain.* He heard the Commander say in a flat, almost unaccented voice, "He looks new to me. He may know Guevara from his lifetime."

"That right?" the guard asked, jabbing his boot into Markham's ribs. "You recognize Che Guevara if you see him?"

"Uh, yeah. He died several decades ago, but I saw the pictures, sure."

"Was it him, then?" Hadrian spat out impatiently. The horses pounded the sand and whinnied at the sharp, imperious note in his voice.

"I . . . I guess it might've been." Markham couldn't rummage through his memory and be sure, but that seemed to be the answer these bastards wanted. Maybe it would get rid of them.

"Anyone with him?" Hadrian demanded.

"Not that I saw." Markham looked into Hadrian's face. A beak nose, sensuous full lips, a mouth accustomed to asking questions, not answering them. Intelligent green eyes set beneath bushy black brows that arched with nervous energy.

"How long ago?"

"Ten minutes, maybe."

"His horse, was it lathered?"

"Yeah."

Hadrian jerked a thumb at a man beside him, who was burdened with a large backpack. "Get on that field telephone! Call ahead to Nuevo."

The man's mouth puckered with concern. "Well, I'll try, but these bumps, this equipment wasn't meant to take that sort of pounding, y'know, Commander. I—"

"Do it!"

Hadrian muttered to himself, "Miserable cur."

Markham whispered to the nearest guard, "What's the nearest town that way?"

"Nuevo," the guard said. "Guevara's got support there. Me, I think we oughtta burn the whole thing. Torch every shack."

The signals man fruitlessly turned the crank on his backpack. It made a *rrrrrttt* sound but nothing more. Hadrian fumed, slammed his palm against the side of his chariot, and finally barked, "Enough! We'll catch him ourselves. Come!"

The guards barely made their leaps into their chariots. The whole lot clattered off in a furious pounding of hooves and excited shouts. Markham got to his feet. *Hadrian.* He wished he had his Britannica handy. No, not a poet.

Markham trudged into Nuevo without thinking what to expect. In a realm where anything, presumably, could happen, he still was not prepared for the tanned and sandy chaos sprawled beneath the unwavering sky glow, unrelieved by slant of shadow or hope of waxing light. Roofs of hammered tin, steaming sewage in old creeks, shanties of warped wood and flapping canvas, lice on the bare necks of infested chickens, gnarled figures cooking on cracked palm fronds held over snapping open fires, scaly old men with twisted yellow faces, children hunched in ditches gnawing at dead animals, smelly old women caked with dirt.

Nuevo was a harbor, the water black and greasy. Wooden-hulled scows bobbed in oily swells, thumping against the creosoted pilings of pine docks. Scum had left its tracery along a quayside of square granite blocks that looked scarred and worn and ancient.

It could all be a hundred thousand years old, he realized. *Stonemasons from Ur, cavemen able to fashion bark canoes, an Australopithicus who could chip flint and stack stone—they all could've had a hand in this place. Hell,* were *having a hand.* Any of the walnut-skinned dwarves laboriously stacking mud bricks could be older than Gilgamesh, wiser than Homer.

Nobody paid the slightest attention to Markham. He passed along the mud-colored walls of a long, official-looking building. Some guards at the entrance wore the same olive fatigues as Hadrian's men, though with rakish tan campaign hats worn at a tilt. They stood at parade rest, swarthy hands cupping what looked like Springfields or some other World War I vintage rifle.

Markham strolled casually by, guessing that to turn back would invite attention. He passed by some high windows framed with chipped brown wood. He only glanced upward at them, but in that moment a hand clasped the wood from inside and strained, turning white in someone's attempt to pull himself up. A sharp, surprised cry. The hand slipped, vanished. A thud as a body hit the floor inside.

He hurried on.

At the corner was a small dusty lot. Three crosses of chunky oak stood there, apparently permanent, canted at angles. On each someone was crucified, head down.

Wasn't that some ancient way to do it, for particularly bad crimes? Markham's scholarly interest stirred and he slowed to stare. Bloated purple heads, engorged tongues lolling from warped yawns. One was a woman, breasts bared. A pine stake had been driven through her vagina and protruded from her mouth. The men—

He gagged and turned away before he could fully see all the effects. Yet passers-by scarcely glanced toward the grotesque figures, contorted with unspeakable—but for Markham not now unimaginable—agonies.

Awful, but not final, he reminded himself. *The poor bastards are probably reentering this charnel house right now.*

The point of executing anybody that way, obviously, was the pain. The experience of the last few—days? hours?—had ground that into his bones. In Hell you always came back, like a ball batted around on a rubber band by a malicious giant. But the *pain*—he shuddered at the memories that came crowding in. How could anybody overcome the automatic human terror of death, coupled with the unbearable, ravaging ways Hell apparently contrived it?

Is this it? I'm to be killed, then let recover, only to die again? Forever? And why? *What did I do to be sent here?*

He lurched against a stucco wall, weak with fevered confusion. For the first time he could remember he felt stirrings of hunger. *So the appetites still exist here,* he thought groggily. *And the means to satisfy them, too, apparently.* He had seen babies eagerly crunch beetles in tiny teeth, old women licking toasted black beans from rusty plates.

He wobbled into the middle of a muddy street.

There were few signs anywhere. He had already asked the way of dozens of people, but none ever replied. There was little talk in the streets, no overheard conversations. *What was it Sartre said? Hell is other people? Well, that's proved wrong. Or maybe it's worse to be ignored.*

Between slumping two-story apartment houses stood a large white building in the classic Spanish style, red tile roof and big wide windows with shutters. Above the broad entrance swooping black calligraphy announced FLORIDITA. Markham, his suit grimy and wrinkled, went in.

He swayed at the entrance of the ample room. A high vaulted arch gave an airy generosity to the warming mixture of brown wood tables, muted red upholstery, and lush hangings of trailing vines. Nobody at the tables looked up.

At least the bartender has to talk to you, Markham thought sourly.

The bartender's fixed smile was like the rictus of a man who has died of a broken back. "A . . . beer." Markham lowered himself onto a stool, feeling every joint and muscle protest.

The bartender nodded and drew a pale amber glass. The man kept up the frozen smile as he placed the fat glass before Markham and then glanced significantly at the cracked wooden bar surface. Markham was suddenly conscious that he had no money. Somehow, it had not seemed important.

"Pedrico, put this *padrone* on my tab," a gravel voice said next to Markham's elbow. He turned. A deep-chested man in a woodsman's shirt and baggy drawstring pants held out a hand. "You just come through?"

"Yes. Several times."

"Sit over here." The man grinned, a sudden white crescent against a tan almost mahogany-deep. His face was furrowed as though a thunderstorm had cut ruts in a soft mound of dark clay. Gray stubble began at his chin and thickened as it ran along the jawline into thick, bushy hair. He led Markham to a corner table.

"Thanks. You're just about the only person who'll even notice I exist."

The old man sat down with a grunt and then knocked back half of a frosted drink he carried. "They spotted you right away."

"As what?"

"New. Full of questions."

"So?"

"Ever have to explain the completely mysterious?"

"Ah."

"And do it again and again? Gets boring."

"I'm not expecting a Welcome Wagon or anything, just—"

"You got the woman."

"What? Well, yes . . . *that* was the welcome?"

The old man chuckled. "In a way."

"She threw me out the elevator door, but before that she . . . offered herself."

"No self there to offer."

"Her body."

"Won't do you much good. She gives it away and it's worth what you pay for it."

"That bad?"

"She's got rid of the clap, I heard."

"A demon with a disease?"

"They're all disease."

"I hardly touched her."

The man's face crinkled as he chuckled darkly. "You're lucky the Agedness wasn't coming on her. There's fungus, brown stuff like shit with roots. Lives in her armpits. Comes out about once a month, grows down the arms. She returns to her true state then, and looks it."

"True?"

"Her real age. One, two hundred thousand years."

"She . . . ages . . . that much?"

"Guy in here a while back, he was ramming it to her when that came on. He's not going to forget that right away."

"How could he bring himself to . . . ?"

"Don't be so picky. This guy, he'd been fighting in Afghanistan. Thought he was in the Muslim heaven at first. Figured the Welcome Woman was a houri."

"Even so—"

"Man was horny! Not that she's any good for that."

"Why not?"

"You'll never get your rocks off with her. Impossible."

"But *why?*"

The old man grinned. "Them's the rules."

"Says who?"

"The Boss."

"Who is . . ."

"Right. Satan. Stay away from him."

Markham paused, took a long drink. The beer was thin and frothy and without any taste. Somehow it seemed like beer when you held it in your mouth, but as soon as you swallowed it was like lifeless, tepid water. This old man wasn't going to lay out a little lecture, but he did have information. Markham decided to get as many facts as possible and reason from there. "So you can't come with the Welcome Woman?"

"Nope. You want a better time, try Angelique. She's the whore over by the window."

Markham covertly studied the slim woman with smoky skin who was chattering amiably to a tight-faced man across the bar. "She . . ."

"There's a special rate if you take a room, too."

"Ah, well . . ."

"Otherwise it's standing up in the alley out back."

"No, I meant . . ." It was ridiculous to be embarrassed, but he was.

"Oh, you won't come with her, either—but she's good at the early stuff."

"Well, how—"

"You don't." The man's face collapsed into a swarm of wrinkles. "Or at least I don't."

Markham finished his beer silently. "I like the way this stuff tastes," the man said gruffly, holding up his empty glass. "Fresh green lime juice. Pedrico uses that coconut water that is still so much more full-bodied and takes the Gordon's gin just right. Bitters to give it color. A hell of a good drink."

The bartender brought fresh ones. "Greg's my name," Markham toasted.

"I'm Hem. Try this."

After the description Markham had expected something good or at least different. But the cold fluid from Hem's glass, while it felt good when it first came into his mouth with a chilling rush, soon tasted like the same days-old water that had been left somewhere too long. "Ah, yes," he managed to say.

Hem gave him a narrow, silent look, and then drank half the glass himself with gusto, smacking his lips afterward. "Yeah, that's the stuff."

"Have . . . have you tried to figure out what's going on?"

The condescending expression on Hem's face was softened by a warmth in the eyes, as if the old man was looking back on some memory. "That's not the point."

"What is?"

"To bear up under it."

"Under what?"

"Whatever the bastards throw at you."

"How?"

"Gracefully."

"No, I mean, how do they do it?"

"Not the point at all," Hem persisted and drank more, throwing his head back with relish and seeming to go into a momentary swoon as the frothy tan drops overflowed and trickled into his beard, clinging as glimmering amber dabs.

"Look, you have to start by figuring out how things work. That's my training. I was—I *am*—a physicist."

Hem laughed. "We don't get a lot of them here."

"But you get some?"

"They pass through."

"Going where?"

"Mostly they end up in the Guard. Or else working for Hadrian's gang."

Markham rubbed his face where the heelprint of a boot still left its bruise. "Why?"

Hem peered moodily into his drink. "Keep the whole business running."

"How?"

Hem's jaw tightened and his mouth compressed as sudden life flared in him. "Boy like you ought to learn, it's not *how* that matters here. It's *why*."

Irritated, Markham countered, "Okay, have it your way. What's this place mean, then?"

Hem leaned close to Markham's face, a cold hard smile playing on his lips as he shaped the words very carefully, as though he had done this to newcomers countless times before. "*Nada. Nada nada. Nada.*"

"What?"

"One single thing. *Nada.*"

"Nothing?"

Ponderously, Hem held up a thumb and forefinger forming an O. "And if you want, you can have two things. *Un doble remordimiento.*"

Markham looked puzzled. Was Hem getting drunk, or was the man's personality slowly emerging from behind a protective shield?

"Two remorses," Hem said. "First, remorse for what you did. Second, for what you didn't."

Markham decided to humor him, like any drunk you meet in a bar. Though Hem did not appear to be drunk, really, only pivoting with Keplerian inevitability about some inner axis concealed from outsiders.

"Okay, what're *you* sorry for?"

Abruptly Hem sat up straight, stopped his clutching at the stem of the high glass. "The sky. I never looked at the sky enough when I had the chance. I liked the way the blue was as hard and cold as good Arab steel. The solid blue and the big white clouds sailing in it. On a good day the sea was like that, good and hard and true."

Markham saw abruptly who this was.

"I . . ."

"There are a lot of suicides here," Hem said slowly.

And Markham remembered. The shotgun placed carefully against the forehead, a cold winter day in Ketchem, Idaho, sometime in the early sixties.

"There are lots of girls from Spain," Hem said dreamily. "Plenty. Ones who got crossed in love or whose fiancés did not keep their promises and did the things to them anyway and then went off without marrying. They poured alcohol on themselves and set fire in the classic Spanish way."

Markham saw that it would be easier, and maybe better too, if he made no sign of knowing. Maybe Hemingway would understand.

"You may enjoy these ladies. They come to town every now and then."

"They don't live here?"

"No, they're in the convents."

"Convents? *Here?*"

"They figure that's a way out."

"Is it?"

A bearish, sad-faced shrug.

"How . . . can anybody . . . get out?"

"Can't."

"But . . . we're still *people*. And this is like Brazil or someplace, not Hell at all."

"Ever been to Brazil?"

"Uh, no."

"Hell's more like Cuba, really. Even got Guevara."

"I heard."

A prick of alertness in the gray eyes. "Where?"

"On the road. A bunch in fatigues asked about him."

"How many?"

"A half dozen or so. Guy named Hadrian in charge."

Hem relaxed. "So it worked."

"What?"

"Guevara's trying to draw Hadrian down this way."

"Why?"

"Hadrian's the"—Hem puffed up his chest and boomed out—"Supremo Commandante! Defender of the Antifaith. Ceaseless fighter against the dissidents. Mean and faggoty and an all-round asshole."

"He was in a hurry."

"Old Hadrian, either chasing D's or chasing ass— literally, in his case."

"What's there to dissent about?"

Hem blinked. "Why, getting out."

"How?"

"Nobody knows."

"Has anyone ever gotten out?"

Hem smiled evilly. "Nope."

"Then how the hell—"

"Look, Satan's got cops and the Fallen Angels and the rest. Guevara figures, knock them over and we can run things ourselves."

"And escape from Hell?"

"That's what he figures."

"What are the chances of that?"

Hem grinned. *"Nada."*

"Then why's Guevara trying?"

"Our *nada* who art in *nada, nada* be thy name."

"Look, Guevara hasn't been here more than a few decades. I remember he died in the sixties, the same as . . ."

Only a quick pained flicker passed over Hem's face, like a storm cloud that moved on and wasn't going to drop any rain this time. "Go on."

"So have the dissidents been operating only that long?"

"No. Hell, I heard Socrates led them when he first came."

"They've been going thousands of years?"

"Sure. Maybe hundreds of thousands."

"Without success?"

This time Hem laughed. "No, this is really the other place." A sudden belch erupted from Hem and he belly-laughed again. "Hey! *Un poco pescado? Puerco frito?*" he called to the bartender. "Any cold meats?"

The bartender scuttled over with a plate of twisted brown things. Markham suddenly felt hungry and ate one. It was tasteless but seemed to fill his need.

"So it's hopeless?"

"I don't know."

"Can't you find out?"

"How, Mr. Professor?" Hem leaned toward him, lips smacking with the grizzled meat. "Look it up in the library?"

"You guessed that I'm—?"

"Sure. I always had the angle on you guys."

"I'm not a literary critic."

"Thank God."

"Nothing happens to you if you say that?"

Hem's eyes widened. "Say what?"

"God."

"Nope. You can swear all you like."

"You call on Him, He doesn't answer?"

"Maybe there isn't any."

"But if there's Hell, there's—"

"Our *nada*, who art in *nada*."

Markham jumped to his feet. "Dammit! I'm trying to find out—"

"Shut it! Just shut it!" Hem lumbered to his feet and bunched a hairy fist under Markham's nose. "You want to argue, you argue with this."

Markham was speechless. In his confusion a small part of him kept on observing and remarking. *A classic macho confrontation with the all-time macho figure, and it just comes over as a dumb drunken quarrel. Great.*

"Look, I . . . isn't there something I can *do?*"

Hem breathed heavily for a moment, staring at Markham with gray eyes that seemed to peer through him, toward a distant something. The man looked tired and out of condition. Against the sullen glow from a big side window his gray hair formed a silvery nimbus about his skull.

"Yeah, maybe. Depends on what you want to find out."

"I'd like someone to talk to who has, well, really thought about this."

Hem smiled without humor. "You mean, thought the way *you* think?"

"I suppose so."

"Some professor?"

"No . . . a scientist. That's what I am." He paused, quelled a rush of emotions with a sip of the beer. "Was."

"There's some physicist Hadrian's got up at Kilimanjaro."

"Who?"

"Does it matter?"

"I need someone who knows modern physics, has kept up with quantum mechanics and—"

"No libraries here."

"If he simply questioned scientists who, who came through, he could keep current."

"I don't think many do show up."

Markham wanted to scream, *Then why am I here?* but he knew that would make Hem mad again to no point.

"Bohr? Einstein? Coleman?"

"Never saw them. I don't hang around much with—"

"Oppenheimer?"

Hem chuckled. "Yeah, he's here."

"Why?" Markham's voice sharpened. "The bomb?"

"People don't come in with tags on 'em."

"How about Feynman? Bethe? Fermi? Teller?"

Hem shook his head. "I don't keep track. Just know this English guy's supposed to be good at a lot of stuff. Hadrian uses him for advice."

"How do I find him?"

"He's under lock and key near Kilimanjaro."

"The mountain's really here?"

To Markham's surprise, Hem looked down at the rough wood table top, fingered a dab of meat. "I . . . call it that."

"Where is it?"

"About twenty miles north."

"How can I get there?"

"Not easy. Have to work around some of Guevara's plans. We must find out when he'll create a certain diversion I know is coming up. Otherwise it's too dangerous."

"Why?"

"Kilimanjaro's dead in the middle of the war zone."

5

A mud-brown village looked across a broad river at the foothills of the big mountain. In the bed of the clear water there were pebbles and boulders and fish swimming among them. Troops went by the last house and Markham stood in the doorway and watched them march toward the rolling thunder up in the hills.

Troops of all times. Detachments of vested longbow men, thick quivers of arrows slanted across their backs. A squad of swarthy, dwarfish swordsmen, beetle eyebrows bunched in concentration. Lines of singing, scimitar-wielding, red-robed women. Haughty grinning grenadiers. Long columns of ruddy Roman shields-and-lances, stepping smartly in the churning dust, clanking and shouting and sporting gaudy yellow ribbons atop beaten iron helmets. Yet among them all were other weapons—flintlock rifles, oiled Springfields, blunt-snouted heavy pistols, sleek crossbows, chunky black grenades, even a stubby iron cannon lumbering forward on wooden wheels behind a sweaty team of Chinese women. Muslims in filmy shirts and leggings plodded remorselessly, swords dangling at leather belts. A brown-skinned officer in blue and gray dashed among the columns, shouting.

The woman who kept the place said the men had been going by like that all day. Their dust powdered the shimmery green leaves of the spindly trees beside the road. They came from all times and kept steadily on, most without looking to the side or talking, just the glazed eyes staring narrowly ahead and keeping to the road.

"What's the officer saying?" Markham asked.

Hem chewed meditatively on a toothpick. "Greek."

"You understand it?"

"No. It's ancient Greek, not modern. Everybody spoke that until about a thousand years ago, somebody told me. A lot of the fighters still do. They don't see any point in learning English, which is what most people switched to."

The dust prickled the inside of Markham's nose and he sneezed loudly. "Where are they going?"

"Up to one of the formations."

"To fight who?"

"Whoever's there."

Hem's eyes looked out from deep hollows, never leaving the ragged parade and the endlessly billowing dust. "The Muslims think if they can just defeat enough infidels, they'll be released to the cool garden oasis where houris wait and water runs and there are dates and grapes for all. The Christians believe they have to prove themselves against the heathen. Those dwarves who went by think they're in some sort of battle for possession of Heaven. The Egyptians believe they're going to rescue the Pharaoh."

"They must have caught on by now that those stories are bullshit."

Hem laughed sourly. "Are they?"

"Of course. This isn't *any* traditional Hell."

"Most others think this is a test, a trial—not Hell at all. They'll tell you straight. What they've got to do is show their stuff."

"Why?"

"They want to do as well as the Greeks at Marathon. Or as well as the Yanks at Shiloh. That's the code they knew and died by and that's what they'll stick with."

"And hope it saves them?"

Hem turned and peered at Markham in the dim bleached light. "What're *you* doing?"

"I'm trying to find out how . . . oh."

Hem slapped the door frame with an abstract, pensive glee, grinning, and the old woman who served watery tepid drinks looked up, hoping for more business. The troops didn't stop often, they were too remorseless. But others did, spectators like Markham and Hem.

"Y'know, I ran into General Cambronne along here once. He was leading a regiment of French regulars, some of them in the Old Guard Cambronne had commanded at Waterloo. I asked him about that story, the one about what he said when the Brits called on him to give up."

"Oh. 'The Old Guard dies but never surrenders,' right?"

"So say the books. Cambronne told me all he said was *'Merde!'* When I was in Paris in the twenties proper people when they did not wish to pronounce it said 'the word of Cambronne.' It means shit of course, shit of purest ray serene. All the truth of the thing is in that one word, not in the big phrases people make up afterward."

"Then *why* are these—"

"It's the only action that means anything, can't you see that? They've got no God anymore, but there's still some chance that if they prove themselves they can get out. The religious Johnnies think that, sure. But the rest of 'em—what was it that Patton said? Something about war being the greatest sport. Well, they're sporting men."

"And if they die?"

Hem waited a long time, staring out at the restless eternal columns. "You've been through that already."

"So they keep coming back?"

"Yeah. It's all they know."

"They like it?"

"Look at them. You think they do?"

Markham studied the faces—drawn and whitened, lined and grimed, mouths twisted and obsessed, eyes advancing with fiery mad zeal.

He hadn't read any Hemingway in decades, didn't remember much except the way the prose turned a spotlight on one luminous point after another, bringing small things fugitive and insubstantial in their own right into sharp focus like an impressionist painting: daubs of light hanging in the vacant airless space of your mind. A pressing sense of hazard, peril, danger oozed through that crisp frozen canvas, constant rehearsal of the final and perhaps only real battle. Hem's carefully chipped sentences had embodied a universe which was not man's alone, perhaps not man's at all, fragile and precarious and yet, when you paid exact attention to it, absolutely solid. Unalloyed. Irreducible.

To all that Hem's response had been a stoic sense of personal integrity, expressed through a cold, proud know-how, detached. He had studied life as if he were watching a painting in the Louvre, trying to enter into it by applying a consistent, systematic method to everything he described.

But now they were all beyond that sharp clear world, well past the looming test of death.

"Let's go," Markham said, shuddering.

"The guide's coming along now."

Hem had paid for a man who knew the way around the main battle zones, to the camp where Hadrian kept his supply depots and administrative offices. There the trading and supplying and manufacture for the incessant war went on. There, Hem said, was the English physicist.

The guide was short, black, with wary eyes. He took his money up front and spoke little. The coins Hem gave the man were octagonal beaten copper. A crude grinning face marked both sides, struck off center.

As the guide counted them a sudden rattling of gunfire came down the road. Markham saw lines of men wavering at the nearest hilltop. Then some antlike figures turned and ran down the hill and others came after them. Thin cries rose. An artillery shell burst on the hilltop and bodies flew above the sudden ball of smoke, turning lazily in air before bouncing down among the rocks.

"Outflanked them," Hem said.

"Why doesn't everybody use guns, at least? Those lancers, they're falling like wheat."

"Guns take factories, people who know how to mine, make machines—a lot. Most people here never saw a gun in their . . . first lives. They prefer to fight with what they know."

The lines broke and men scattered everywhere. They tried to reach the road but their enemy poured forward, the swordsmen coming ahead and chopping them down from behind as they ran. Markham could hear screams, shouts. The columns on the road milled, surprised, and did not form up.

"Shouldn't we . . ."

"Yes. Let's go around this."

They moved quickly to the right, behind a long straggly line of Arab archers. The guide said they would get clear easily. Markham kept up his loping run and after a few minutes saw that the man was right. The engagement swirled in confusion on the hillside, a knot of smoke and rushing figures.

They cut down a narrow draw and scrambled across a stream, leaping among a jumble of rocks and logs. Halfway across Markham felt something soft beneath his feet and saw that they were running across a jam of bodies that had drifted downstream and fetched up among the debris of combat. The bodies were so plentiful that they stacked three deep against the rocks. *So you don't just vanish when you die,* he thought.

They reached a stand of fragrant eucalyptus. He said, "The victors in this battle—does anything happen to them?"

Hem said, "Nah. They go on to the next battle tomorrow."

"So even if you win the rat race, you're still a rat."

Hem shrugged. "These fought even when they thought they had only one life. Why shouldn't they fight now?"

"Why don't you?"

"I'm no rat."

Something fat and leathery flapped overhead, wheeled, and dove toward the distant clamor. Great wings supported what looked to be a swelling black intestine. "Satan," Hem said. "That's the form he prefers when he's feeding."

"On what?"

"Soldiers he feels aren't eager enough for the battle."

Markham watched the huge thing descend upon a luckless band atop a far hill. Satan picked up a struggling figure, bit off a piece, and—apparently finding it not to his taste—flung it aside.

Hem ignored this and peered at clouds scudding toward the stubby snow-crested mountain he called Kilimanjaro. "Looks good for the next few hours. Storm moving in."

6

Three hours later, according to his Seiko, Markham lay in the gloom beneath roiling skies and appreciated the shelter of the storm. Rain-soaked, muddy, sore from falls and sudden wild dashes to escape artillery bursts, he peered ahead. A drop traced itself down his brow, hung on his nose. Insects buzzed and stung at the nape of his neck.

Things rustled in the weeds. Markham tensed and knew there was nothing he could do. Earlier he had seen an emaciated brown man get bitten by something long and yellowish, an incredible slick shiny snake with lashing tail. The man had rolled and kicked and died with an awful rattling cough, even before the snake could uncoil and glide into the bushes.

Artillery muttered over the horizon. Clouds boiled in, bringing sounds of clanging steel and distant anguished cries. Markham turned his head slowly as Hem had said, using peripheral vision. Nothing.

"Move on up," Hem whispered.

Markham wriggled on, mud's liquid fingers tugging. Their guide had abandoned them a hundred meters behind, pointing in the gloom toward the jumbled buildings of Hadrian's Office of Military Supply.

They had reached the right place at what Hem's informant said was the right time. Che Guevara planned to capture Hadrian somewhere a few kilometers away in some complicated maneuver. That would provide distraction and allow Markham and Hem to slip in this way. The attempt should have started half an hour before—though what anyone meant by time here Markham had not discovered, since there was no daily cycle to give it meaning or measurement.

"Sounds like some rifle fire over that way," Hem said.

Quick snapping sounds, then nothing. "It's probably had time to draw away most of the guards."

"Let's go, then," Markham whispered.

He and Hem slipped from shadow to shadow.

The unmoving glow above could not penetrate the hovering rain clouds. "You hear anything?" Hem asked.

Markham listened. Then he did. A scrabbling of nails on a rocky outcrop, a dark mass oozing out of shadow, coming fast—*A dog?*—and before he could think it hit him. He rolled, felt a wet hot mouth and then sharp teeth coming together on his fingers. He bit his lips to stop from screaming. The thing grunted with eager hunger. Something broke in his hand.

He rolled the thing against the ground, slamming it hard, and managed to twist the head away with his left hand. A corrosive reek of musk and acid filled his nose. Its mouth free, the thing said clearly, "You. Die. Now."

Markham grabbed at matted bristly hair and wrenched the thing away, keeping the mouth back with a punch to the throat. He felt a dull impact transmitted through the bulk of it and saw Hem stab down again, then again. The weight came on Markham fully and he realized the thing he held was a large misshapen dog-man, four sinewy legs tapering to sharp claws, head narrowing to a snout and slack, drooling mouth. He pushed it away with disgust.

"One of Hadrian's breeding programs," Hem said thoughtfully, wiping his blade on the dog-man's coat.

"Good God."

"I should've mentioned them. A good sign, though."

"Why? If there are more of these—"

"Means Hadrian's pulled his men off this post

right now. He must be using them for personal guards, worried about Guevara."

"So?"

"Means we'll have less to go through."

He was right. They crawled another hundred meters and this time were ready when a black shape came lumbering at them. Hem caught it in the throat with a single quick jab. Markham had his knife out—bought from the guide—but wondered if he could use it properly. They duckwalked toward the first low wooden frame building when a voice called from startlingly nearby, "Jumbar! Here ole fella! Jumbar boy!"

Ole Jumbar isn't in the watchdog business anymore, Markham thought with satisfaction. He lay down to let the man pass.

A crunch of boots on gravel that seemed only inches away. Markham saw a moving patch against the sky. The knife was firm in his hand. He leaped up, lunging—and grabbed the man around the throat, silencing him. He dropped the knife and twisted the man down into the mud. Hem came swarming over them, swearing in a quick angry whisper.

"No!" Markham cried, but he felt Hem's arm come down and plunge a blade to the hilt in the man's chest. The body jerked, coughed, rattled— and went limp.

"Why in hell didn't you cut his throat?" Hem whispered.

"I . . . I thought . . . I could keep him quiet."

"And if he got his mouth free? Want to bring everybody?"

Markham still felt all the prohibitions against

killing, though he didn't want to say that. Hem seemed to understand, but said nothing. He motioned and they trotted toward a squat wooden frame building, one of the few whose windows spilled warm yellow light onto the muddy field.

Markham inched open an unlocked door and looked inside. A lone man hunched over a table, scribbling. Markham slipped inside.

The man looked up. His mouth formed a startled pouch below darting, intelligent eyes. The face held a look of concentrated energy, yet the man said nothing as Markham approached and whispered, "Just keep quiet."

"In faith, you much surprised me."

"I'm looking for a scientist," Markham said as Hem slipped into the room. "An English—"

"I be the only such abouts."

"I've just . . . arrived here."

"Come ye in."

The man appeared about forty, dressed in green fatigues. His skin was bone white, as though he never went out, and his long face had a look of pensive, dreamy power. Markham approached the table and glanced at the familar sight of pages covered with equations. "I labor most times to set right Hadrian's turgid shops and yards, to manufacture the implements of retribution for use against the armies of darkness engendering. These restful hours I pursue mine own works."

"You're a physicist?"

"Aye, as much as these rogue Moors and heathen let me be."

"Your name?"

"Isaac. Isaac Newton, late—very late—of Cambridge and London."

Good grief. "I . . . sir, I have come to you for help. You are widely regarded as the greatest intellect of all time."

"Stuff and drivel." Newton threw down his quill, spattering pages with ink. "Many pass through with such words slithering from their rubied lips, but I think it is one more Mephistophilean ruse."

"No, honestly, you are. You started modern science. You've heard of Einstein? He—"

"I've met a conjuration of that name."

"You know of his, ah, advancements beyond your work?"

Newton sniffed. "I heard of melting clocks and sliding sticks."

"It's more than that, I assure you. But my real question is, sir"—Markham gestured wildly, his head aswarm with questions—"what *is* this place?"

Newton looked sternly at him, ignoring Hem. "All mankind is of one author, and is one volume. When one man dies, no chapter is torn from that great book, but translated into a better language."

"Uh, what?"

"This is but another edition. A fresh tongue. A proving ground, God wot."

"To prove . . . what?"

"The Lord's eternal lesson. We are cast here amongst shameless Papist logicians, slimy Portugals, wily wenches fit solely for rutting, blackamoor armies, dark dread powers—all to find our own writ way."

"To . . . what?"

"The Lord's great mercy."

"But we're in *Hell.*"

Newton frowned. "So it would seem to the unattended eye. I assure you, though, fresh traveler full of gapes—this is no damnation. Such destiny would make the reason reel."

"What is it, then?"

"A fool's test."

"And if we pass?"

"Heaven then, for the quick-eyed."

"And the rest?"

"More dour fretting. Here we feel the sharp bite of guilt, for life brief and naught done."

"You're . . . sure?"

"As sure as I fix on the rheumy ancientry. Bookish learning, the pen's fair incessant wallow—that be our exit from this nightless inspection."

"Then we can find a way out?"

"With proper twist to the ken, aye."

"Using science?" Markham gestured toward the mounds of sheets that sprawled across the ample pine table. An oil lamp cast sharp shadows across endless henscratch lines.

"Oh nay. Nor vain tattle, waffling poesy, or any other airy art."

Markham shook his head. "But science is the only way I ever knew to understand the world."

Newton gave him a warm, broad smile, yet the eyes remained intent, unyielding. "So thought I, long ago. But a man might as well study rubor, calor, tumor, and cholor—they are equal afflictions. Science sleeps here."

Markham glanced to the side, saw that Hem was leaning against the door, grinning slyly. "What changed your mind?"

"The eye," Newton said softly, a bony white finger spiking upward.

"You mean . . . the sun?"

"Ha! 'Tis no sun. It never moves."

"We could be locked to it by tides, like the moon."

" 'Tis an eye that watches all below."

"*Whose* eye?"

"Satan lives among us here, bleak-spirited and vexed, powerful and lightning-swift. It be not he above."

"So?"

"The *Lord* witnesses. The Lord judges. His single all-seeing eye, cloud-shrouded ever. And it falls to us to riddle our way into His good light."

"Riddle?"

"To fathom heavens that the mere present man's eye cannot glimpse."

"Look, you just *said* nobody sees the eye through the clouds. So what heavens are there to, uh, fathom?"

"The astrological pattern, fat with truths."

Dizzy, Markham leaned on the table, disturbing a sheet. Newton leaped up, snatching at it. "No! You'll not see the traceries!"

Markham had glanced at a sheet, and saw that elaborate signs and emblems of the zodiac covered them. He remembered that Newton, though the greatest of scientists, had in fact devoted most of his career to theology and alchemy. The man's mind had been broad and not always able to discern what was science and what was sheer humbug. He had also been deeply suspicious of others stealing his work. That led to a nervous breakdown. Abandoning his Cambridge chair, he had become Warden of the Royal Mint, a scourge of counterfeiters. That surprising administrative ability, combined with sharp intelligence, was undoubtedly why Hadrian used him here.

Newton rushed around the table, spitting oaths. "I knew you when you appeared! Last time it was offers of gold, of ambergris and musk, of unicorn's horns, was it not? I see you, Quathan the Unrepentant. Begone!"

"No, you don't understand. I'm a scientist, a natural philosopher like yourself."

"Necromancer at best, deceiver!"

"I studied your laws in school! I, I—"

"Such laws as were, rule not here. Aristotle's rude rub holds in this flattened land. Things left alone do not glide serene—they stop, velocity eaten by friction's waste. For such are we—waste."

"But you founded true astronomy. You could apply your laws here, or something like them. By careful observation . . ." Markham's voice trailed off. "You've already tried, haven't you?"

"Only astrology functions here. Reading signs, divining portents—that is the true learning."

"You can make real, rational predictions that way?"

Newton's face twisted into a congested mask. "Newcomer, on Earth you and I knew that Reason led to understanding, but Death ruled. Here Death can merely return you to Hell. Otherwise it is powerless. If there is a divine transition from this place, it must come from Reason—but not the narrow notions of mechanistic science."

"But that's all we have!"

"So?" Newton's eyes became crafty. "Yet I know what your scientism did after my departure."

"We advanced, built on your foundations—"

"And rid yourselves of God! Swept Him from the world's stage. Ordained that the equations ruled, that the mere will of man or God was as nothing compared to them."

"Well . . ." Markham began uncomfortably.

"Having displaced human will from the natural world, Doctor Scientist, now explain *this* place." Newton swept an arm in an all-encompassing circle.

"Well, what can we study, how—"

"We must rely not on forces and fluxions, but upon the innate sympathies and antipathies of occult knowing."

Markham could not help himself. He had had a lifetime of dealing with cranks at cocktail parties, with otherwise reasonable people who believed in fortunetelling or ancient astronauts or dead superstitions. "That stuff is nonsense."

"Is it? Well!" Newton's eyes now blazed and jerked with fevered energy. His bony fingers clamped the table, long arms braced to defend the field of scribbled scraps. "You'll not learn how I read the heavens through blankets of sulfurous cloud—not until I have finished my researches! Tell the Devil *that* if you dare."

Markham sighed. "I'm not from the Devil. I don't give a damn—literally—about your astrological garbage."

"Then get thee hence on any account, conjuration! What a sorry thing you be."

With that Newton abruptly began to mutter to himself and stir the sargasso of papers. Markham could hear ". . . if only I'd not . . . the trinity, had I but believed truly in Father, Son, and Holy Ghost . . . or not castigated so Flamsteed for that data

. . . or Leibniz over discovery of that trifle, the calculus . . . this is the third temptation of a week, by my troth . . ."

Markham followed Hem's beckoning hand to the door. "We better go before the next round for that guard," Hem said. "Somebody'll notice."

Out, into muggy air beneath a cold gray mass of mottled clouds that hugged the hillsides.

As he stumbled down a steep slope, letting the bushes scratch him, Markham knew there was a kernel of truth in what Newton said, an idea . . . It slipped away.

Clearly any mechanistic physics was inadequate to deal with a place where ancient evils reigned. Somehow this filled him with joy, though he could not say why. If he got a moment to think . . .

"Patrol over there. This way!" Hem whispered. They bent and crawled through scraping manzanita.

Hem, Newton, Hadrian . . . what are the odds on meeting them? Maybe Hell has most of the famous . . . a place for unique, consuming sins . . . but then why me? I was nobody special. Some good physics, minor transgressions, nothing lurid. Why me?

They worked their way down an arroyo and into dried creek bed. The going was easier and Markham felt good to be trotting doggedly away from the confusions that Newton had planted in his mind. It was better to act than to fret endlessly. Maybe he had been wrong, you couldn't figure this place out by mind alone, it was a *stage*, where dead players trod. . . .

They passed through low scrub trees and up ahead there was only gloom. They ran for ten minutes. Markham panted, trying to keep up. Hem was older but had a solid, steady pace and puffed easily.

"*Alto!*"

The shout from the trees made Hem duck and roll away, into the bushes. An arrow whistled by. Markham froze, then dove for cover—only to find two big men with gleaming shortswords blocking his way.

Hem got no further. Quickly a squad prodded them into a clearing nearby and a scowling man came striding over, whispering, "Who this?"

Hem said, "We're just passing through."

"You are from Hadrian?"

"No, we're leaving the battle."

The man laughed. "Cowards? You run?"

"Let's say we bore easily," Markham said.

"I say you are Hadrian men."

The accent, the flinty eyes, scruffy beard— Markham saw suddenly that this was Guevara. *Hell is for the famous. Maybe that's the ultimate sin after all. But there were plenty of spear carriers— literally—here. So maybe they were famous ten thousand years ago. But then why me?*

Hem said casually, "I drank with you once, remember?"

Guevara peered through the dusty light. "Ah yes. The writer. Two Americans we have here, where they should be not."

Hem said contemptuously, "Hell is free. Perfectly free."

"Not for all," Guevara said. He snapped his fingers and a short fat man came hurrying over. Markham could see there were about twenty men with weapons forming lines in the gloom. A short distance away three held a man captive, hands tied. Markham recognized Hadrian's long, fleshy nose. The face was withdrawn, somber. Blood dripped slowly from his nose and spattered a luxuriant white tunic.

"Tickle them," Guevara said.

The fat man in filthy fatigues took out a knife and without hesitation casually jabbed Markham in the ribs.

Guevara asked, "Where? You from where?"

Markham kicked him in the balls. Someone grabbed him from behind and pulled his arm up so that it twisted in the socket. Markham shifted right and Hem came down on the man's back and then there was the fat man's face in front of him and he punched at it. The fat man stabbed with the knife but missed and then they were all rolling hard on the ground, the dust filling Markham's nostrils.

Somebody kicked him in the side and then he was on his feet again, hands pinned behind him. Guevara stepped near, smiling. "You are confessing your opposition to the revolution."

"What revolution?"

"Against all. You are newcomer? *Si.* You would join then? To revolt! To fight our way through Hadrian and the devils and all."

"Then where'll you go?"

Guevara gestured expansively. "Beyond."

"You know a way out?"

"We will find one."

"You're condemned to perpetual revolution?"

Guevara's mouth tightened. "You try to be funny."

Markham felt heady from the curious elation that had been slowly gathering in him since he had left Newton. In his life on Earth he would have been cautious of a man like Guevara, but now he saw this man as negligible, the macho posturings a mere show.

"Not as funny as all this empty ritual."

"You are friend of Hemingway?"

"Sure."

Guevara smirked at Hem. "You escaped Cuba before we had chance to slit your throat."

Hem smiled coldly and said nothing.

Guevara looked at both men, calculating. "This time I make no mistake. I not trust you."

"Trust us with what? Just let us go, dammit."

"When the rescue party following Hadrian fans out, they question you, find which way we go."

A sinking cold feeling ran up Markham and he tensed painfully, fighting the old fear. "Take us with you, then."

Guevara shook his head dismissively. He waved a hand and said to the short man, "Do these."

Guevara said it with such obvious ease that Markham knew he had given the order before on this mission, would give it again with equal unconcern.

From Markham's experience, he could see Guevara's logic. Though the dead returned to Hell, they reappeared elsewhere, and later—well after this skirmish would be over. A simple way to get rid of troublesome types.

The short man was quick and came in with the knife low, tilted up, eyes fixed and feet shifting lightly in the dust. Markham strained against the hands holding his arms behind him. The fat man plunged the knife into his belly and for an instant he felt the impact but nothing more. Then the slow cold ache of it came into him and he convulsed with fear and then the hands were no longer holding him and he ran straight at the fat man. His fist lashed out and caught the man solidly on the cheek. The face fell away and he was running hard, shouts all around him, the pain now a low slumbering ache and his bunched muscles feeling good to be used and to breathe deeply and to run.

Someone chopped at him with a sword but he ducked and lurched to the side, feeling light on his feet and quick. The faces swept past in a liquid way as if under water and he heard feet pounding behind him. When he came to a narrow lane free of brush he looked back expecting to see Guevara's men pursuing but it was Hem, doggedly loping behind.

He went that way for a while. It felt good and there might be Guevara's murderers behind him and anyway he could not feel the pain this way. It sat there, a glowing smoldering ember waiting to burst into fire but he could keep it that way if he didn't stop.

But then the fire grew in his lungs and his heart racketed in his chest and he slowed.

Hem was far behind. Maybe Hem had called to him but he was not sure. He was trying to think of something but it would not come clear and solid in his mind. He remembered a movie he had seen, *Barry Lyndon*, and how at the end, in a final freeze frame of a crippled sour man getting into a carriage, some cold modern typeface said, "Whatever you may think of these people, they are all equal now."

But it wasn't true. Nobody was equal here, they were all following their own trajectories, shaped by their obsessions.

Somehow that seemed to matter and as he ran on and felt the wetness running down his legs he knew finally what Newton meant.

Markham came to some rocky ground and scrambled over some boulders. He could not see well, there were purple specks swarming in his eyes, so in a way he was not surprised when his foot slipped from the blood and he felt the boulder give way. It lurched aside, teetered—and was gone, thumping below.

He clutched for something, anything—caught a shrub—lost it—raked fingers across a smooth rock face—clasped at a dusty ledge—thrashed madly— and was gone—

—falling straight down, tumbling. He caught a glimpse of a narrow box canyon, the ground swelling up so fast he could not cry out—

He woke sometime later.

This time they would not let him die so quickly. He tried his legs and saw the left shinbone jutting out, a white blade like a knife thrust clean through him. The left arm too was turned wrong and he could not move it.

The pain did not seem to matter so much this time. It was just another thing that got in the way of thinking.

Hem came from out of the shrouded dusky radiance and said, "Damn fool. I told you not to run when you're wounded."

"You're just pissed 'cause I beat you."

He had meant at running but Hem took it differently. The big rough man looked at Markham's wounds and nodded. Markham studied Hem's face and knew that whatever happened Hem would not die, could not die. That thing had been denied Hem and would be forever. The thing he had prepared for in life he could not have here.

Hem squatted down and said, "That bunch wouldn't have followed us anyway. They've got to make tracks themselves."

"Ye- . . . yeah."

"Let me see."

"I'm all right."

"The Hell you are."

"*Oh.*"

"Pretty bad?"

"I'm getting better at it."

"Breathe deeply. It helps."

He did and then a slow seeping weakness came up from the gut and he felt it in his chest and in his arms.

"They got you too." He pointed at Hem's shirt where a red splotch grew.

"Little bastard slipped it into my ribs as I went past him."

"They used the old falling number again."

"It work?"

"No. I'm not scared of it. They're running out of ideas."

"They've got plenty."

The clouds above were thinning but not breaking up. He saw as he moved to ease the low ache in his gut that more light poured through the clouds from the Eye or the star or whatever it was, but the foggy bank would not break and let him see what lay above them. He would never get to stare directly into the Eye.

He was far away now even though he could feel the gritty hard sand he lay on and there were no problems at all. It was going to be bad this time and he knew that but it did not matter now. He had the fear of death in him that the devils had used and he knew that fear would not go away but he had learned how to risk death now and know what the risk was worth. He had learned something from Newton, even if he did not fully comprehend all of it. He had beaten *them*, whoever or whatever ran this place, just by facing the thing he feared.

Hem was saying something but he could not hear very well now for the ringing.

Church bells? Sure, church bells in Hell.

It was just the endless chiming of shock and blood loss in his ears, he was sure of that, his reductionist self hovering there ready with an easy explanation. Always ready.

He felt the damp air and tasted it and it came into him.

The thought that had been trying to get through finally did then Markham nodded to himself with professorial pride, glad to finally see.

They are all equal now. And equally important.

The swarm of tics and traits that was each human personality, that came out of swimming mystery and persisted . . .

"It's not over," he said.

. . . science had brushed that aside, enshrined instead the mindless physical world as the provider of order . . .

Hem laughed. "It sure isn't," he said gently.

. . . what was important was not some nebulous World Mind or Spirit of the Universe that was a hollow echo of the old dead God . . . not some flaccid compromise substitute, some abstract idea served up by embarrassed modern theologians . . .

"Y'know, when I come back . . ."

"I'll save a beer for you."

". . . I think I'll take up hang-gliding."

No—it was *you* and all your fragile vexing memories and hates, loves and dreads, that mattered.

"Screw science," Markham said. "I like this better."

Dimly he saw too that because a choice of actions still persisted, Hell could not be final. His mathematician's habits immediately gave him a vision of an infinite series of airless alabaster hyperspaces, each folded one into another, and the raw white ping-pong ball of Self bouncing among them all . . .

He relaxed completely on the pine-scented sand and prepared to let himself be carried off in the jaws of jackals, off to greater adventures and places unknown in the bowels of the Great Beast.

THE PRINCE

by

C. J. Cherryh

The foundations shook. The lights went out. The computer went down.

"Dannazione—!"

Lights went up again. The monitor came up on a blank screen and the disk drive hummed away, hunting idiotically for vanished instructions.

Dante Alighieri was already on his way down the hall, down the stairs, through the grand hall, and into the First Citizen's glassed-in garden portico. *"I scellerati! I maledetti—!"*

"Sivis, sivis Graece modum, Dantille." Augustus waggled fingers, waved a hand, and anxious sycophants shied aside as he swung his feet over the side of the couch. *"Noli tant' versari—"*

"Gone!" Dante waved a fistful of papers. *"Gone!"* The steam seemed to go out of him. He drew one breath and another and gasped after a third. "I had it. I *had* it—"

"Indubitably," Niccolo drawled from a chair to the side.

Dante's dark eyes went wide. White showed around his nostrils and along the line of his lips. Then the eyes suffused with tears and the lips parted in a sob after breath. "If I could remember—if I could only remember—but that machine, but this place, but those lunatics, *ma questi*—"

"I know, I know, my dear boy." Augustus put out his hand and patted the poet's hand, which was clenched white-knuckled on his knee opposite him. "You have to be patient, you know. You have to expect these things."

"It is," said Niccolo, extending his feet before him, ankles crossed, "the nature of this place."

Dante bowed his head into his hands. "The damned lights fail, this insane power that comes and goes—" He looked up again, at Augustus's face, at the half-dozen sycophants. At Niccolo and Kleopatra and the visitor-youth who stared wide-eyed at the mad poet. "I was so close. They *know*, don't you think they know? And the lines are gone, *two hundred lines*—"

"You'll remember them again. I'm sure you will."

"If it made any difference," said Niccolo.

"Damn you!" The poet leaped up and for a moment violence trembled in his hands, his whole body. Then his countenance collapsed, the tears fell, and Dante Alighieri turned and ran from the room.

"Do you know," Niccolo said to no one in particular, "I did once admire the man."

"Shut up, Niccolo," Augustus said.

Niccolo Machiavelli stretched his feet the further and made a little wave of his hand. *"Dimittemi."*

"Sorry won't mend it. Dammit, Niccolo, do you have to bait him?"

"The man's dangerous. I tell you, *Auguste*, you ought to have him out of the house. Visit him on Louis. *Two* madmen ought to get on well together. They can commiserate. Bestow him on Moctezuma. They can plot strategies together."

"Be still, I say!"

A second flourish of the hand. "You always had a fondness for the arts. It served you well. This man will not."

"Niccolo—"

A third lift of the hand, this time in surrender. *"Signore."*

"Out!" That was for the sycophants, the collection that hovered and darted like gnats throughout the Villa. Petty functionaries and bureaucrats in life, they haunted the place and came and went in perpetual facelessness, trying for points. One scurried up with papers, a pen.

"If the Imperator would—"

"Out!"

The sycophant fled. The newly arrived youth, who had come wandering into the downstairs hall with some sort of petition, gathered himself to his feet and tried for the door.

"You," Augustus said, and transfixed the fugitive in midstep. *"What's your name?"*

"B-B-B-Brutus, if it please you, sir."

"Di immortales. Which?"

"W-w-w-which?"

"Lucius, Decimus, or the Assassin?"

"A-a-a-assass-in?"

"S-s-s-sounds like the First Lucius," Niccolo said.

"Shut up, dammit, Niccolo. *Which are you, boy? Uterque?*"

"M-Marcus. Marcus Junius Brutus."

"Ye gods." Kleopatra got off her couch, on the other side. Niccolo sat stiff and with his hand quite surreptitiously on the dagger at the back of his belt. And the Akkadian got up with his hand on his sword.

"What's wrong?" young Brutus asked, all wide-eyed. "What's the matter?"

"You just got here, did you?"

"I—don't know." Wide eyes blinked. "I—just g-g-got this notice—" Brutus reached into his robe and Sargon's sword grated in its sheath. Brutus stopped cold, a terrified look on his face. "Did I do something?"

"Never mind the paper," Augustus said. "I've seen them. Official directive. An assignment of zone. Where have you been all this time, boy? Down-stairs?"

"I—don't know. I—I think I'm d-d-d-dead—"

"How?"

"I don't know!"

"The Administration has a sense of humor."

"Quid dicis?"

"Never mind." The house shook. The lights blinked again. Augustus raised his eyes ceilingward as the lights swayed. A wild sob drifted down the corridors. *Damn!*—from far up the hall.

"Viet Cong," Niccolo explained. Young Brutus

looked pathetically confused. "The park. *Viet Cong.*
They make overshots. Plays merry hob with the
power lines —You don't know about that either."

A slow shake of the head. A steady gaze of quiet,
helpless eyes.

"Sometimes," Niccolo said, "you really know
it's Hell."

"The man who lost something," Brutus said over
lunch in the garden court. "What did he lose?"

Niccolo blinked, looked at the boy across the
wire and glass table—Kleopatra had joined them,
demure and dainty in a 1930s cloche and black
veil. And Hatshepsut. It was an unlikely associa-
tion, the Greek with the Egyptian, the Egyptian in
a lavender 2090s bodysuit and with a most distressing armament about her person. But they were
all a little anxious lately. Niccolo kept to his dagger: and a tiny 25th-century disruptor, when armament seemed necessary.

"Dantillus," Brutus said.

"Dante. Dante Alighieri. Born long after your
time." Niccolo sipped his wine, waved off a hovering sycophant who proffered more. The sycophant
persisted, sycophantlike. Niccolo turned a wither-
ing look on the fool, who ebbed away. "Never trust
them," he muttered. "Always ask for the whole
bottle."

"Check the cork," said Kleopatra, and Brutus'
wide eyes looked astonished.

"But what did he lose?"

"Oh," said Hatshepsut, "*ka* and *ba*, I think."

"*He psuche,*" said Kleopatra. "*Kai to pneuma.*"

"*Animus et anima,*" Niccolo said with a twist of

his mouth, and smiled. "His soul. At least that's what he calls it. —*Dammit*, man!" He rescued his glass from a sycophant who oozed up to the table so subtly it almost succeeded in pouring.

"More wine," said Hatshepsut. "The whole bottle."

The sycophant was gone on the breath.

"You see," said Niccolo, "Dante Alighieri was very devout. He's sure it was a mistake that sent him here." He laughed, with a second bitter twist of his mouth. "Isn't it always? That rascal Cesare Borgia made it upstairs—his father was a pope. And here I sit, because *I* wrote a book."

"You think that's why," said Kleopatra, sipping wine. Her eyes were enormous through the veil. A diamond glittered on her cheek, beside a perfect nose. "I daresay that's what drives poor Dante mad—*thinking*, you understand. He was quite unreasonable from the beginning—began writing out all his works by hand, absolutely certain that he had offended—*ummn*—the Celestial—by some passage of his work. And he went to the computer to speed his reconstruction. Now *that's* become an obsession. Dante and that machine, hour after hour. Checking and checking. Redoing all his work. He gets terribly confused. Then the computer goes down. Poof! One has to feel sorry for him."

"I don't," said Hatshepsut. She leaned elbows on the table. "The man was a fool. *La divina Beatrice*. To put divinity on a lover—*that's* a mistake! I had a lover try to *take* it once; chiseled his way into my monuments— Sssst. Let me tell you, I was a god. So was my friend here—well, goddess; times change. Augustus was, of course, but the silly Romans only did it after they were dead. *I* was a real god, beard, atef, crook, and flail, the whole thing; I held my power and I died old. Now I know why I'm here. Politics. Niccolo's here on politics. So's Augustus. And if Dante's here, it's *still* politics. Nothing else."

"Dante's become quite a nervous man," said Niccolo. "He's certain he's wronged someone important." He shrugged. "On the other hand— Perhaps he *doesn't* belong here. I'd truly watch what I told him."

"You think *I* belong here?" Brutus asked in dismay.

"But you have a paper," Niccolo said softly. "It says you do. Just don't trust Dante. The man was brilliant. Never mistake that. But he's not able to accept this. Some never seem to. Not to accept where one is—that's quite mad."

The sycophant arrived with the wine, another with glasses. Niccolo turned and took them, slapped an intrusive hand.

"—As for instance, I survived where others did not. I survive here. I keep company with gods. And a surfeit of sycophantic fools." He waved off a corkscrew and supplied his own from his wallet. "You never know. Poor Cl-Cl-Claudius was deified with a dish of mushrooms. Cesare Borgia had a certain touch." He inserted the prongs and pulled the cork. "Most anything can be deadly. Poison on the glass rim. On one side of a knife both parties share. One has to trust someone sometime." He poured a glass and handed it toward the youth. "As for instance, now."

* * *

"He *what?*" Julius Caesar swung down out of his jeep in the driveway, swept off his camouflage helmet, and dusted a hand on his fatigues. "I don't believe it."

"Nevertheless," said Sargon. The Akkadian leaned on the fender while the khaki-clad driver got out and stood staring. "Marcus Junius Brutus."

"There were seven hundred years of Marcus Junius Brutuses."

"The last. Augustus said to tell you." Sargon set his jaw and his ringleted beard and hair shadowed his sloe-eyed face in angular extremes. "He's seventeen."

Julius looked at his driver. Decius Mus gnawed at his lip, took the rifles out, and slung them over his shoulder as if he had heard nothing at all. "Dammit, Mouse—"

"He doesn't remember," Sargon said. "I told you: he's seventeen."

"Oh, *hell.*"

"Yeah," Sargon said.

Octavianus Augustus paced to the window and gazed outward where the Hall of Injustice towered up into Hell's forever burning clouds. Looked back at Julius, who sat in a spindly chair, booted feet crossed. Mud was on the boots, flecks of mud spattered on Julius's patrician face. Julius always brought a bit of reality with him; and when he was under the roof Augustus felt like Octavianus again; felt like plain Octavius, jug-eared adolescent scholar.

Get out of Rome, Julius had advised his widowed niece Atia once upon a time, a dangerous time of civil unrest; and sent her whole family to obscurity in Greece. But there had been letters from Julius. There had been the long understanding: careful tutelage of her son Octavius, the pretenses, the cultivation of this and that faction—not least of them the army. To meet with Julius under these circumstances, in the quiet of his private apartments—it brought back the old days; brought back secrecy; and hiding; and as always when uncle Julius talked business, Augustus Pater Patriae, First Citizen, felt his ears a bit too large, his shoulders a bit thin, felt his own intellect no match for the raw scheming charisma that was Julius.

Augustus was a god, posthumously. Julius sneered at gods and worshiped luck. His own. Julius deliberately created his own legends. Even in Hell. And Augustus felt helplessly antiquated, in his light robes, his Romanesque villa, before this man who took to modernity like a fish to water—

Julius spurned the *most* modern weapons. Not to be thought ambitious. Of course.

"It's us they're aiming at," Augustus said finally. "This little gift comes from high Authority. The refinement, the subtlety of it: that argues for—" Augustus' eyes shifted toward the skyscraper that towered at the end of Decentral Park. And meant His Infernal Highness. The Exec.

"Well, whoever set this little joke up has certainly bided his time," Julius said. "If it was planned this way from the start, that lets Hadrian out as originator—Brutus was in storage a damn long while before *he* got here. Has to be someone who predated us."

"I've wondered—" Augustus' voice sank away.

He came back and sat down, hands clasped between his knees, in a chair opposite his great-uncle. A boy again. "How high up—and how far back—do the dissidents go?"

"Making the boy a catspaw for that lot?" Julius rubbed the back of his head where a little baldness was; it was a defensive habit, a nervous habit, quietly pursued. "Damn, I'd like to know how long he's held in reserve and where he's been."

"No way to find that out without getting into Records."

"And deal with the fiends. No. That's vulnerability. Open ourselves up to his royal asininity—"

Hadrian, Julius meant. Supreme Commander. Lately kidnapped by the dissidents. So much for High Command efficacy. Augustus flinched at the epithet. "He's in favor—"

"Asses are always in fashion. They make other asses feel so safe."

"*Absit mi!* For the gods' own sake, Gaius—"

"Isn't it the way of empires? You set one up, then you have to let the damn bureaucrats have it. Only thing that saved Rome, all those secretaries, with all those papers—no one after us ever did run the government. Couldn't find the damn right papers without the secretaries. The thing got too big to attack. Even from the inside. It just tottered on over the corpse of every ass who thought he could shift it left or right. Same thing going on down at the Pentagram right now. The dissidents work for the government. They don't know it; but they do. Whole thing runs like a machine." Julius ticked his hand back and forth. "Pendulum. It gets the great fools and the efficient with alternate strokes.

Now here's Hadrian gone missing—you think the government's really going to miss Hadrian? Not before snowfall. You think it cares, except for the encouragement it affords fools? His *secretaries* know where all the damn papers are. The Exec'll put some other ass in if they lose him. If they get him back they'll let him serve a while before they advise him to retire—he's lost prestige, hasn't he? But appoint me in his place? Not a chance in Hell. They'll pick some damn book-following fool like Rameses."

"You think all of this is interconnected."

"You miss my point. *Chaos* is the hierarchy's medium. They don't plan a damn thing. Half the chaos comes from the merest chance some insider with a capital *S* has a coherent plan. The rest of it comes of every damn nut outside the system who thinks he's just figured it out. The waves of the bureaucracy will roll over it all eventually. But you have to think of that chance: that very briefly, someone in a Position wants to neutralize us. Beware the bureaucrats. Beware the secretaries."

"*Prodi*. You escaped them."

"Oh, no, no, no, *Augustulle*. What do you think, that geniuses masterminded my demise? It was the bureaucrats. The fools. And who survived it all? *You* killed the conspirators and inherited all the secretaries. And where are those same secretaries?" Julius waved a hand toward the wall, the window, the Skyscraper. "Still at it. All those damn little offices. You wonder why I stay out in the field? The army's the only bureaucracy you can sit on. I *really* don't want to find his imperial asininity. I'd *like* the damn dissidents to send Hadrian's head in. That'd take him out of circulation a while. I'm terribly afraid they won't. But someone in those offices is either afraid I'll take out the dissidents—or thinks I might use this operation to gather troops for myself—"

"Of course you're not doing that."

"Frankly I'm not. I always preferred Gaul. It was much safer than Rome. *Wasn't* it?"

"You never were a politician."

"Never."

"Niccolo says kill him."

"Pah. Kill him! What would that stop? I tell you: what they've done in sending this boy is damned effective. I'd rather face a regiment."

"Than kill him? *Pro di*, when the State's at risk, one life—*any* life—"

"Now that's Niccolo talking. No. I'll tell you another thing. I have a soft spot." Julius picked up his helmet. Looked at it and fingered a dent ruefully as if it held an answer. "Maybe it's my head, what do you think?"

"I think he's a problem you want to ignore." Augustus got to his own feet with a profound sigh. "I'll tell you where the soft spot is. It's age that gets to you. It's battering down the fools time after time and finding they're endless. It's getting tired of treachery. There's a point past which Niccolo's advice has no meaning. There's this terrible lassitude—"

Julius looked up at him, a stare from deep in those black eyes, and Augustus/Octavius flinched. "Do you think they know that—the secretaries?"

"Like rats know blood when they draw it. They're playing a joke."

"Does it occur to you that they're playing it on him as well—on Brutus? Maybe he's offended someone."

"Dante."

"Offended *Dante?*"

"No. *Offended someone.* That's how they manage us, you know. There's always that nagging worry. Who it could offend. Who might know. How far the ripples might go. Dante's obsessed with it. It's a disease. It's the chief malady in Hell. I have it. You have it. We're all vulnerable. *Prodi, win* the damned war!"

Julius smiled that quirkish smile of his. "I do. By continuing to fight it."

"Damn, as soon argue with Mouse!"

"No one argues with Mouse. He doesn't *want* anything. He knows this is Hell. You and I keep forgetting it, that's our trouble. They make it too comfortable for us long-dead. And then they do something—"

"Like this."

"They find something you want. It doesn't take a great mind to do that. A fool can do it. What they can't see is where it leads. And how it leads back to them. Mouse teaches me patience, *Augustulle.* A man who *chose* this place of his own volition has nothing they can hold him by. I have no intention of winning my war. Or of killing this boy. Now I know about him what I should have known all those years ago."

"That he's your son?"

"That, I knew. No. *Now* I know how to hold him."

"Like Antonius. Like Antonius, brooding over there with Tiberius and his damned—"

Julius quirked an eyebrow. "*You* were my trouble with Antonius, *Augustulle*. You still are. Antonius refuses to come where you are. And my only Roman son knew I couldn't acknowledge him. For my reputation's sake. For that bitch Rome. I'll tell you another secret. I never expected to live as long as I did. It's the women; the Julian women—gods, if we could persuade my aunt in here. Old aunt Julia pushed and shoved Marius; did the same to me; and trained my sister, who taught your mother, who trained you. Brutus didn't have a Julia, that was what. Just the little society-minded fool I got him on. I turned him away. And lo, in fate's obscure humor, he turns out to be the only *Roman* son I ever sired. I always thought I had time. You, off in Greece—you were insurance."

"You'd have killed me if you and Calpurnia—"

"*Prodi*, no. What was Alexander's will? *To the strongest?* I knew which that was. You don't hold a grudge, do you? *Don't* create me another Antonius, nephew. Brutus, I can handle."

Augustus opened his mouth, trying to find something to say to that. But Julius turned and left, closing the door gently behind him.

The floor shook to a distant explosion. The lights dimmed and brightened again.

Julius never paused in his course down the hall. The troops had the Cong baffled. The Cong made periodic tries on the villa. It was perpetual stalemate.

It was a raison d'être. And a power base.

He snapped his fingers and a half a dozen sycophants heard the sound and converged beside him as he walked along. No sycophant ever resisted such a summons.

"I want," he said, "the young visitor: in the library."

He walked on. There were other orders to pass. Some of them were for Mouse.

"He's out of his mind," said Sargon.

"His son," Kleopatra said, drifting on her back. The pool was Olympic-sized, blue-tiled. Kleopatra righted herself and trod water while Sargon sat on the rim and dangled his feet in. "Son, son, son. Dammit." She swam off, toward the other end, neat quick strokes, and Niccolo, standing chest deep, wiped his hair back and gazed after her.

"Ummnn," Niccolo said. While Kleopatra seized the baroque steel ladder and climbed out, black and white striped 1980s swimsuit and a very little of it. "Doesn't *look* like a mother, does she?"

"Caesarion."

"Very touchy. *Very* touchy." Niccolo waited till the diminutive figure had walked away toward the dressing rooms, lips pursed. Then: "Half a dozen children and estranged from all of them."

"This damned boy is setting the house on its ear."

"He'll do more than that. It's a master stroke. Marcus Junius Brutus. Julius' natural son. Augustus had more than one reason to kill him, didn't he? Brutus couldn't have *claimed* his paternity and built on Julius' foundations without acknowledging himself a parricide. But Augustus could take no chances. Brutus murders Julius; Augustus takes out Brutus—Kleopatra's brats all side with their dear papa Antonius, completely his. Even Julius' other son, the noble Caesarion. Dear, *ambitious*

Caesarion: Augustus killed both of Julius' natural
sons, you know. So in Hell Julius sides with his
heir Augustus; Kleopatra sides with Julius, completely ignoring Augustus's little peccadillo in mur-
dering one of her children— Isn't love marvelous?
While Marcus Antonius sulks in Tiberius' merry
little retinue, drinking himself stuporous. *There*'s
the man who wanted most to be Julius' heir.
There's the man who handed Julius his soul to
keep; and Julius just used it and tossed it. Do you
know the worst irony? Antonius still loves him. He
loves Kleopatra. And those kids. And his sister and
her little crew of murderers and lunatics. Antonius
loves everyone but Augustus, who destroyed him.
And lo! Brutus—who always was the greatest threat
Antonius understood. This just might bring the
poor fellow back."

"Neutralize Caesar."

"Someone in the Exec's service planned this one.
Someone *Roman*. Someone who understands enough
to know where the threads of this run."

"Tiberius?"

"Tiberius was never subtle. Try Tigellinus. Try
Livia. Try Hadrian himself."

"Before he was kidnapped?"

"*If* he was kidnapped. What if *he* ran the dissidents?"

"You dream!"

"I put nothing beyond possibility. I'm surprised
by nothing."

"*Brutus* certainly surprised you."

"Only in his youth. He would arrive someday.
That he hadn't only meant that he would. It was
irresistible to someone."

"Maybe he just served out his time in the Pit, eh?"

Niccolo leaned his arms back on the rim of the pool. His eyes half-lidded. "The Pit is a myth. I doubt its literal existence."

"Then where do they go? Where *are* the ones we miss?"

"In torment, of course. Wondering when *we're* going to show up. And when it palls, when at long last it palls and we all stop worrying—" Niccolo made a small move of a scarred hand. "*Eccolo*. Here they are."

Sargon's hands tensed on the pool rim. He slid into the water and glared.

"There are people we *all* worry about finding," Niccolo said. "Look what they've done to Brutus. *Innocence. Ignorance.* Whips and chains are a laugh, Majesty. It's our *mistakes* that get us. The Pit is here. We're in it."

"You have a filthy imagination!"

"Intelligence is my curse. I am a Cassandra. That is *my* hell, Majesty. No one listens *all* the time. Always at the worst moment they fail to heed my advice." Niccolo rolled his eyes about the luxurious ceiling, the goldwork, the sybaritic splendor. "I will not even solicit you. I *know*, you see, that if I gain you, you will fail *me*, Majesty, Lion of Akkad. That is the worm that gnaws me."

"Insolence ill becomes you. *You* are the worm that gnaws this house. Sometimes I suspect *you*—"

Niccolo's dark brows lifted. "*Me*. You flatter my capabilities. I have no power."

"Remember you're in Hell, little Niccolo. Remember that everything you do is bound to fail.

That is the worm that gnaws you. Power will always elude you."

"I adopt Julius' philosophy. Cooperate in everything. And *do* what I choose. Which is little. Fools are their own punishment and they are ours."

"Fools are in *charge* down here!"

"That's why they suffer least. Are you content, Lion? Does nothing gnaw at *you?* No. Of course not. You're like poor Saint Mouse. The one virtuous man in Hell. The one incorruptible soul. He has no hope. But you do. Why else do you live in this house? You were no client king. You ruled the known world."

"Flatterer. I also adopt Julius' philosophy. And you will not stir me, little vulture. No more than you stir *him.*" Sargon leaned into the water and swam lazily on his back. "I am immune." His voice echoed off the high ceiling and off the water. "Better a foreign roof than Assurbanipal's court. If you want intrigue, little vulture, try your hand there. My own ten wives are *all* there. Not to mention the heirs. Why do you think I'm *here?* Not mentioning all the other kings, and all the other queens and concubines. Don't teach *me* intrigue, little vulture. Take notes."

He reached the ladder. He climbed up to the side, water streaming from dark curling hair and beard and chest. And Niccolo smiled lazily, not from the eyes.

"I am writing a new book," Niccolo said. "Dante inspires me. I am writing it on the administration of Hell."

"Who will read it, little vulture?"

"Oh. There will be interest. In many quarters."

Sargon scratched his belly and wiped his hand there. "Damn, little vulture. They'll have you in thumbscrews if you go poking around Administration."

"For instance, do you know that Julius exchanges letters with Antonius?"

Sargon stopped all motion.

"Mouse takes them." Niccolo turned and heaved himself up onto the rim of the pool, turned on his hands and sat, one knee up and hands locked about it. "I wonder what he's going to write today. He will write. Mark me that he will." He smiled, not with the eyes. "He'll have to tell Antonius that Brutus has come, you know. Antonius would never forgive him if he didn't. And never's such a damned long time down here."

"Damn your impertinence to the Pit. I had a wife like you. I strangled her. With my own hands."

Niccolo spread wide his arms. "I could never equal your strength, Lion. I should never hope to try."

Sargon glared a moment. Then he seized up a towel and wiped his hair and beard with it. Hung it about his neck with both hands, and there was a glint in his almond eyes. "Come along, little vulture. I have uses for you. How many others do? Hatshepsut? Augustus? —Hadrian?"

"How should I betray a confidence? Lion, do you attempt to corrupt me?"

"Impossible."

The lights flickered. A screen went dark, and Dante leaped from his chair. "Ha!" he cried, "*ha!* I got you, you thrice-damned sneak!" With a note of hysteria crackling in his voice and a maniacal stare, man at cyclopic machine. "Thought you got me! I had it saved! *Saved*, do you hear me?" He jerked the recorded disk from the drive and waved it in front of the monitor. *"Right here!"*

"Do you really think they hear you?"

He dropped the disk and spun about, hair stringing into his eyes. He wiped it back, blinked at something that did not, for a change, glow monitor-green, and straightened a spine grown cramped with myopic peering at minuscule rippling letters. That something which did not glow was a man in 20th-century battledress. Was the owner of a pair of combat boots that flaked mud onto his Persian carpet. Of a large black gun at his hip, a brass cartridge belt, brass on his shirt, a black head of hair, and a face that belonged on coinage.

"Caesar."

"Marvelous machines." The Imperator-deified walked over to the computer which had come up with READY, and picked up the disk.

"Don't—d-don't." Dante Alighieri perspired visibly. Knotted his large, fine hands.

"Oh?" Julius tapped a few keys. DRIVE? the monitor asked. "Wondrous," Julius said. "Do you know, I need one of these." He looked the disk over, one side and the other. Slipped it into the drive. Called up MENU.

"Please—"

"I did quite a bit of writing myself, you know. I still keep notes and memoirs. Old habits. You're sweating, man. You really oughtn't to work so hard."

"Please." Dante flipped the drive drawer, ejected

the disk into his hands. "Please. I'd hate to lose it."

"The great epic? Or your little list of numbers?"

"I—" Dante's mouth opened and shut.

"*Never* trust the sycophants. I'll *give* you a number, scribbler. I want you to run with it. I understand you're quite talented."

"*Io non mai—*"

"Of course you do." Julius reached out and gathered a handful of the poet's shirt. "*Prodi*, you do it all the time, *mastigia*. With our equipment, on our lines, with our reputation. Let's play a little game. You like numbers? Let me give you the one for the War Department."

"I—I—I—"

"It even works."

Brutus paced the library, paced and paced the marble patterns, up and down in front of the tall cases of books and scrolls. He waited. That was what the message had told him to do. He paced and he worried, recalling innuendo, Niccolo's small barbs, and the brittle wrath in Kleopatra's eyes. He had amused the Egyptian: Hatshepsut. There had been mockery in the way she looked at him. There had been invitation.

And he was very far from wanting *that* bed or another bottle of wine with Niccolo Machiavelli or another of those looks from Octavianus Augustus né Octavius, plebeian—who regarded him as if he had coils and scales and still dealt with him in meticulous courtesy—*wise*, he thought of Octavianus; *wise man*—with instinctive judgment. And he would not give a copper for his life or his safety with the others without whatever restraint Gaius Octavianus Augustus provided.

Did he order me to wait here? Brutus wondered in confusion. *He knows me. I don't remember him. With the adoption suffix on his name. I didn't catch the new clan. And gods, what clan has Augustus for a cognomen? No, it's got to be a title. Imperator, they called him. A war hero. And a god, prodi! And goddesses! And Dantillus and Niccolo— Are they serious?*

They're laughing at me, that's what. They hate me. I threaten them. Why?

What am I to wait on here?

He found the wine uneasy at his stomach, and his skin uneasy in the chill air, in this awful half familiarity with things-as-they-were. He did not like to look out the window, where a building towered precariously skyward, vanishing into red, roiling cloud. The sight made him nauseated. It would fall. It would sway in the winds. What skill could make such a thing?

Is it like this, to be dead? What happened to the world, that books are mostly codices and lights come on and off by touching and how do I know these things and why do these people I never met in my life all know me?

Is this what it is, to be dead? Are these shades and shadows?

Is this man Niccolo one of us?

Is he a god like Hatshepsut?

Am I?

What did I die of? Why can't I remember?

The door opened. A man in clean, crisp khaki

walked in, a handsome man of thirty with dark hair and lazy amusement in his eyes.

"Is it you?" Brutus asked—for he doubted everything around him. *"O gods, is it you?"*

"Et tu," Julius said, and closed the door behind him. "My son."

Brutus drew a gulp of air. Stared, helplessly.

"We've had this interview once before," Julius said. "Or have we? Massilia?" Julius walked toward him, stopped with head cocked to one side and hands in his belt. "You'd surely remember."

"I remember."

"Well, gods, sit down. It's been too long."

Brutus retreated to the reading table and propped himself against the edge with both hands, trembling. "My mother—told me—"

"So you said in Massilia."

"But—when did I die? You *know*, don't you? Everyone knows something I don't— *Prodi*, can't someone be honest with me?"

Julius gave him that long, heavy-lidded stare of his. The mouth quirked up at the side the way it would and the lock that fell across his brow the way it would. This was the Caius Julius Caesar who had gone over the wall in Asia; made scandal of the king of Bithynia; set the Senate on its ear.

Are all those things gone, above?

"So," Julius said. *"Honest* with you. You stand here less than twenty. Ard you don't remember anything."

"Me di—"

"That might be a benefit."

"Why? What happened? Where did I—?"

"—die? That's a potent question. What if I asked you not to ask yet?"

"I—"

"Yes," Julius said. "*Hell* of a question to hold in check, isn't it? Hell is doubt, boy, and self-doubt is the worst. Doubt of my motives—well, you must have made some sort of mistake up there, mustn't you? Or here. You can die in Hell too, you die down here and you can come back right away or a *long* time later. When do you think you came?"

Brutus stood away from the table edge, waved a helpless hand at sunlight no longer there. "I was riding along a road, there by Baiae, just a little country track, it was just—an hour or two— Then—I woke up—*di me iuvent!*—on a table—this— this unspeakable old man—"

"The Undertaker. Yes. I do well imagine."

"Did I fall? Did my horse throw me?"

"You weren't to ask, remember. For a while."

"It was something awful! It was something—"

"Can't let go of it, can you? Especially self-doubt. I tell you that's the worst for you. Be confident— look me in the eyes, there. See? Better already. Straighten the back. Fear, fear's the killer. Kills you a thousand times. Somebody put that in my mouth. *Nice* writer. There now—" Julius came close and adjusted a wrinkle in Brutus's tunic. "You just take what comes. You and I—well, there're worse places. Assuredly."

"Is my mother here?"

"I really don't think she wants to see me. I don't hear from her. Never have. One thing you learn down here, boy, is not to rake up old coals. People you think you might want to see—well, time doesn't exactly pass down here. Oh, there are hours in the day—eventually. Sometimes you know it's years. Sometimes you don't. Whatever time it's been, you're not the boy who was riding down that road outside Baiae, now, are you? Death is a profoundly lonely experience. It changes everyone. But— You don't have that, do you?"

"I *don't!* I haven't, I can't remember—"

"Without that perspective. Gods. Poor boy, you can't well understand, can you? You just—"

"—blinked. I blinked and I was *here*, on that table, with that nasty old man, that—*creature*. I—"

"Can you trust me?"

Brutus took in a breath, his mouth still open. His eyes flickered with the cold slap of that question.

"Can you trust me?" Julius asked again. "Here you are. You never liked me much. I've told you that the dead change. You don't know what direction I've changed. You came to me at Massilia and I never did figure out exactly what you expected of me. We talked. You remember that. You asked were you truly my son and I said—"

"—only my mother knew. *Pro di immortales*, was that a thing to say to me?"

"But *true*, boy. Only she does know. I had to tell the truth with you, the absolute truth: it was all I could give you. Self-knowledge. I had to make you know your situation. And what certain actions could cost. Protect your mother; protect your father's name—the name you carry; protect myself—yes; from making the feud with the Junii worse than it was. Politically I didn't need it. Maybe it was misguided mercy that I was as easy on you as I was. It was a hard trip for a boy to make. It alienated your father's family, humiliated your mother; and if it weren't for your mother's relatives and that little military appointment you got after that interview, the scandal would have broken wide open. It was a damned stupid thing you did, coming to me. Too public. Too obviously confrontation. And you're still the boy who made that trip, aren't you? I see it in your eyes. All hurt, all seventeen, all vulnerable and full of righteousness and doubt. And you needing so badly to trust me. Have you an answer yet?"

"Damn you!"

"You said that then too. Well, here we are, both of us. Damned and dead. Can you trust me? Can you trust life and death made me wiser, better? I know you. You're a boy looking for his father. And you've found him. You've got all this baggage you've brought to lay at his feet and ask him to do something magical to make you not a bastard and *not* whispered about in your family and not at odds with your relatives, and not, not, not every damn thing that was wrong with your existence when you rode to Massilia. A lot of problems for a seventeen year old. You think I could have solved them with a stroke."

"You could have done something."

"Well, you're a *few* months older, at least. In Massilia that winter you wanted everything. Let me give you the perspective of my dying, since you lack your own: everything and anything I did with you that day was doomed to fail. You were the only one in that room who had the power to do anything. Do you know—you still are?"

"Dammit, don't play games with me!"

"Not a game. You're seventeen. It's the summer after. You haven't figured it out yet. I failed to handle your existence. Your mother failed. Your father of record failed. They found a compromise that let you live ignorant until he died and you were old enough to pick up the gossip. Then it started, right? Must've been hell, you and the Junius family gods. Manhood rites. *That* must have been full of little hypocrisies. February rites: praying to Junius ancestors, not that they heard it. Hell on earth. All your seventeen years. And I regret that, boy. But what could I do that late? Make it a public scandal instead of a private one?"

"Was I a suicide?"

"There you are, back to that question. So you considered suicide after talking to me. Maybe you considered killing yourself all that long ride home. Am I right?"

"Yes." A small voice. Brutus rolled his eyes aside, at the wall, at anything. "I *didn't* kill myself. Not on that road, that summer. I'm sure of that, at least. I was happy—I loved a girl—"

"Good for you. So you did find an answer of sorts. I told you, it had to be your own answer. Your existence was centerless as long as you looked to me to justify you; as long as you looked to your mother or to Junius. You were your own answer, the only possible answer. Do you understand me now?"

"I was the only one who cared."

"Not the only one who cared, son. The only one who could *do* anything. You could have killed yourself. Or me. Which would have been even worse for you. Or you could go back to Rome, go out to Baiae and be seventeen and in love. How was she?"

"*Dammit*, do you have to put your lecherous hand on everything?"

Julius made a shrug, hands in the back of his belt. "It probably made a difference in your life—one way or the other. *Prodi*, you were so vulnerable."

"*Was* she. *Was* she. *Is! Is! Dammit*—"

"You're dead. I assure you, you're dead and so is she. Whoever she was. And remember what I said about the dead changing. You're late. I've been waiting for you—thousands of years. Now do you see what you're into?"

"*Di me iuvent.*"

"You're a lost soul, son. One of the long wanderers, maybe. This is Hell. Not Elysium. Not Tartarus. Just—Hell. And it rarely makes any sense. Do you trust me yet?"

Brutus stared at him in horror. "How can I?"

"That's always the question. Here you are. Here you'll remain. I offer you what I couldn't in life. But the problem of your existence is your problem. You want me to embrace you like a father? I can. I can't say I'll feel what you want me to feel. I know you won't. Remember that you're a long time ago for me. And you're a long way from Massilia."

"*Gods!*" Brutus sobbed. And Julius obligingly opened his arms, invitation posed. "*Gods!*" Brutus fled there, hurled himself against the khaki shirt, put his arms about his father, wept till tears soaked the khaki and his belly was sore. And Julius held him gently, stroked his hair, patted his back till the spasms ebbed down to exhaustion.

"There," Julius said, rocking him on his feet, back and forth. "There, boy—does it help?"

"No," Brutus said finally, from against his chest. "I'm scared, I'm *scared*."

"You're shivering. It was awful, I know, the Undertaker and all."

"It's not that."

"Me? Am I what you're afraid of? A lot of us are to be afraid of. Marcus Antonius, for instance. But he's not in this house. I warn you about him simply in case. You want a commission, dear lad? I can manage that. I'll show you the best side of this place. Gaius doesn't bite. Octavianus. Augustus. My niece Atia's boy—I adopted him. You see? I *needed* a son. It came down to my niece's son, finally. Caius Julius Caesar Octavianus Augustus—nephew of mine's got so damn many names and titles I can't keep up with them myself. And Mouse. You'll like Mouse. He lived a long time before us. Vowed himself to hell to save the country—charged Rome's enemies singlehanded—"

"Decius Mus!" Brutus reared a tear-streaked face and looked Julius in the eyes. "*That* Mouse!"

"Damn good driver. Not much scares him. I told you you can get killed down here. It still hurts. I really appreciate a man with good nerves. Got a lot of good men. Mettius Curtius. Scaevola."

"Marius?"

"Poor uncle Marius got blown to local glory. Haven't found him since. Little fracas with Hannibal—gods, two hundred years ago as the world counts it. Mines. You know mines? Of course not. A little like *liliae*. Worse. Hell, they invented a lot of ways to kill a man up there." He slapped Brutus's shoulder. "You want to dry that face? You want to stay here by yourself and rest a while, or do you want to take a tour around with me? Mouse has got the jeep, but he'll be back. You know cars? Did you walk here?"

"I—I—" Brutus made a helpless gesture at the view out the library window. "I thought this was another part of the building where I woke up. But I don't know. I walked down a hall—"

"Well, things like that happen here. Don't try to figure them. You've figured out the lights, the plumbing's fancier, but ours *worked*. You can ride wherever you like, horses we've got—but you'll want to learn to drive. Augustus isn't much on modernity, but he makes up for it on quality. He has an excellent staff, never mind the sycophants—"

Something roared overhead. Low. Brutus flinched and ran to the window. Julius stayed where he was. "They *fly* here too. I don't advise taking that up. Awfully chancy." There was a boom from the other side of the house, a series of pops. "Fool's overflown the Park. The Cong take real exception to that."

"I'm going mad!"

"No, no, no, it's just change. Novelty. I tell you, it's attitude. Doubt's your enemy. Disbelief is another. Believe in airplanes. Believe in yourself. Believe in visiting the moon and you extend yourself. I believe it happened. There's a limit to what I believe—I just like to have a *little* touch with the ground, you know; like feeling the mud under my feet, like the smell of gasoline—"

"What's gasoline?"

"It runs jeeps. Come along, come along, boy. *Gods*, there's so much to catch you up on—"

"What in the name of reason is he up to?" Kleopatra cried. A sycophant bobbled her nail polish and she shoved the creature down the chaise longue with her foot, sent a bright trail flying over the salon tiles in the sycophant's wake. Ten more took that one's place, mopping polish, seeking after the gesticulating hand, in a susurration of dismay and self-abasement, while the stricken sister wailed and snuffled hardly audibly. "O *fool, fool—!*"

"They'll never improve," said Hatshepsut. She lay belly-down on a marble slab while a masseur worked slowly on her back.

"I don't mean her! It! I mean *him!* O, damn! I don't believe it. He can't. He *hasn't* acknowledged that boy."

"It hardly makes any difference, does it? *Everyone* knows. Ummmn. Do that again. You're better than my architect."

"Dammit, he can't, he can't, I won't have it!" Kleopatra fisted a freshly lacquered hand and pounded the cushion. "He—" Her eyes fixed beyond, incredulously. Hatshepsut rose up on her elbows, looking toward the window, where a jeep pulled into the drive, and her mouth flew open as wide as Kleopatra's, whose lacquer-besmirched hand was instantly enveloped by frenetic sycophants.

"Ohmygods."

"Who?" Augustus cried. *"Who?* I'll have his—"

"Not publicly," Niccolo drawled, and carefully

drew back the curtain, peering down onto the drive as Mouse got out one side and a stocky, curly-headed man in tennis shorts bailed out the other. "Look at that. Even Mouse looks perplexed."

"The hell he does." Augustus came and took a look of his own out past the curtain. The handsome, lop-eared face showed a hectic flush. "What in the name of reason is he thinking of?"

"Antonius?"

"My uncle, dammit!"

"Ah." Niccolo smiled, a fleeting cat smile, long-lashed eyes lowered in contemplation of the scene on the driveway. "On that man I take notes, I never presume to guess him."

"*Antonius?*"

"Your uncle."

"That little bastard downstairs got him once. That *ass* out there tried to get *me*— He's got Kleopatra's brats over at that pervert Tiberius'— *Prodi!* He's got *Caesarion* in his camp!"

"Whom you murdered."

"A lie."

"*Auguste*, all statecraft is a lie and lies are state-craft, but split no hairs with me. This earless ass in your driveway is a schism in your house and a damned uneasy pack animal. I don't think he'll bear patiently at all. And I wonder what he'll do to young Brutus."

"Wine," said Sargon from the far side of the room. "It worked with my ass of a predecessor. Of course—I could just shoot him."

Niccolo turned and lifted a brow. "Like Sulla?"

"Not on my doorstep." Augustus turned from the curtain and snapped his fingers. A horde of sycophants appeared, saucer-eyed. "Get me a Scotch. Where's Caesar?"

Some sped on the first order. A few lingered, feral grins lighting their eyes. These had more imagination. Not much more. "Dante," the whisper came back. "Brutus," came another.

"Mouse went to Antony," said a third, not too bright.

"Out!"

It wailed and departed.

"Be civil," Niccolo said, "my prince. Learn from your uncle. Aren't we still guessing what *he's* up to? Welcome your enemy. Forgive him. If the divine Julius wants a minefield walked, why, he sends for Antonius." Niccolo tweaked the curtain further aside and stared down his elegant nose at the drive. "Ah, there, now, one question answered. There comes Julius and young Brutus. Now, there—they meet. How touching. Father with son on his arm. Antonius' gut must be full of glass. He *counts* on Caesarion. He's been trying to seduce Caesar and Kleopatra out of here for *so* long, and he so hopes Caesarion will prove the irresistible attraction— Look. An embrace, a reconciliation, Julius with Antonius."

"Watch for knives."

Niccolo grinned. "None yet. Antonius is too devoted, Julius too convolute, the boy too innocent. And look—now the divine Julius draws Antonius aside, now he speaks to him while Mouse holds young Brutus diverted with the jeep and the gadgetry and the guns— O fie! Fie, Saint Mouse, where is your virtue? Adoration, positive adoration shines in young Brutus' face—boy meets the hero of his youth. Meanwhile the divine Julius is whispering apace to mere mortal ass—Antonius glowers, he glares, he swallows his wrath—oh, where are sycophants when they might be useful?"

Something whistled, distantly. Boomed. Power dimmed. *"Maledetto!"* wailed from down the hall.

"Got him again," Sargon said.

"I can't!" Kleopatra said, and fidgeted as a sycophant buttoned her silk shell blouse. Another fastened her pearls, a third adjusted the pleats of her couturier skirt. "I *can't* face him."

"Yes, you will." Hatshepsut shut her eyes and, leaning forward, submitted a bland, smooth face to the ministrations of clouds of sycophants armed with kohl pots and brushes. The sable eyes lengthened, took on mauve and lavender tint about the lids that accorded well with the mylette glittersuit. Fuchsia beads hung in her elaborate Egyptian coiffure. Some of them winked on and off. So did the diode on the star-pin she wore. And the ring on her hand. And the circlet crown, which swept a trail of winking lights coyly over one strong cheekbone and back beneath the wig, and into her ear where it whispered with static and occasional voices in soldierly Latin. "Ssss. Aren't they friendly? Talk about the weather, talk about the house, talk about the boy—all banal as hell."

Kleopatra rolled her eyes. "Oh, *gods.* How can I put up with this?"

"They're coming this way."

Kleopatra's red lips made a small and determined moue. Her tiny fists clenched. Hatshepsut took an easy posture, arms folded, as a half-dozen sycophants suddenly deserted them to dither this way and that around the door.

It opened. Sycophants on the other side beat them to it while the sycophants inside were undecided. A trio of men who knew better stood behind a boy who knew not a thing.

"How nice," Kleopatra said with ice tinkling on every word. "A whole clutch of bastards."

"Klea!" Julius said.

"Do come in. I was just leaving."

"Maybe—" Brutus said, stammered, his young face blanched. "Maybe we ought—"

"Not likely," Julius said. "I want you upstairs, Klea. Both of you."

"The hell."

"Klea." The man in tennis shorts looked soul-in-eyes at her, advanced holding out his hands. "I've come to make peace. You, me. Augustus. Brutus."

She looked past him to Julius, whose face carefully said nothing.

"And to what do we owe this?"

"She's difficult," Julius said. "She's always difficult." He put his hand on Brutus's shoulder. "Klea, this is a boy. This is a nice boy. *Don't* be difficult."

"I—" Brutus said. And shut up.

Kleopatra cast a look Hatshepsut's direction. Hatshepsut lowered elaborate eyelids, lifted them again in a sidelong glance, and Kleopatra walked deliberately past Julius with a shrug of silken shoulders. There was a sudden and total absence of sycophants. "Well, well, well. Tell me, *mi care Iuli*—just what *did* bring you back from the field?"

Julius's brows lifted. Kleopatra walked on, sharp echo of stiletto heels on tile, sway of petite hips and pleated skirt. "Come now," she said, snagged Brutus by the elbow, hugged it to her and drew him a little apart, conspiratorially. "These are my husbands. My second and third. How do you like the villa?"

"I—" Brutus cast a desperate look over his shoulder to Julius and Antonius and Decius.

"He doesn't have the perspective," Julius said. "He remembers a road outside Baiae. He was on vacation. Two blinks later he's here. *Think* about it, Klea."

Kleopatra froze a moment. Took her hands carefully from Brutus' arm.

Brutus looked from one to the next to the next. Last and pleadingly, at Decius Mus.

"Come here, boy," the hero said. Held out his hand. Brutus retreated there, to the firm grip of Mouse's hands on his shoulders.

"Let's talk reason," Julius said. "Upstairs. The plain fact is, Klea, we're under attack."

"Brilliant," Niccolo said, ear inclined to the library doors as he leaned there with his shoulders. He rolled his head back to face Sargon, who stood with arms folded, sandaled feet square, and a keen curiosity on his dark-bearded face. "Brilliant. Julius has Brutus in there as hostage. Augustus, Kleopatra, Antonius—all sitting there on best behavior, knowing full well that any one of them could blurt out something that might jog Brutus the innocent right over the edge— And Hatshepsut sits silent as the sphinx—the cooling influence: he has her there, an outsider-witness to keep this loving family from too much frankness; while the silent, the redoubtable Mouse is a damper on everyone. *No* one bares his weaknesses to that iceberg."

"It's not only his own life Julius's gambling in there," Sargon muttered. "Someone'll have to kill that boy if he's not careful. And *is* Mouse incorruptible? Beware a man of extremes, little vulture. Mouse is a passionate man. Ask his enemies."

Niccolo looked back and raised a brow, turned his ear to the door again. "More of family matters. The politeness in that room is thick enough to stop a man's breath. Antonius vows selflessness, with tears in his voice he swears he's changed profoundly; Augustus swears he wishes to sweep all complications away—as he has come to love, he says, Kleopatra as his sister—as he will regard Antonius as his friend and this engaging young stranger as his younger brother—oh, and Augustus means it, Lion, he always means such things. And will mean them to the day some offense inflames him—then, *then*, he strikes without a qualm. There is no liar, Lion, like a sincere and reasoning man."

"A plague on his reason. What's the old fox got in his mouth?"

"Julius won't be hurried. That's a certainty. He's ranked his pieces, made his move— You ought to have taken this invitation to conference, Lion."

"I? I'll be waiting when the sun comes up on these oaths and protestations. They'll come to one who wasn't witness to their oaths, when they want to break them."

Niccolo made a grimace of a smile. "Ah, well, to *you*, Lion, they come for moral advice; but to *me* they come only when they've set their course. And come they will, to us both—to me when they wish to be rid of this young leopard. To you when they wish to justify it. Even in Hell we must have our morality."

Sargon chuckled softly. "What's the boy doing?"

"Silence, of course, silence—a *tabula rasa*, blank and oh, so frightened. Julius plies him with such a wealth of trust as would daze any prodigal son— and the leopard cub yet is leopard enough to look for blood on the old leopard's whiskers. But being cub, being cub quite lost and desperate, he nuzzles up to any warmth—if *Hatshepsut* clasped him to her bosom he would call her mother and weep for joy."

"He'd be far safer."

Niccolo laughed, merest breath. "Oh, with either of *us* he'd be safer, Lion, at least his life would be. —Ah! Now, now, we get to business! Attack, says Julius: he names enemies—"

Sargon stepped closer, applied his own ear to the door, royal dignity cast aside.

". . . an executive-level operation," Julius was saying. "We've got the fool Commander in dissident hands; and what put him there was a ragtag nothing having a chance dropped into their laps— administrative blundering or a leak in the Pentagram; or you can draw other conclusions. *Hadrian*, son. Publius Aelius Hadrianus, so damned modernized he's forgotten his own name. Supreme Commander of Hell's Legions. Remember you're thousands of years late. Hadrian ruled Rome—*ruled*, exactly so. He was—never mind what he was. There's a group of rebels—just think of the civil war and you've got it. The rebels grabbed Hadrian while he was gadding about on another of his damn tours; the headquarters is in its usual mess; you walked into a situation, boy. The Administration's embarrassed; the dissidents have scored a big one. And you can count on an embarrassed Administration to make some moves to distract *anyone* they don't trust. That's one level of thinking. There are others. There's one level that says we may have personal enemies that want to take advantage of the chaos and the Administration's lack of attention. You want to ask a question, son?"

"I—"

"It's a confusing place. Seventeen and you don't know any real facts about how your own country ran, you didn't understand why Rome tore its own guts out—"

"I know about Marius. *And* Sulla."

"Well, think of it like that, then. Gods help you, we're thousands of years old; you're seventeen. You wonder what you're doing in this room? You have to learn. You're going to learn." The sound of footsteps crossing stone. "There's something in the wind. *Antoni*, tell them what you told me."

"Rumors," Antonius' voice said. "That's all I can call it. Talk. The dissidents—they're laying plans for some kind of strike—Klea—Klea, forgive me—Caesarion—"

"What? What about Caesarion?"

"He's left, Klea, he's—gone. He's joined them."

"Oh, my GODS! Joined the dissidents?"

"I didn't want to tell you, I wanted to tell you—down there—I—"

"Do something!" The sharp impact of stiletto

heels on the stone. "Zeus! You're his father! DO SOMETHING!"

"That," said Julius's low voice, "is why I think we're in trouble. From both sides of this affair. Caesarion moves to the dissidents. And—"

Upstairs a door opened and closed. Footsteps pelted down the hall upstairs and down the steps— Niccolo heard it coming, turned in utmost vexation and Sargon hardly a moment slower, as a disheveled black-clad figure came bounding down toward them and the door, papers in fist, trailed by a chattering horde of sycophants. *"L'ho fatto! L'ho fatto! Scusi, prego, prego, scusi—"* as he came barreling up to the doors. "Here, is he here?"

Yes-yes-yes, hissed the sycophants, fawning and whisking right on through the closed door so brusquely Niccolo sucked in his gut in reflex. Sargon retreated in dismay as Dante shoved the doors open and charged on, papers in hand. Sargon's mouth stayed open, his feet planted. But Niccolo Machiavelli strolled on through the doors as smoothly as if he had been following Dante Alighieri from as far as upstairs, right into the library and the conference.

Dante never stopped. He walked right up to Julius and waved a paper in Julius' vision. "There, there—it's *here*—"

It evidently had import. Niccolo's brows both lifted as Julius took the paper in his own hand and read it carefully, as Julius listened to the poet chatter computerese at him and jab with a pencil here and here and here at the selfsame paper. And the people in the room had risen from their chairs,

Sargon had trailed through the door, everything had come to a thorough stop.

"Out!" Julius snapped suddenly; but that was for the sycophants, who went skittering and wailing and tumbling over one another in panic flight from the room. No one else budged, except Dante Alighieri, who ventured another poke with the indicating pencil at the paper that trembled in Julius' fist. A quick whispered: "There, *signore*, there, I'm quite sure—"

Julius flicked pencil and hand away with a lift of his hand. "We've found who sent you here," he said, looking straight at Brutus. "How's your current events, son? Six eighty-five from the founding of the City. Your year. Who's the man to fear—in all the world: who's worst?"

Hesitation. Brutus stared at Julius like a bird before the serpent.

You, that look said. It was painfully evident. Then:

"In Asia. Mithridates."

"The butcher of Asia," Julius said. *"Mithridates* is one of our problems—he's the one who plotted this little surprise, holding you out of time. And if he's sprung it—" Julius gave a sweeping glance to all of them. "If he's spent this valuable coin, it's for no small stakes." Julius shook the paper, as if it were legible. "Rameses has moved up to acting commander."

"Ummmn," said Sargon.

"Ummn, indeed," Julius said. "We've got imminent—"

Something whistled over the roof, whumped in a great shattering of glass that rocked the floor

and sent shards of the great library window flying
in a dreadful glitter of inward-bound fragments in
the same instant that everyone dived for cover;
everyone except the poet—Niccolo grabbed him
on his way down, landed on him, and lay in the
shower of glass nose to nose with Dante Alighieri,
in utmost shock at the reflex that had betrayed
him to heroism.

"Prodi," Augustus murmured from under a table. Another strike whumped down. "Efficiency.
What's Hell coming to?"

*"Pol! Iactum habent isti canifornicatores ter
quaterque matrifoedantes Cong!"* Julius scrambled
up in the glass shards, hardly quicker than Mouse
and Sargon and Antonius, with Brutus and Hatshepsut a close third. Augustus elbowed a glass-
hazarded way out from under his table and Kleopatra staggered up on tottering heels, smudges
all over her haute couture. Niccolo delayed, mes-
merized by his own stupidity and the utter shock
in Dante's eyes. *"Agite!"* Julius was shouting.
"Up and out! *Move!"* And Sargon's hand landed on
Niccolo's collar and hauled him up by one hand,
shaking him.

"Out!" Sargon yelled, "Julius is right, they've
got the range—*move,* man!"

Niccolo spun loose and ran when the rest started
to run. From somewhere Hatshepsut had gotten a
deadly little pistol, Julius was waving them out of
the imperiled room, which swirled with smoke
and windborne dust—

Julius passed him then, headed down the hall
through which sycophants rushed and screamed
in terror. He overtook Antonius, grabbed Antoni-

us' arm and shouted at him: *"Get over that hill, get that brood of yours moving—* Take the Ferrari! Klea, have you got the keys?"

Kleopatra stopped against the wall, rummaged her black handbag. Came up with keys. Antonius snatched them and ran, as the house quaked to another explosion and Augustus stopped and looked in anguish at a crack sifting dust from the hall ceiling. Mouse tore by him and hit the stairs downbound, while Sargon and Hatshepsut hit the same set going up.

Niccolo opted for the latter, grabbed the banister, and ran the steps two at a time.

Weapons, that was what the others were after. Their private arsenals.

He had another concern that sent him flying up that stairway like a bat out of hell—

He reached his own apartment, thrust the key in the lock as the floor shook to another shell somewhere in the rose garden. He ran inside, fumbled after more keys, unlocked one desk drawer and drew out the disruptor, unlocked another and snatched up a notebook which he thrust into his shirt.

Then he ran, as another impact shook the villa, somewhere in the vicinity of the swimming pool. Down the hall, Sargon and Hatshepsut were headed for the stairs, Hatshepsut with a laser rifle, Sargon with an M-1 in his hand and a 1990s flex-armor vest above his kilt.

Niccolo overtook them on the second turn, as plaster sifted from the ceiling and the chandelier swayed to another hit.

*   *   *

The Ferrari shot out of the garage in a squeal of tires on gravel; slewed as the man in the tennis shorts spun the wheel and hit the gas. Dirt rained down, and bits of sod.

"He's clear!" Kleopatra cried, and got her head down behind the driveway wall again as dirt and clods and rosebush fragments pelted their position. "You damn dogs!" Her face was smudged and white when she lifted it, and she had a .32 automatic braced in her hand as she peered over the rim of the driveway's bricks. "Let me try," Brutus was saying, while Mouse backed the jeep around and Augustus and Julius swung the rear-mounted launcher into action.

"Don't fire!" Julius yelled at Kleopatra. "Get down, you'll draw attention."

She ducked. "Shells," she told a gibbering sycophant which turned up next to her. "In my bedroom in the top of the closet, in the shoebox—go, fool!"

It gibbered, and whether that was where it was going was anyone's guess. It yelped as it reached the stairs and Sargon and Hatshepsut and Niccolo Machiavelli came tearing out. It scuttled.

"All of you," Julius yelled, "get the hell out of the driveway! Sargon, take left flank round back! Klea, Brutus, get to cover! Mouse, get back inside, take that second-story center window, and save it till we've got targets. And get the hell back down here if they get you spotted!" He dropped a shell into the launcher and it whooshed off in an arcing streak toward Decentral Park, over a rhododendron hedge, a stand of oaks, kicking up a cloud by the time Julius swung the mount over a degree and Augustus popped another one in, laying stitches down a line.

Kleopatra ran low, barefooted over the grass, and scuttled in behind ornamental rock and an aged stand of pine. Brutus hit the ground by her side, eyes wide, about the time a shell landed in the front of the drive and blasted gravel and shrapnel that tore through the thicket, ricocheted off the ornamental boulders, and shredded bark off the pine. A barrage of shells left the jeep-launcher.

"Pro di, pro di," Brutus mumbled in a state of shock. His face was ashen. *"Di—o Iuppiter fulminator maxime potens—"*

"Catapults," Kleopatra said. "Keep *down*, boy!"

Another shell hit. The jeep-launcher returned fire in a steady stream as fast as Julius and Augustus could drop rounds in. Kleopatra risked a look up, just as a cloud of fire erupted in the smoke beyond the park oaks.

"Got the bastards!" she yelled, and remembered to her embarrassment who was beside her, as somewhere a motor began to grind toward them and an incredible long snout poked through the rhododendrons across the street, with crunching and cracking of branches: a Sherman tank, lurching and crashing its way up to street level.

Brutus gave a moan and froze like a rabbit as black-clad Cong followed that juggernaut, attackers pouring out of that gap in the rhododendrons, around either side of the tank. Kleopatra took aim, both hands braced on the rocks, and sent rounds into the oncoming horde. Bullets spanged back, and she ducked and Brutus yelped and ducked as the tank ground on across the pavement toward the lawn.

The ground exploded massively as the treads crunched the curb and hit the grass.

"Mine," Kleopatra gasped, huddling with her arms over the shuddering teenager. "Ours."

Brutus just gulped and tried to keep his lunch down.

Another tank broke through.

Hatshepsut steadied the laser on the rim of the flowerbed and took cool aim at the tank as Sargon blasted away at the black-pajamaed horde that tried to storm their position. Steady fire came from Mouse's position up in the second-floor window.

Niccolo took aim of his own, no good on heavy iron atoms, his little pistol, but effective enough against water-containing flesh. Cong dropped and writhed.

Then a Fokker roared over, and a screaming whine ended in a whump and a deluge of rosebushes and rhododendron.

"Damn!" Sargon yelled, and Hatshepsut rolled over and got a shot off after the plane as it headed for a turn. "Range," she complained. "Damn scatter— Where's the Legion, dammit? Where's Scaevola? Asleep?"

"I imagine," Niccolo said, picking off one and the next targets, "the Cong have *them* pinned. Air support. This is a—"

A shell hit the front porch.

"Mouse!" Brutus cried. *"Down!"* Kleopatra

snapped, and fired off a series of shots, paused and had to reload. Not hide or wisp of the sycophant with the shells. The box she had picked up in the garage was near empty now.

Cong poured through the bushes, and the plane came around for another pass as Julius and Augustus sent missile after missile on as short a trajectory as they could: "We've got to pull it back," Julius yelled and scrambled over the seat, got the jeep into motion backward and then in a gravel-spitting turn around and over the lawn, headed behind Kleopatra's position and the cover of the pines and rocks.

About this time an incoming round hit the retaining wall of the driveway and sprayed the front ranks of the Cong breakthrough at that point with brick, geraniums, and shrapnel.

"Fall back!" Kleopatra yelled, elbowing Brutus into motion ahead of her. *"Get to the jeep—we're getting out of here!"*

The boy moved, got to his feet, and ran for his life. Kleopatra sprinted after him, low as she could, while Augustus got the launcher swiveled round again and sent a ranging shot over their heads into the park.

A returning shell hit the pines—hit the gravel nearby, and Kleopatra went skidding, blinked in astonishment at pain in her back and at the wild-eyed boy who had staggered to one knee, blood starting from half a dozen wounds as he scrambled up and ran back for her.

"Dammit!" she yelled. She had died the focus of heroic fools. She had no more appetite for futilities. She thrust herself up to her knees, grabbed her gun and got that far before the boy got to her, snatched her into his arms and swung into a lumbering run with shots kicking up the pine needles and the fragments everywhere around him.

"Age! Agite!!" Julius yelled at them, while Augustus lobbed another shell overhead. Julius flung himself into the driver's seat, put the jeep's flank between them and the Cong. Augustus abandoned the launcher to haul Kleopatra up and over the side into the floor of the jeep. "Get in!" Julius yelled at Brutus, while shots spanged off the bodywork and the launcher. Augustus came up with a grenade and threw it as Brutus clawed his bloody way into the passenger seat: then the jeep cut tracks out of the lawn as Julius hit the gas and turned. Shots whining past their ears and Brutus took a wild look back over the seat rim at a wave of Cong running past the pines.

Then the sky went up in a sheet of flame and the whole of hell lurched. Julius swerved the jeep wildly out of control and stabilized it again as the air shock rolled over them and bits of trees and rhododendron and worse stuff began to rain down.

"Ran into their own fire!" Augustus was screaming. *"They blew up!"*

In truth there was a billowing cloud where the pines had been, and that group of Cong was a scattered few survivors staggering about in the smoke. Julius swerved and blasted the horn, taking the jeep across behind the house, jouncing and bumping across flowerbeds and the remnants of the rose garden, dodging shellholes. And Sargon and Niccolo and Hatshepsut came straggling disheveled and dusty from the portico of the east wing, firing back as they ran.

Another huge impact rocked the park beyond the house, blew out a last corner of glass from the second story and toppled a cascade of roof tiles.

Then a gathering babble howled beyond the house, as the Cong regrouped their forces.

A second bedraggled pair came staggering out the back door, through the patio. Mouse and Dante Alighieri—holding each other up.

"He got into Pentagram communications," Mouse gasped as they and Sargon's company reached the side of the jeep. "He fed in attack instructions on the Cong's coordinates and the Pentagram zeroed in a couple of *their* rounds right into them. There may be more rounds incoming—"

"Get in!" Julius said. They were already climbing; Sargon boosted Niccolo and Hatshepsut up to hang on over the fenders, scrambled up himself and turned the M-1 behind. The overloaded jeep bounced and wove its way around the craters in the lawn, headed away at speed as Cong poured in a black wave around either side of the house and Sargon, Niccolo, and Hatshepsut sprayed fire across their ranks.

That was when Antonius and Agrippa showed up over the hill in front of them and Mettius Curtius and the First Cav. came rumbling over the rise of the west, with Scaevola and the Tenth Legion hard behind.

The harried Cong veered north, toward open parkland and the urban outskirts.

About this time Attila's division arrived over

that hill, on the bizarrest instructions from the Pentagram he had ever gotten.

"Prosit," said Augustus, lifting his glass. It was a bizarre setting, even for Hell, the red-and-white-striped canopy in the shell-pocked rose garden, with the salvaged furniture—but there was not a window left in the villa and sycophants were in frenzied activity inside, sweeping and patching. *"Prosit heroibus nostris omnibus!"*

"Quite," said Kleopatra, lifting her glass with her left hand. She was in a rose satin dressing-gown, all in flounces, her right arm in a tasteful beige silk sling. "To our heroes!" Inside the villa a plank fell. Saws buzzed. Glass tinkled.

And Kleopatra included Marcus Junius Brutus in that sweep of her glass, so that Brutus hesitated with his own drink in hand, his young face aflame and his eyes filled with a new worship.

Dante Alighieri stood up and stammered out a *"Grazie."* Mouse, accustomed to honors, simply gave a bland nod of his head. And Sargon stood up and raised fragile wine glass in herculean fist.

"To us!" Sargon said with royal modesty, and Hatshepsut added, lifting hers: "To all us heroes!"

"Prosit," said Julius, and drank that one too. And laughed.

But Niccolo Machiavelli walked away from that gathering with a troubled heart, in the mortifying recollection of Dante Alighieri's face nose to nose with him on the library floor.

He had betrayed himself, the most consummately rational man in Hell, as a fool among the shrewd and the calculating—all of whom had advantage to gain from their actions; but he had had none, had absolutely no ulterior motive in that leap which had preserved Dante Alighieri (and gotten him painful slivers of glass in several sensitive portions of his anatomy). He glanced back, at the poet and the boy-assassin basking in the warmth of praise from the powerful; and flinched and walked away in the ruin of all his self-estimation.

A WALK IN THE PARK
Nancy Asire

The plumbing was broken again, but that was nothing new. Every other Friday a pipe broke, the stool stopped, or the sink backed up. Or was it every other Thursday? Keeping track of such things in Hell was a fruitless enterprise: just when the rules started to make sense, the Management changed them.

Telephones were another joy. The small, olive-skinned man scowled at the receiver, slapped it against his palm twice hard enough to sting, returned it to his ear, and listened. He heard the ring on the other end: if the static ever died, he might be able to hear enough to carry on a conversation—*if* anyone answered.

"Plumbers Unlimited," said a toneless voice. "Your name and your problem?"

"Kitchen pipe's broken," he said. "I've shut off the water."

Static. "—name?"

"Bonaparte. Napoleon Bonaparte."

More static. "—sorry, sir. I'm going to put you on hold."

"But—"

Too late. There was a click on the other end, instantly followed by some of the most obnoxious Muzak he had ever heard. He glanced up at the clock on the kitchen wall and watched the minutes tick away. *Oh, God. If I've been placed on Terminal Hold—*

"Hello?" The toneless voice was back.

"Did you have a good dinner," Napoleon asked, "or simply go out for a few drinks?"

"No need to get testy, sir," the voice sniffed. "Kitchen pipes. Let's see—" Static. "—only do pipes on Mondays."

Three days of making coffee water in the bathroom? "Then do it on Monday!" He slammed the receiver down, closed his eyes, and leaned back against the wall.

The doorbell rang. He grimaced. If it was more of those Hari Krishna idiots soliciting donations—

He walked through the dining room into the living room. With a sidelong glance at the entry hall and front door, he went to the picture window. Even then he could not see who stood on the step. A hedge ran alongside his driveway: on its other side a large orange moving van was pulled up in front of the house next door. The Axis Moving Company. New neighbors? It was hard telling who was moving in. Not that he would miss De Gaulle—the fellow was a terrible bore.

The doorbell again: he turned around and stubbed his toe on one of the paperback books lying on the floor. He stooped, picked it up, and looked around for a place to set it down. There were books everywhere—the chairs were stacked with them, the table in front of the window nearly buried. He frowned at the mess, shrugged, went to the entry hall, and opened the door.

For a long, long moment he stood motionless. He darted a quick look at the moving van, then back again, staring at the figure on his doorstep. His caller was tall, elegantly thin, and dressed in one of the best genuine red British general's uniforms Hell could provide.

"Why," he asked of no one in particular, "why out of all the people in Hell does it have to be you?"

Wellington stared. The height was right—short, barely topping his shoulder. But the age was wrong—younger by ten years. Thinner, a full head of hair, olive complexion: and those unnerving eyes. Gray-blue, deepset under level brows, they never missed a thing. Wellington's heart skipped a beat. Could it be—could it possibly be—?

He swallowed heavily. "Napoleon? Is that really you?"

It was Wellington all right—dressed to the nines and snooty as ever. Napoleon sighed quietly, shifted the book from one hand to the other, and leaned up against the door jamb.

"Come off it, Wellington. Who do you think I am?"

Wellington lifted one eyebrow, stepped back slightly and gestured. "Wearing *that?*"

"That what?" He looked down at his faded jeans and thoroughly broken-in sneakers. "You know I detest dressing up. Now, are you coming in or staying out? You're letting in all the cold air."

Wellington glanced over his shoulder at the moving van. "I suppose the movers can handle it. I hire only the best."

"Huhn. That I'm sure of." He gestured with the paperback and Wellington walked into the living room. "Next-door neighbors. Ha! Someone somewhere must have a rotten sense of humor."

"What's going on in here?" Wellington stood in the center of the room, both eyebrows raised as he looked around at the clutter. "My word! Were you robbed?"

Napoleon shut the door. "Robbed? What are you talking about?"

"This." An elegant hand waved.

"My books? I'm running out of space." He followed Wellington into the living room and set the book down on top of the precariously balanced pile on the chair nearest the door. "You didn't come over here to discuss my library, Wellington. What do you want? A cup of sugar?"

Wellington was busy looking for a place to sit down. "Uh . . . no. I actually had no idea that you—that we would be living next door to each other."

"Here." Napoleon walked over to one of the emptier chairs, set the resident books on the floor. "Sit, will you? You're enough to give a man an ulcer."

The right eyebrow rose. Wellington brushed off the chair and sat down, maneuvering his sword around to his side. He removed his black cocked hat, glanced around for somewhere to set it, opting at last for the book-strewn table beside the chair.

"God, Wellington. A sword yet. Have you got rats in your house or what?"

"One has to preserve one's dignity."

"Mon dieu!" Napoleon sat down on the clear end of the couch and looked closely at his visitor. Wellington never did anything without a reason. His appearance could be interpreted as anything from spying for the Management to simple loneliness. "You rang my doorbell for a reason, Wellington. What was it?"

"Mere neighborliness. Introducing myself, you know. I didn't know *you* were living here. Where's Josephine?"

"I haven't the slightest idea. Probably whoring her way down the South Shore. Why?"

"No reason. I'm just surprised to find you living alone. Marie-Louise?"

"Last time I heard she was dealing blackjack at Fred's Casino." Napoleon cocked his head and stared. "Good Lord, Wellington. What are we playing—Twenty Questions?"

Wellington stiffened and drew his head back. "Just being polite." He glanced away and scratched at the end of his long, thin nose. "I still can't believe it."

"What?"

"You . . . me. Next-door neighbors."

Napoleon shrugged. "Oh, well. I'll get over it."

"Eh? *You'll* get over it? How do you think I feel? Even after all these years I can't understand why I, of all people, ended up here!"

"In my living room?"

Wellington closed his eyes briefly, his face bearing the expression of one hugely wronged. "No. Here. In Hell."

"You displeased someone. We've *all* displeased someone. That should be obvious by now."

"But—" Wellington shook his head. "What did I do? What could I have possibly done to deserve this? Now, you, on the other hand—"

"Wellington. You're my guest. Guests don't insult their hosts the minute they walk in the door."

"Sorry. That was a bit mean of me, wasn't it?"

"Nothing out of character." Napoleon leaned back on the couch and studied his visitor. "It's rather strange we haven't run into each other before now. Even our tours of duty were at different times, but that could have been planned. Where were you living?"

Wellington crossed his legs, flicking at an invisible dust mote on his snow-white trousers. "Uptown. Penthouse. Rather nice, though a bit run-down."

"Huhn. Penthouse. That sounds like you. Why'd you move?"

"I had no choice." Wellington's frowned. "I got

a notice in the mail that my lease was up and that I'd be moving to new accommodations. Can you imagine that? The ruddy nerve!"

Forced to move? That's odd. I wonder if De Gaulle was given a choice? "Oh, well. You'll like it here about as much as anywhere. Even the neighbors aren't bad, except Goebbels. He lives on the other side of me. Spies for the Management and makes a general nuisance of himself. Everyone else is basically harmless. The only major drawback we've got to contend with is the park across the street."

"The park?"

"I should say, the Viet Cong in the park. It gets noisy at times."

"Oh. Well." Wellington blinked and looked around the living room. "You'll have to come over and see my house once I've had it redecorated. It isn't all that bad. But whoever used to live there had truly abominable taste. Pretentious, in a word."

"Even for you? That was De Gaulle. You know how *he* is."

"Never met the man, but he obviously has all his taste in his mouth."

Napoleon laughed. "I think I'm going to enjoy having you living next door. I'd forgotten how humorous you can be." He lifted a hand. "No, no. That wasn't a snide remark. Besides, if nothing else pans out, we can always keep the other neighbors busy trying to figure out why we don't kill each other off."

The Rule Book was a morass of the most tangled laws, ordinances, and regulations that had ever blighted the universe. To make things worse, instead of being printed in several volumes, the book came in one huge binding. It was so heavy Napoleon had not moved it from the dining-room table for years, just shared his dinner with it.

He flipped through a few pages, ran a hand through his hair, and sighed. It might take decades more of sifting through the legalistic jargon to find the loophole he sought, but one of the things he had learned was the value of patience.

He leaned back in his chair, took a long swallow of coffee and found it had gone cold. Loopholes had to be there. No law had ever been written without at least one loophole. Lawyers would have starved to death otherwise. Justice was not the issue. Wellington agonized over how he had ended up in Hell. The thought had tortured Napoleon at first, too, until he had realized that was his own particular punishment—not knowing why. Once he had recognized the trap for what it was, he gave up wondering. The fact simply *was*. There was no use in puzzling over why one was here: the object now was to find a way out.

Such a Way Out possibly lay hidden in the gargantuan book before him.

He turned a page. An explosion rocked the house, rattled the china—small flakes of plaster drifted down from the ceiling on the print. Napoleon sighed, shoved his chair back, and walked to the living-room window. *Damned Cong! Can't they aim any better than that?*

This time there was no pothole in the street, no crater in the front yard. The sea of dead leaves whirled about in the wind and then was still. He rubbed his chin and looked out across the lawn and street into the park. Decentral Park everyone called it, and it was as large or larger than its earthly namesake. He stared over into the tangled brush and trees. Nothing moved but the Vietcong were out there somewhere, obviously more confused than usual.

Unless, he thought uneasily, *it's the dissidents.*

Furious knocking sounded at his door. He walked to the entry hall and peered through the lower window; Wellington stood on the doorstep, so angry his face was white. Napoleon opened the door.

"What's wrong, Wellington?"

Wellington waved a hand toward his house. "It's those idiot Cong!" he yelled, walking into the living room, a few stray leaves entering behind. Napoleon closed the door, leaned back against it, prepared to listen to some tale of craters in the sideyard or driveway. "Blew a hole right in my living-room roof! Can you believe that? My living-room roof!"

Napoleon blinked. The Cong had always had poor aim, but this was ridiculous!

"Complain," he suggested. "Call the Hall of Injustice. Yelling at me won't solve anything."

Wellington paced from one end of the living-room to the other, threading his way in and out of the piles of books on the floor. "I tried that," he snapped. "The phone's dead! The lights are off! The—"

"Use mine, then." Napoleon motioned across the entry hall to his telephone in the study. "It generally works."

"Thanks."

Wellington went to the telephone, picked it up and punched in the number. He glared at the receiver and turned to Napoleon, his face now reddened with rage.

"Slap the receiver in your hand a few times." Napoleon mimed the procedure. "Sometimes that solves the problem." He walked to the living-room window, heard Wellington pound the telephone against the wall. *God! He still can't follow directions, can he?* Leaning his forehead on the glass, he tried to see over into Wellington's front yard. Yes. The shell had hit the house: shingles and pieces of wood lay strewn about among the dead leaves. He shifted uneasily from one foot to the other. Events such as this and their resultant complaints usually brought the Authorities swarming. The last thing he needed was Authorities camped out on his doorstep.

Wellington slammed the receiver down in the cradle and stomped into the living-room.

"Inept clowns! It's a wonder Hell hangs together with the stupidity of the—"

"Wellington. Shut up. Do you want us to be drafted again? I just got out of that idiot collection of yahoos they call the army and I don't want to go back again, not for a long, long time."

Wellington glanced around. "D'you think your house is bugged?"

"It's hard telling. I just don't take the risk." He walked back to the dining room; Wellington followed. "What did they have to say at the Hall of Injustice?"

"You mean what *didn't* they say? I talked to one person who said he couldn't help me; he transferred me to another fellow who said he was no longer in charge of shelling from the park but that he would put me in contact with someone who was. This woman said she was a vacation replacement and wasn't all that sure how to handle such things, but that she would transfer me to her supervisor. I got placed on hold and finally talked to the supervisor who told me she was involved in something far more important, but that she would let me talk to someone who could help me." Wellington waved his hands. "It was the first person I talked to, and he said he was going to lunch, to call back later."

"Huhn. Typical." Napoleon gestured at a chair by the dining-room table and took the one near it. "Sit, Wellington. It doesn't look like you're going to get much done for a while."

"But it's cold! Bloody cold!" Wellington jerked the chair back and sat down, one neatly booted foot tapping nervously on the floor. "I can't be expected to live in a house with no lights, no heat, and a hole this big in the ceiling!"

"Oh, move in with me until you get your place fixed."

Wellington stared. "Move in with you?"

"Look, Wellington. I know the place isn't up to your usual high standards of neatness, but it *is* warm and," he spread his hands far apart, "I don't have a hole in my ceiling this big."

"But—" Wellington gnawed on his lower lip. "Oh, all right. I think we can live in the same house for a few days."

Napoleon rolled his eyes. "For a few days. It had better be only for a few days." He pointed toward the front door. "Go get whatever you want to bring over. And"—he caught at Wellington's sleeve as the other stood to go—"keep this in mind. One lousy crack about my cooking, and you're out on the street!"

Wellington had brought surprisingly few things with him when he moved in. Napoleon had expected a full contingent of servants, the best crystal, and other creature comforts. Since he was going to spend more than just a day or two with his house guest, Napoleon had even moved most of the books out of the living room. Now he could barely turn around in the study, but it was better than listening to Wellington complain.

The Iron Duke was presenty ensconced in a chair before the television, one of the few appliances in Hell which rarely broke down. Napoleon made a face and looked back at the Rule Book. *I wish the damned thing would short out! If I hear "Danny for Dogcatcher: A Paid Political Announcement" one more time, I'll throw up.* Political announcements aired with nearly the same frequency as used-car ads. He flipped to another page and squinted at the minuscule print. *No, I'll go blind first, reading this idiot book.*

The commercial for Ed's Used Cars played for the fourteenth time, complete with banjos and howling dogs. Napoleon tried to ignore the blather in the background but that grew harder by the minute. Wellington, however, appeared unconcerned, or unconscious. Napoleon frowned toward the elegant figure lounging in the chair. *God! He's likely asleep. Either that, or his brain's finally turned to mush.*

"And now," the resonant voice of the television announcer blared, "we bring you the late afternoon movie, 'Godzilla and the Wolf Man Meet Buck Rogers in the Twenty-fifth Century!' "

"That does it!" Napoleon shoved his chair back from the table and stalked into the living room. "Wellington, would you *please* turn that nonsense off!" Wellington looked up, his eyes innocently round. "How do you expect me to concentrate when—"

The doorbell rang.

"It's for me," Wellington said, standing and pulling his uniform coat into tidy lines of neatness. "I'm expecting company."

"Good. Why don't you go out somewhere?"

Wellington looked down his nose, sniffed something unheard, and went to answer the door. Napoleon glared after. *Patience, patience. He's only going to be here for a few more days.* He walked across the living-room and flipped off the TV. *God! Let it only be a few more days!*

The visitor was speaking Spanish, his voice very quiet. Wellington had probably learned the language during the infamous Spanish campaign. Napoleon peered at the door, but Wellington blocked his view; he was left with the impression of a short, dark man clad in nondescript clothing. He shrugged. Wellington being Wellington, he was probably ordering some Spanish sherry.

"I'm going out for a while," Wellington announced, taking his cloak from the coat-tree by the door. He threw it around his shoulders and left, slamming the door behind.

Napoleon shook his head. The silence in the house was wonderful. He went into the kitchen, checked to see if the newly fixed pipe was behaving itself, and poured a fresh cup of coffee. Leaning back against the counter, he sipped contentedly at his cup. *Wellington's not really such a bad fellow but he* is *trying on the nerves*.

Suddenly, he remembered Wellington's odd reluctance to move in. "I think we can live in the same house for a few days," Wellington had said. Napoleon cursed softly, his coffee gone sour. He set his cup down and began to pace up and down the kitchen, hands locked behind his back. Wellington never had told him why he had lost his lease on the penthouse. Or why he had ended up moving next door. Add to that several hushed phone calls in the middle of the night along with other oddities. And now this visitor.

Napoleon's heart skipped a beat. He stopped pacing, turned and walked quickly into the livingroom. The drapes were open: he paused, went to the end of the window, and carefully peered out behind the curtains. Wellington and his Spanish-speaking visitor were nowhere to be found. But Napoleon could see the head and part of one shoulder of someone standing down by the evergreens at the far end of the driveway. Whoever stood there was hidden by the branches and the dark light of early evening.

He let the drape fell back. *The Authorities? Oh, God! What's Wellington got himself wrapped up in now? Not the dissidents! Not that bunch! Especially now that Hadrian's disappeared.* A cold chill ran down his spine. *And me. The twit's got me mixed up in this, too. He's living in my house! Aiding and abetting and all that!*

He quickly reviewed what he had in the house that could incriminate him if the Authorities ran a search. Not much. That was one of the advantages to having a near eidetic memory. *But Wellington? Lord knows what he's dragged in.*

The doorbell rang.

Napoleon froze, glanced quickly around the room: nothing looked out of place. "Here it comes," he muttered, walking toward the door. "The fertilizer's hit the ventilation system!"

He paused briefly, turned on the entry hall light, and opened the door.

It was the Authorities, or at least one of them—a tall, saturnine fellow, bundled up in a rumpled trench coat that had seen better days. A dark hat was pulled down over the man's eyes, and there was a suspicious bulge under the fellow's left armpit.

"General Bonaparte?"

"Yes?"

The Authority glanced at Napoleon's sweater, jeans, and sneakers. "You're out of uniform," he said in a voice cold as his eyes.

"I'm retired. Please, come in. It's cold outside."

The Authority came into the entry hall and looked into the living-room. His dark eyes moved from place to place, scanning and cataloging the room's contents. He glanced back.

"Arthur Wellesley's living with you, isn't he?"

Napoleon drew a deep breath, shut the door, and schooled his face into an expressionless mask. "Wellington? Yes, he's living with me. Has been for the past few days." Before the Authority could speak, he assumed his most official air. "I'm glad you stopped by. Something has to be done about getting Wellington's house fixed. And getting the Viet Cong out of the park. I've complained about them a number of times, as has Wellington. They shelled his house and his roof still has a hole in it. The damage report went in days ago but neither of us has seen even a hint of a repair crew. We both served in the army for years. Service of that type should have its rewards. Certainly you could arrange to get Wellington's house fixed sometime soon."

The Authority stared, his thin face frozen into an expression of astonishment. He gathered himself and frowned deeply. "General Bonaparte. Please let me remind you that *I* represent the government here, not you."

"That's obvious," Napoleon said lazily, allowing none of his anxiety to show, "because if I did, there wouldn't be any Cong left in the park."

The man's face reddened. "Just because you're some hot-shot general doesn't give you the right to—"

Napoleon lifted one eyebrow. "Why did you want to talk about Wellington if not to get his house fixed? You just said you represent the government, and last time I checked, the government was in charge of housing."

"Don't change the subject, General! We're talking about Wellington, not his house. He's had some strange visitors, and now they're coming here since he's moved in with you."

"Oh?" Napoleon's mouth went dry. "I haven't noticed anyone stranger than usual in the neighborhood. There's the Cong in the park, Caesar goes by in his jeep every now and again, and there's always the door-to-door salesmen."

"May I ask where Wellington is?"

"Out. I think he went off to buy some sherry."

The sense of menace in the room grew more intense. Napoleon kept his stance relaxed, his expression overly polite. The Authority stared at him for a long moment, then turned away. He opened the door, paused, looked back over his shoulder, and smiled thinly.

"If you value your well-being, General Bonaparte, let me remind you what the penalty is for consorting with dissidents."

"Dissidents! I wouldn't be caught dead with such riffraff."

The Authority smiled again, even colder this time. "You just may be caught dead somewhere, General, with or without dissidents, if you don't show the government a little more respect. Good evening."

Napoleon waited until the Authority had disappeared down the driveway, then shut the door and stood resting his forehead on it.

"Dammit, Wellington! If you've got us both in trouble with the Management, *I'll* kill you before they do!"

He straightened, took a long, deep breath, walked back into the kitchen and flipped on the overhead light. His coffee had gone cold: he tossed it, refilled the cup with fresh, and bolted it down, burning his tongue as he did so. Where was Wellington? He closed his eyes wearily. Not the dissidents! Not even Wellington could want out of Hell badly enough to consort with the dissidents. And yet—

He frowned, set his empty cup in the sink, and went to the front closet. His greatcoat was shoved to the end, buried behind several of Wellington's cloaks. He yanked it off the hanger and threw it on. Checking his jeans pocket to see if he had his keys, he turned off the lights. For a moment he stood in the darkness, looking out the living room window, but saw no one. He opened the door, shut it behind him, made sure it was locked, and set off down the driveway.

It was never entirely dark in Hell—the sky always had a reddish tinge to it. Napoleon turned to his left, walked down the street, head bowed, the cold north wind coming straight out of the park. Bare, gnarled tree limbs rattled above him, stark against the lurid sky.

He looked around as he walked through the dry leaves skittering out of the park. The neighbors' houses were much like his own: stone, rough wood, large windows, yards with split-rail fences or rows of shrubs. Across the street, the park stretched off into the distance, a tangle of vast expanses of trees and brush. Unkempt; it was still better than living close to a lot of other places he could think of.

The wind moaned through the trees in the park; he heard the distant angry voices of the Viet Cong, but all else was quiet. The neighborhood was deserted, the windows of the houses glowed with lamplight: everyone seemed to be indoors, likely at their evening meals. Even Attila's house was quiet—he was off with the National Guard for the weekend, and his wives were probably going mad without him around to yell at.

Napoleon rubbed his chin and kicked a pebble off to one side of the street. *All right. Think it out. Is Wellington involved with the dissidents, or does it only appear that way? And if he is involved, what in the name of all the fiends in Hell am I going to do about it?* He could hardly turn the idiot in, though that would be the safest thing. No. Whatever had happened in the past, he and Wellington at least knew and respected each other. Death had not changed that.

He heard voices coming toward him down the street. He turned, darted off into Louie (XVI) the Locksmith's front yard, and burrowed in behind a low-hanging pine tree at the end of the darkened driveway. His heart skipped a beat. It was Wellington's voice—Wellington talking to the mysterious Spanish-speaking visitor.

He tried to make some sense of what they were saying, but could not hear enough words. Italian and Spanish were distant cousins, but even if he had known more than a smattering of Spanish he

could not have understood. The wind was too fit-
ful: what was said, too quiet.

At last Wellington passed him in the street, not
more than two paces away. He waited, hidden by
the pine tree. There were times when being short
was an asset.

When no one followed, he stepped out from behind the tree, quickened his pace, and caught up
with Wellington.

"All right, Wellington," he hissed. "What's going
on?"

Wellington jumped nearly a foot to one side. His
face tight with anxiety, he whirled toward Napoleon, hand searching for the sword he usually
wore.

"Cut the dramatics," Napoleon said. "You've got
a lot of explaining to do, and I suggest you start
now. I've just had a visit from the Authorities, and
you were the subject of conversation."

Wellington stared, his face still pale in the dim
light. "The Authorities? Asking about me? Whatever for?"

"Damned good question. Now answer me this.
Why did you have to move? Who's been calling
you in the middle of the night? And, even more
importantly, who was your visitor?"

"Wait a minute here. I haven't done anything—"

"That's not what the Authorities think. Now you
either spill it, Wellington, or you're going back to
your own house, great big hole in the roof and
all."

Wellington stared a moment longer, then turned
and started walking down the tree-lined street.
Napoleon hurried to catch up.

"I haven't done anything *that* bad," Wellington said. "Nothing worse than most people."

"Those phone calls, the fellow you went out with tonight—they weren't Cubans, were they?"

Wellington was silent for a few breaths. "Yes, they were. What of it?"

Napoleon's heart lurched. "Jesus, Mary, and Joseph! You aren't involved with the dissidents, are you?"

"God, Napoleon!" Wellington stopped suddenly. "I may look dumb sometimes, but I'm not! The dissidents! I'd be insane to get caught up with them!" A look of horror crossed his sharp features. "You don't mean to say—the Authorities don't . . ."

Napoleon sighed quietly. "Yes. They do. I'd be willing to bet on it."

"Oh, God." Wellington's shoulders slumped. "If I'm guilty of anything, it's dealing with the black market. The people I've spoken with *have* been Cubans, but that's because I've been trying to get my hands on some good brandy, some decent cigars . . ."

"Cigars?" Napoleon closed his eyes wearily, then looked up at Wellington. "They're after you, Wellington, and knowing the Authorities, they'll shoot first and interrogate later. Thoroughly."

"But I'm not guilty of consorting with the dissidents!" Wellington's voice took on a self-righteous tone. "I'll bloody well—"

"You're not going to do a damned thing. If I've learned anything at all about the Authorities, they watched me leave. I don't think they trailed me. And that inept clown I talked with tonight—he's not going to report back to his superiors before he takes you in. He's the type who wants all the glory for himself."

"They've probably staked out the house," Wellington said. He glanced down the street, then back again. "You know the neighborhood—I don't. What do you suggest?"

Napoleon rubbed his chin. "Get back to that yard I hid in, the one with the fence running across the front. There's a pine tree close to the street. Hide behind it. I'm going back home. If I can, I'll send those idiots off on a chase they'll remember for years."

"But—"

"Move, Wellington." He grinned in anticipation. "That skinny little bastard threatened both of us. And I'm not going to let him have the satisfaction of thinking he got away with it."

Wellington turned and walked quickly back to the house Napoleon had pointed out. The pine tree stood at the edge of the yard and looked like a more than adequate hiding place. He glanced over his shoulder—Napoloen's retreating figure had all but vanished into the darkness. He shrugged, grimaced at the thought of possibly getting dirty, and slipped in behind the pine tree.

He sneezed once and then again. This would not do, not at all. He fished around for his handkerchief, pulled it out of his sleeve, and blew his nose. And sneezed again. He held his breath, then tried breathing through his mouth. That was somewhat better. All he needed to do was to give his position away because he was allergic to this type of pine tree.

He peered out through the branches. The street was deserted, fading away into darkness. He disliked leaving his fate in someone else's hands. What if it was a trap? So far Napoleon had been a good neighbor, but— He cringed inwardly. There was always the problem of Waterloo.

No. The past was over. They were both trapped here in Hell and it made little difference in the end who had won what battle where. Besides, he admitted in a fit of honesty, if Grouchy had not been so fond of strawberries and Blücher had not turned back from his retreat— He sneezed again. Waterloo would have been *his* defeat, not Napoleon's.

He shivered in the chill. The Authorities? They couldn't possibly think he was involved with the dissidents! He always made it a point to play by the rules when he could. Rewards for good behavior? Anything was possible.

One thing's for bloody sure. I'll have to give up dealing with the black market for a while. He sighed wistfully. *Pity. They've got the best damned cigars in Hell!* Everything sold in the shops was of shoddy workmanship—all the better to torture the consumer and the repairmen. Perhaps later, when things had settled down, he could reestablish his contacts with the marketeers.

He wiped his nose; another sneeze threatened, then subsided. He had no idea what Napoleon was doing, but trusted to the other's plans.

Not much choice, is there? If he gets me out of this mess—I'll throw a party, that's what I'll do. His heart sank. *But where will I ever come up with the brandy and cigars?*

As Napoleon neared his house, he quickened his pace, glanced back over his shoulder, and tried to appear as furtive as he could. He paused briefly at the end of the driveway: if his sixth sense was working at all, the Authority and his men were stationed in the bushes by the sides of the house. Glancing once more behind for good measure, he walked up the driveway, fishing for his keys. His house was quiet; the porch light should have turned itself on by now. The bulb had obviously burned out—another damned inconvenience.

"And where have you been, General Bonaparte?"

The tall, thin figure of the Authority stepped out from the shadows. Napoleon set his face to an expression of shocked surprise.

"You startled me," he said accusingly. "Where have I been? Out looking for Wellington, that's where."

"Oh?" The Authority's face sharpened, his eyes narrowing slightly. "And why, may I ask, were you hunting for him?"

Napoleon moved a few steps closer: as expected, the tall man faded back a bit. "Wellington's not involved with the dissidents. If anything, he's scared to death of them. Now I'm not saying that *they* aren't after him. With the situation what it is at General Headquarters . . ." The Authority flinched. "If Wellington's had strange visitors, I'd chalk it up to his sometimes outré taste in drinking companions."

"You don't expect me to believe this claptrap, do you, General? If Wellington isn't guilty, why'd you go off after him? He can talk for himself, can't he?"

"I was going to advise him to call you people and explain things. But I couldn't find him." Napoleon let his shoulders fall, then glanced quickly back down the street. Out of the corner of one eye, he saw the Authority look in the same direction. "Now, is there anything else that—"

"Why are you so worried about what's going on back there?"

Napoleon started, tried to appear surprised that the man had noticed. "Uh . . . no reason."

The Authority's eyes narrowed and his hand crept toward the bulge under his left armpit. "Don't give me that. What's back there?"

"I'm not sure." He looked down at his feet, then up again. "I think it may be a band of dissidents."

"What?" The Authority reached inside his coat and withdrew the gun from its shoulder holster. His thin face sharpened even more. "And why do you think that?"

"I heard something like Spanish being spoken off in the park. And I think I saw several fellows in fatigues darting in and out of the trees."

The Authority's eyes narrowed to slits. Cold menace poured out from him, but this time it was directed elsewhere. He waved broadly with one arm and several trench-coated men materialized from the shadows.

"Take us there!"

Napoleon drew himself up and crossed his arms.

"You're *ordering* me to take you there?" he asked in clipped tones. "I may be retired, but I *do* remain on the best of terms with the Supreme Commander and his staff."

The second mention of the Supreme Commander, alluding to the kidnapping and the rest of it, gave him the results he had hoped for. The Authority glanced hastily around at his men.

"If you'd be so kind as to tell us where you saw these dissidents, General. . . ."

"Well, if that's all you want," Napoleon said, rubbing the end of his nose to hide his smile, "I'll be glad to take you there."

The Authority's jaw tightened but he remained silent. Napoleon turned and led the way down the driveway and out onto the darkened street. He noticed even more trench-coated footpads slink out from the hedge between his yard and Wellington's. Soon, he was not only followed by the Authority, but twelve gun-toting flunkies. *Marvelous*, he thought. *A parade.*

The street lights had not come on yet; he tried to calculate odds but gave it up as hopeless. The only thing he could hope for was the opposition's familiarity with their own turf.

Three houses to the west of his and across the street, he reached a familiar section of the park. Bushes and tangled undergrowth grew close to the edge of the street; beyond, trees clogged the darkness. "There," he said, pointing into the park. "I saw the dissidents there."

The Authority licked his lips and looked sidelong at his men as they waited behind. Napoleon could read the man's thoughts like the morning newspaper. He would not call for reinforcements, not this one. He wanted all the credit for himself.

"My thanks, General." The Authority beckoned his men closer. "I'll remember your help to my superiors."

Napoleon bowed his head and walked across the street away from the park. Behind, he heard the Authority issuing orders to his men: the brush rattled noisily as they disappeared into the night.

Napoleon stifled a laugh and kept walking. The yard where Wellington hid was only two houses away, a perfect vantage point. He quickened his pace, reached the yard and turned. There was no one left on the street now; the Authority had not even thought to leave someone behind in case there was trouble.

The street lights flickered on—a garish sodium glare. It would make little difference. Ten paces into the park and primal darkness reigned.

After a quick look around, Napoleon walked up into the driveway. "Wellington," he hissed. "Get out of there and watch this one, will you?"

A sneeze answered him, then another. Louie's pine tree rustled as Wellington crept out from behind it. Napoleon looked up, grinned, and pointed.

"Any moment now," he predicted.

"Any moment now what?" asked Wellington. He drew his cloak closer and dabbed at the end of his nose with a rumpled handkerchief. A few pine needles had lodged in his hair: he meticulously picked them out. "Napoleon. What have you been—?"

Shots rang out in the park; excited voices yelled in an unintelligible language. There were screams, more shots, and a medium-sized explosion. Then all was quiet.

"Good God, Napoleon! What was all that about?"

Napoleon put his hands in his coat pockets and rocked back and forth from heel to toe. "A little bit of strategy," he said. The wind switched and blew the acrid smell of explosives into the yard. "I don't think we'll be seeing the Authority or his men for a long time. They just took a walk in the park with the Viet Cong."

Wellington stared, then a slow grin spread across his face. "Damn," he said, amusement rich in his voice. "You haven't lost your touch, have you?"

"I hope not." The wind blew sharper now—dead leaves ran before it. "Come on, Wellington. It's cold. Let's go home."

THE HAND OF PROVIDENCE

David Drake

Hermann and Reinhard hid in the ornamental shrubbery, cursing under their breath at the way the branches spiked them, while liches like ambulant skeletons pulled down a couple on the grounds of the Villa of Augustus.

The woman was a Scot who had been a queen and who did not, in Reinhard's opinion, deserve what was happening to her. The man was named Patton, and he deserved much worse.

"There are more of them now than for . . ." said Hermann and shrugged, "for many years." The slide of his Model 97 trench gun was loose enough to have a little play, and his left hand worked it silently back and forth that fraction of an inch.

Three liches were standing hipshot at the edge of the clearing, leaning on spears and chittering as another trio ringed the couple on the lawn. The man drew a pair of heavy handguns and pointed them at a liche whose head and limb seemed bare bone but whose torso had an integument like horn or seared parchment to give it substantial bulk.

"There aren't many," said Reinhard as he looked from the liches to his own pistol and then to his companion. Each of the hidden men would have been 36 if he were alive—had been 36 when they died, millennia apart—but there was little physical resemblance between them. Reinhard Heydrich was tall and fair, his face aristocratically long and his frame slim without being in the least frail.

"Perhaps we could—" he continued tentatively, waiting for a cue in the expression of his companion.

"I could have used you," said Hermann, who had been chief of the Cherusci until the Cherusci butchered him with long-bladed swords, "to send to Varus as a counselor. There would be a *thousand* of them, all around us."

He indicated the brush about them with a bob of his head and his olive-drab cap, intended for insulation beneath a helmet and worn now with its earflaps velcroed over the top. His moustache was broad and black, and his frame was so solidly muscular that he looked short even though he was within an inch or two of six feet. "Not that he needed it," the chieftain added thoughtfully. "Varus."

Beyond, the encircled man began firing rapidly with the pistol in his right hand, though the revolver in his left managed only one shot and that skyward. The liche behind him took a cautious step like that of a horse testing its footing. The woman screamed and dodged sideways, the motion drawing the liche in a lunge and a sweep at the woman's throat with the spear it held.

The man spun. He had not hit the liche at which he had been firing, but he now put a gun against the bare skull of the creature finishing with a short grip on its spear the job of decapitating the woman. The shot scattered fragments of the empty calvarium and disarticulated half the jawbone. The liche collapsed over its victim, crumbling away while the woman still thrashed and spouted in her death agonies.

One of the other liches bounded the three meters separating him from the gunman, skewering him from the base of the neck and upward through the brain till stopped by the crossbar which kept the blade from sinking too deeply. The pithed victim's arms slapped at the air, flinging away his handguns, as the liche lifted him by the spearshaft and began to walk toward its waiting companions.

The woman had ceased to move. The remaining liche wired her ankles with the casual expertise of a farm wife wringing a chicken's neck. With its spear shouldered and the woman dangling upside down from it like a hobo's bindle, the liche followed its fellows. All five of them disappeared into the undergrowth.

There was no sign of the liche which had been shot. The scene was marked only by the pistols, the woman's wig, and the grass spattered with blood from the victims' throat and nostrils respectively.

Hermann stood up, wiping a speck of dust from the 17-inch bayonet of his shotgun with a nonchalance belied by the film of sweat on his broad forehead. "You see, when I tell you to wait, you must wait."

"I never questioned your instincts," Reinhard said coolly as he stood also, reholstering his pistol while holding the flap back with his left hand. "We'll have further need of them, I'm sure, before we locate Hadrian."

"The Leader," said Hermann in what he thought was agreement as he began striding toward the facing wall of the villa, a double tier of pillars. There were fleeting motions within the archways, but they seemed more ephemeral than secretive. There was no sign of anyone whom either man would have termed a person, and the shouts of the woman when the liches first broke cover had apparently gone unremarked from the building.

"Hadrian," Reinhard snapped in correction, but his companion gave no sign of having heard.

Hermann advanced across the cleared area at what seemed an awkward shuffle, but he covered the ground faster than Reinhard's legs could scissor along at a walk and keep up. The black uniform Heydrich wore suited his trim figure very well, but it was cut too tight for unimpeded motion. Still, they could not very well have driven up to the front entrance of the villa and expected to gain their present ends.

There were ornamental yews around the base of the building, concealing the fact that the pillars were set on a stone footing a meter above the ground. Hermann, who wore loose cotton breeches and footgear from a time beyond Reinhard's own— as light as socks, but impervious to thorns—leaped onto the colonnade with no more discomfort than the slap of crossed bandoliers against his bare chest. Reinhard, by contrast, had the alternative embarrassments of having to ask for help, or chancing a fall on the coping and sprawling on his face.

He took the second option and sprawled as he knew he must. *Accursed* trousers.

It struck him, not for the first time, that the punishments one received in this—place—were sometimes earned by lesser sins than those for which weaklings prayed to be absolved.

There was nothing on the portico or in the hallway off it which they next entered. Motion, perhaps, and fear—sycophants, fluttering away with tales of slaughter on the lawn, of armed intruders, of cobwebs permitted to accumulate between the pillars of an upper hallway. They were souls without personality, the sort of trash that accreted to nodes of power like Augustus or Hadrian . . . though they did not include Hadrian's own soul, whatever he might have feared on his deathbed.

Reinhard's boots sent a series of echoes down the hallway as he paused, arms akimbo, and waited for a considered response by the residents of the sprawling villa. A helicopter passed overhead with rotor blades clopping like a sign saying KICK ME. Various automatic weapons attempted to do so in a distant whisper. There was a crash behind the two poised men. They jumped, Hermann slashing at the empty air with his glittering bayonet. A patch of fresco had been shaken from the vaulted ceiling, though the vibration causing the damage had been scarcely noticeable.

"Hughes Tool," Reinhard said as he turned again,

reaching for his breast pocket and pretending that the motion had not started as an attempt to draw his pistol. "Well, they don't seem to be coming for us."

He began to unfold the photocopied architectural plan he had brought from the microfilmed files at headquarters. "We will do what we need, and leave; and because we have not embarrassed Augustus openly, he will not find it necessary to hinder us." Smirking to his companion, Reinhard added, "It works as well with, shall we say, husbands and fathers, you realize. No embarrassment, no trouble."

"Who cares about trouble?" Hermann snarled, but he was nervous under a concrete roof in a way he had not been in the brush. His bayoneted shotgun kept questing in abrupt little jerks at an angle to his line of vision as if he hoped to take something unawares. "Besides, Augustus is afraid to die. Even here. And he knows I'm not afraid to kill."

Reinhard swore and crumpled the crackling plan.

All Hermann's bravado disappeared as he snatched the paper from his companion and tried to smooth it with his one free hand. "But it's blank," he said in puzzlement. "We're lost!"

"We're not lost," Reinhard snapped. "Yes, the *accursed* copy has faded after a few hours, no more. But I have seen the plan, and we will follow my memory of it."

Hermann grunted something that might have been assent, because he followed Reinhard as he strode down the hallway with heels rapping loudly but too precisely to be certain proof of anger. As they strode along, Reinhard looking for the staircase that would give access to the back upper portico, the Cheruscan chieftain batted at frescoes with the iron buttplate of his shotgun.

The hallway—it wasn't the one Reinhard had intended to follow—ended with a trompe l'oeil staircase painted on the solid wall to the left and a real staircase to the right, concealed behind a curtain which Hermann ripped from its rod with an upward, disemboweling stroke from his bayonet.

"That's correct," said Reinhard as if his pause had been for effect. He preceded his companion up the stairs at a quick jog, knowing the Cheruscan was not comfortable on them. This would be a useful reminder of who was in charge on this search for Hadrian, a task for which Reinhard had enlisted Hermann only because of his muscle and the fact that his personality made a useful foil on occasion for a trained intellect.

Hermann's weapon clattered repeatedly on the sides and ceiling of the helical staircase, slowing him and giving Reinhard a moment to take in his surroundings at the upper level, a portico indeed but an interior one surrounding a skylighted banquet room on the ground floor. He did not remember a banquet room on this side of the villa. Unless they had gotten mixed up in their directions *out*—

"Well, where's Machiavelli's room?" demanded Hermann, his face red with marginally suppressed anger and his whole head and front flecked with bits of plaster from the staircase. Momentarily, Reinhard wondered whether the villa had taken its vengeance for the battering Hermann had given its hallway. This place was accursed.

Of course.

The essence of leadership is decision. "We will go—" the taller German started to say, with no certainty of how he would complete the sentence, when a small man in robes stepped muttering onto the portico from the nearest room to the right and, in his concentration on reaching the stairs, almost walked into Hermann's chest.

"*Scusi, sig—*" the little man began, rebounding more from surprise than from contact.

"*Niccolo,*" Reinhard said in pleasure tinged by an equal surprise.

Unbidden, Hermann's free hand caught Machiavelli by the wrist. The shotgun reached around from the other side, so that the bayonet's point stuck out ahead of the Florentine and its unsharpened back edge lay like a finger of death against his right ear.

"What are you doing?" Machiavelli sputtered. "What are you doing *here?*"

"You didn't come to Headquarters when summoned," said Reinhard with a sad smile toward his own long, slim fingers, perfectly manicured and uninvolved with anything that might be happening to the little man at this moment.

"You had no *right,*" the Florentine said, his voice dropping into a whisper. "You weren't even supposed to know of my, my connection, I was *promised . . .*"

He twisted his head left, whether to speak to Hermann or to turn away from bare steel, and said, "Arminio—"

The Cheruscan released Machiavelli's wrist in order to grab the smaller man by the face itself.

His hand was so big that the thumb and middle finger clamped near opposite earholes and squeezed hard enough that the palm threatened to break the Florentine's nose. "Hermann, now, little Roman," the chieftain said in a voice as implacable as his fingertips. "Can you remember that, I wonder?"

He straight-armed Machiavelli, raising the shotgun with the same motion so that the Florentine could crash against a pillar and sprawl backward onto the mosaic flooring.

The look that Machiavelli gave them as he raised himself onto his elbows was not anger, Reinhard thought, and not even fear. It seemed to be resignation and no more, though perhaps with deliberateness curtained behind it as it was sometimes in the eyes of the Jews and Gypsies he had seen when he inspected the camps built to his design at Auschwitz, at Buchenwald and Belsen and so many other sites . . .

"Your pardon, Messer Hermann," said the Florentine softly. "It was not my intention to offend you, Prince of the Elbe. Perhaps you would permit me to lead you into a room"—he shifted his weight onto his left palm and elbow so that his right hand could indicate the door from which he had stepped onto the portico—"where we would less probably be interrupted to your distress."

Reinhard nodded crisply. "Of course," he said. "We don't wish to handicap your important services, Niccolo . . . but you must recognize that the priority now must be locating the Supreme Commander so that he can be released. Yes?"

"Of course," said Machiavelli as he rolled to his feet quickly to avoid Hermann's hand which reached down to lift him with as little delicacy as it had spilled him there. Robes swirling and the cap he had snatched back from the floor crumpled in his hand, the Florentine pulled open the door. It was mounted on pivot pegs rather than true hinges, and they squealed angrily as Machiavelli dared not.

The taller German motioned Machiavelli inside ahead of him. "I wonder, Messer Reinhard," said the little Florentine as he followed Hermann's instinctive precedence into a badly lighted study, "how it chances that you found me, ah, in this building. Augustus himself directed you?"

"He had a map," said the Cheruscan as he lifted an apple from a bowl of fruit on a sidestand. There were gray patches on the yellow skin. "We followed it," he continued, punctuating the syllables with a crunching bite from the apple. *"Pah!"* He spat the piece in bits and spray toward an open basket of scrolls by the room's one upholstered chair.

Machiavelli made a quick motion toward the scrolls, with a pained expression and his mouth open to cry a protest. "Ah, Messer Hermann," he caught himself in time to say, his head bobbing approval. "I see, of course. But it had been my belief"—and as the Florentine's tone began to fawn even more abjectly, his eyes swung sidelong in query to Reinhard—"that the architectural drawings of this villa on file at Headquarters were faulty. That this wing, in fact, was not shown."

He paused. Hermann took another bite of apple, and though he masticated it stolidly this time,

Machiavelli sidled to interpose his body between the Cheruscan and the scrolls.

"In fact," the Florentine added, braving Heydrich's cool smile, "I thought when I examined the plans myself that such was the case."

Dared one thank Providence in such resort as this, Reinhard wondered. Aloud he said, "Surely you don't think that the Insecurity Service has no other source within this place, Niccolo? Or that you could ignore a summons from me?" The sentence, like a cat's foreleg, had claws at the end.

"There's liches out there," remarked Hermann as he began spitting seeds one by one toward the wall, aiming for the frescoed head of St. George being throttled by a smirking dragon. "More than usual. More than I ever saw before. Killing people."

Machiavelli nodded tightly, afraid to speak and afraid of being beaten for dumb insolence . . . or because one or the other of his interrogators chose to fill empty time with blows. "Yes, *signori*," he said, "Death is very terrible, even here." He attempted a fitfully ingratiating smile which faded before Hermann's apparent disinterest and the other German's own wolfish grin.

"You like to learn things, Niccolo," Reinhard said as he lounged against a wall. "We know you've learned where Hadrian is, for instance."

That was a lie, but the head of the Insecurity Service had good reason to suspect that Machiavelli knew something. The very dearth of information in his reports was a signpost, and the way the agent had ignored increasingly strident summons showed that he had hidden motives.

Which was axiomatic with Niccolo Machiavelli, of course.

"Now, I *suggest*," the fair-haired German continued pleasantly, "that you tell us where to find Hadrian. Because if you don't speak, or you lie to us, Niccolo"—he shook his head in dismay at even the thought of such a pass—"then you'll have an opportunity to learn why those the liches carry off never seem to return the way others slain here do. Eh?"

"There's a pack of them outside, little one," said Hermann, reaching out with apple-sticky fingers to turn Machiavelli toward him. He touched the Florentine's jaw gently, instead of crushing it the way that touch reminded the victim he could have done. "We fought our way through them, because you didn't come when we called."

It was important to remember, thought Reinhard, that Hermann was not the oaf his build and normal manners suggested, and that his use of "we" in reference to the Service of which he was a part—a small part, Reinhard would have said—suggested a dangerous turn of mind.

"Masters," the Florentine blurted as he bobbed his head violently, "it was only my hope to have, you realize, something more concrete to offer, something more worthy of your perusal. I haven't a place, you see, but only a source—and I haven't had the opportunity to follow up on it."

"The guts, you mean," said Hermann as he released the little man and wiped his bayonet on the apron of cat fur, the cat being not his own totem but rather the totem of a tribe hostile to him during the days he was alive and a chieftain.

"Yes, as you say, Messer Hermann," agreed Machiavelli. "The liches. So I have not talked to Poe myself or even gone out of this villa in weeks."

Reinhard knew that the little Florentine was afraid, because Niccolo was *always* afraid: it was the wellspring of his personality, whether described as "logic" or as "cowardice." But if the head of Insecurity had *not* known that, he would have suspected the look that flashed across Machiavelli's face was something quite different.

"So," Heydrich said, rubbing his uniform with his palms in a vain attempt to cleanse the black fabric of the smutches it had picked up when he fell, "you think that Poe—Poe the journalist, you mean?—has knowledge of where the Supreme Commander is being held?"

Machiavelli sucked his lower lip in as he searched for a phrase. He raised an index finger and said, "I have sources within *Là-Bas*—as you know, *signori*, as of course you know."

Hermann snorted. "You've tapped the composing room's mainframe," he said with casual assurance on a subject that comported ill with his dress and physique. "Fine, tell us what you learned."

"Yes, *signori*," said the Florentine, guarded again as he looked from one questioner to the other, as if to see whether they were handing masks back and forth to wear alternately. "The composing-room computer. And they started to set a story titled 'The Answer to the Secret for Which All Seek,' bylined E. A. Poe—yes? And then, nothing, the file wiped, that number of the journal appearing with no story about secrets, no story by Messer Poe— and no story by him since, two weeks later."

"He drinks," said Hermann, the words dismissing but the taut consideration in his face hinting otherwise. "He binges. No surprise that he hasn't made a deadline in two weeks."

"It was a hoax, I would say," Reinhard went on appraisingly. "Another of his lies about how to leave here forever, not so?"

"Of course, Messer Reinhard," Machiavelli said with a dignified bow, "but—would Huysmans have spiked a false story, do you think? Because only the publisher could have killed the story in that way, wiped it after typesetting had begun."

"That doesn't prove Hadrian's whereabouts were the subject of the story," Reinhard said sharply, his tone making him angry because it implied that he was treating Niccolo as a peer with whom he had to argue points rather than laying them down. "A title like that could be anything. Could *be* the path out of this—out of Hell."

"Yes," agreed Machiavelli. "And if it were that, *signori*"—he bowed to Hermann also, undismayed by the Cheruscan's black frown—"would it not be, I thought, information worthy in its own right?"

The two Germans looked at each other. Hermann shrugged and took from the basket a banana whose lower half was covered with opalescent fuzz. The Cheruscan watched the fuzz turn to slime where his fingers brushed it as he said, "You should get out more, little Roman. You'd get a better sense of this place and your worth to it."

He faced Machiavelli and smiled. "Perhaps you ought to visit Poe right now, liches and all. Hey?"

Hermann's left hand reached out with the piece of decaying fruit, directing it at Machiavelli's forehead—unless the Florentine chose to step aside and sacrifice the container of scrolls. Trembling, Machiavelli held his ground, though he closed his eyes and stiffened rather like a man waiting for a fluctuating current to be applied to his genitals.

Reinhard struck the banana to the floor, careful not to touch Hermann's fingers as he did so. The Cheruscan had certain reflexes to deal with what he considered a physical challenge. . . .

"Come," Reinhard said sharply, "the task is one to be done properly, Hermann. Therefore, our task, not that of a"—he sneered for effect, but the disgust was real enough—"little greaseball from below the Alps."

"All right," said Hermann without affect. "I don't mind leaving here." He stepped forward and opened the door with his foot, a thrust rather than a kick but firm enough to pop the latch mechanism and strew it onto the portico. The Cheruscan shuffled out of the room holding his weapon by the slide and small of the stock, ready to use it as a stabbing spear but not a gun.

Reinhard nodded in dismissal to the Florentine and started to leave the room himself.

"Messer Reinhard," Machiavelli said.

The tall German turned, letting his face smooth again to neutrality. "Yes, Niccolo?" he said.

"About those the liches—take—not returning," Machiavelli said, "That is true, is it not?"

To ask for truth here, thought the head of the Unsicherheit Dienst. But aloud he said, "To my knowledge, Niccolo. You've been—here longer . . . but of course, you don't get out much."

"Reinhard!" Hermann bawled from the portico

and another door banged. The Cheruscan had apparently gotten lost as he started to leave, even though the stairway was the next portal over.

"Have you ever wondered, Messer," the Florentine continued with unexpected intensity, "whether *that* is the real path out of here? Whether the liches are agents of the—Other Power—who choose those who are to be translated from this region to a, to a higher one?"

"Reinhard, if you leave me here, I'll have your guts for breakfast!" called Hermann from somewhere outside on the portico.

"No," Reinhard said softly, remembering the pair he had just seen being killed, remembering the accounts of others: relatively good, relatively bad . . . all of them damned, and no link beyond that. "It's random, Niccolo, just like everything else here."

"Yes, Messer," Machiavelli said with a sigh.

"What happens to you won't be random if you've lied to me, you know," the German added.

Hermann's 12-gauge shotgun blasted, the sound echoing among the pillars and across the faces of the portico. He must have started in the wrong direction and become completely disoriented in this forest of stone. *"Reinhard!"*

"Yes, Messer," the Florentine said, bowing. "Never will I lie to you."

A lie and they both knew it; but that was the way of the world as well as of Hell, thought Reinhard as he strode onto the portico, hoping that his companion would not shoot him by accident or deliberation.

*   *   *

Hermann paused and mopped his forehead with the cotton shell of his cap. "You should have had Valdstejn pick us up on the grounds," he said. "This *park* . . ."

"The radio didn't work," Reinhard snapped, also bleeding from innumerable scratches. The hike from their vehicle to Augustus's villa had seemed less enervating.

"The radio *never* works," the Cheruscan rejoined, accurately enough. "You should have *told* Valdstejn to drive up to the house as soon as we were inside."

"We—" Reinhard began in exasperation.

Hermann pinched the taller man's lips closed. Reinhard's shock was so great that he almost missed the Cheruscan's words, "Wait—what's that sound?"

The head of Insecurity relaxed with the realization that Hermann had acted from need, not pique. Not that the act would be forgotten, but . . .

There was a sound, wheezing—polka music, surely. The direction was . . . "Come," Reinhard said, pausing a further moment to draw his pistol and hold it skyward as if it were a foil at the beginning of one of his Olympic fencing bouts. "It must be Valdstejn, but why he's playing music . . ."

For all his bulk, Hermann passed his companion in the clawing brush and made surprisingly little noise in doing so. At these ranges, the bayonet was probably as effective as the shotgun on which it was mounted, but the Germans had not really expected trouble. As recently as two days before, the park had been off limits to anyone who didn't wear sandals made from tire tread and inner tube. Then the cluster bomb which the Insecurity Service had arranged for the VC to capture had quieted things down no end by detonating in the middle of their encampment. Odysseus ought to get a medal for setting that one up.

The air cushion jeep they had left parked with its driver was still there. A liche sat on the plenum chamber, bony legs dangling as it grinned and played an accordion. Valdstejn's submachine gun lay across a seatback, but there was no sign of the driver himself.

Hermann began sidling toward the vehicle, his weapon slanted forward to slash or stab.

"Wait," Reinhard said as he aimed at the liche's chest. The creature seemed to be unarmed, but they saw only the one and the strains of the "Thunder and Lightning Polka" would have concealed the creeping approach of a further regiment. Ten feet away, an easy shot, but when the gun fired the others would—

The muzzle blast of the 9-millimeter automatic deafeningly punctuated the accordion music, but it did not put an immediate period to the wheezing sounds. Dust puffed from the liche's parchment-like skin, and the chest dimpled as the sternum shattered within. The creature slid forward, still grinning, pulled by the weight of the accordion which moaned discordantly. The liche began to crumble away in concentric circles spreading from the bullet's exit hole.

Nothing further broke the silence save the rasp of Hermann's garments against the brush as he pivoted, ready to engage anyone—anything—that appeared in answer to the shot.

Reinhard ran the three paces to the jeep and swung himself into the driver's compartment. There

was sign of Valdstejn, blood on the seat cushion
and the instrument panel, but no more. The magazine of the driver's submachine gun was empty,
and the weapon stank with powder residues and
lubricant heated by rapid fire.

Petcock open, torque converter disengaged . . .
turbine ignition, a thump and a building whine as
the rotors began to spin up power.

"Get in, damn you!" Reinhard shouted and cursed
himself internally for a clumsy choice of words
that betrayed his own perturbation.

"I don't think there're any more around," Hermann said, kicking at the accordion which remained
while the liche drifted into dust around it.

"Do you want to wait until there *are?*" Reinhard
demanded loudly enough to be heard even though
he locked the torque converter forward as he spoke
and fed power to the lift fans. The ground-effect
vehicle trembled.

Hermann stepped into the tonneau, clearing the
front seat by tossing Valdstejn's weapon off into
the brush. Empty, the submachine gun made a
bad club, while the Winchester the Cheruscan carried was a very good spear. "Where're we going?"
he asked as he settled himself with the care of a
man boarding a hand-hewn skiff.

"New Hell, of course," Reinhard snapped. "To
discuss the matter with Mr. Poe."

If, his mind added silently as the fans forced a
slapping path through the brush, the Providence
that has followed us so far permits.

The mixture of snow, slush, and slime coating
the cobblestones of this portion of New Hell was

no impediment to the air cushion jeep, but the bearings of the accursed turbine began to squeal and shake the frame. The vehicle was running like hell, drawing a lopsided snaketrack down the center of the street. Reinhard switched off the headlight to reduce the load on the laboring turbine. The halogen bulb was giving poorer illumination than the feeble gaslights spaced along the blocks of the subdivision.

"We're looking for a tavern," Reinhard said, trying to curb the desperate frustration which always gnawed him when machinery chose to fail. "The Vulture, if I recall the file entry. It's close to the offices of *Là-Bas*, and those are the logical places to check first."

"We should have gone back to Headquarters, if you're in doubt," said Hermann, who had lowered the earflaps on his cap. Neither man was particularly afflicted by the climate here, which closely resembled that of Germany: wretched, in varying fashions and degrees.

"There've been liches here," the Cheruscan added as he squinted over the side of the jeep at the surface of the road.

"Watch for a tavern sign!" the driver snapped.

There was a rumble of engines from ahead of them, a wedge of five or six lights bobbling toward the jeep at low speed.

"Gypsy Jokers?" Hermann asked idly as he wiped the side of his bayonet against his bare shoulder to remove touches of snow.

"I think this is Pagan turf," Reinhard said. "Unless there's been a renegotiation. That's all under Hoover, so I don't—yes, Pagans."

The troop of motorcycle police split to either side of the jeep. When the leader recognized the head of Insecurity, he gave a one-finger salute which Reinhard returned stiff-armed. The troop passed at a thunderous idle. They were mounted on side-valve Indians with suicide shifts and either straight pipes or turnouts. All the bikers wore golden torques, and their robes and long hair fluttered in the wind of their passage.

"There's an inn sign up there," Hermann said when the air cushion vehicle had struggled far enough from the motorcycles for his voice to be heard at a normal volume.

"Wh—" Reinhard began, and the jeep's headlight split the night with full, sharp-edged vigor. "This *accursed*—" the tall German shouted as he raised his gloved fist to smash at the light switch which had chosen to disobey him.

"That's him," said Hermann, pointing over the windscreen with his shotgun. "That's Poe."

A man had huddled beside a housefront while the troop of Pagans passed. Now he stood, weaving, thrown into sudden relief against stone steps and rusty iron railings by the powerful headlight. The hand which he threw before his face to shield his eyes held a flask of glazed earthenware.

Reinhard swore again, pivoting the tiller with one hand while he switched belts on the torque converter with the other. "Watch him!" he shouted needlessly, for his companion had already risen with his left and gripping the top of the windscreen and his right pointing the bayoneted shotgun as if Poe were a pig he intended to stick.

The turbine ran flawlessly again. Its thrust

snatched at the reversing pulleys and sucked the jeep to a stop hard enough to flex the rubber skirts.

Hermann vaulted over the hood. He skidded full-length on the mucky cobblestones as his quarry bleated and began to run.

Poe was surprisingly sure-footed, Reinhard thought as he too jumped from the vehicle and almost turned up the slick heels of his boots on the treacherous footing. Experience, he supposed. The little journalist ducked into an alley instead of running the half block back to the tavern from which he had presumably come. Either he was moving with drunken randomness, or he had realized that the alley was too narrow to pass the jeep.

Cursing horribly in German and Latin, Hermann rolled to his knees and thumbed back the exposed hammer of his shotgun.

"Don't *kill* him, you—" Reinhard cried as, with a shriek of abject terror, Poe rushed back out of the alley. He stumbled. The liche following him with a two-handed sword raised the weapon as inexorably as a metronome clicking off lives.

The jeep's fierce headlight limned the sword on the house front as a black shadow, the liche's bones as dense gray, and the horny skin as a saffron blur surrounding the bones. Hermann fired, and light flooded unimpeded through a fist-sized hole in the creature's chest. Poe moaned and cradled the bottle in his hands as the sword jangled to the cobblestones beside him.

Six more liches sprang from the alley mouth. They carried barb-headed spears, some of them fletched at the butt to stabilize them if they were thrown. Their feet clicked on the stones.

Gloved, Reinhard's hands were clumsy as he unsnapped his holster and drew the pistol he had not expected to need with Poe.

Hermann lurched to his feet and closed his eyes. He held the shotgun at his right hip, with his right index finger on the trigger while his left hand pumped the slide. As the empty case tumbled away, the bolt slid back and cocked the external hammer. The hammer spur bloodied the web of Hermann's right hand which had ridden forward on the grip with the recoil of the first shot. The big German did not notice the pain. At this moment, he would not have noticed a spear being thrust through his lungs.

When Hermann's left hand slammed forward, chambering a fresh round with the trigger held back since the previous shot, the Model 97 fired again. The Cheruscan pumped the action four more times, emptying the magazine of its buckshot charges in a quintet of red flashes from the muzzle.

Had the liches been flesh and blood, there would have been carnage. As it was, there was chaos. At point blank, the buckshot did not spread appreciably, though the trench gun had a cylinder bore and an 18-inch barrel. The weight of the bayonet and its mounting (which had prevented use of an extended magazine tube) made the gun muzzle-heavy and kept it from pointing skyward by the end of Hermann's blind ripple of fire. The gun rotated somewhat around the axis of the Cheruscan's body, however, sweeping left to right across the debouching swarm of liches.

Each charge ripped the creatures it hit like round shot through sails, tumbling the leaders into the path of their fellows with grins and clattering spears. The brownstone front of the house which acted as a backstop for the targets spattered back the lead with spurts of sand blasted from its own surface.

Poe continued to squeal and the Cheruscan was howling. It might have been a challenge, but Reinhard suspected the sound had more to do with the hatred of firearms which hellish familiarity had not caused Hermann to lose.

There were pieces of liches, liches crawling, and a single liche upright with his spear poised to skewer Poe. Hermann lunged forward and rammed his 17-inch bayonet home until the muzzle slammed against the creature's left nipple. The loose parts of the shotgun jangled, and Hermann's blood-slippery right hand slid hard against the hammer again.

The liche had been thrown off stride, but for a moment it tried to force back against the Cheruscan's weight. Then it collapsed and began to crumble about the hole punched through it by the narrow bayonet.

Two of the creatures which had fallen during the gout of buckshot were still struggling forward, one of them despite the fact that its right leg was no longer articulated to its shattered pelvis. Reinhard fired, missing by eight inches a target almost close enough to touch, but the steel-jacketed bullet howled away from the cobblestones like a circlesaw biting a nail, slicing through the liche's torso in its passage. The creature's remaining three limbs splayed and dropped it flat.

Steadied, though his eyes were flecked with afterimages of the bullet sparking from stone, Reinhard shot the remaining liche as it rose with its spear drawn back to throw.

There was no longer any sound on the street, but the muzzle blasts and ricocheting projectiles were still deafening in the memory of the three humans now blinking at their surroundings.

Poe raised himself to sit, knees spread, in the filthy slush. "Oh," he said. He raised his flask for a drink. The jeep's headlight showed with brutal certainty that the lower half of the container had been smashed away by a bouncing pellet. "*Oh* . . ." The journalist was very drunk already.

"Edgar, *Edgar*," Reinhard gasped with a concern that would have been difficult to fake as effectively. He lifted Poe with one hand under the armpit, after making the initial mistake of trying to grab the journalist with his right hand also— though he still held a cocked pistol in it. "We were sent to save you from this terrible danger!"

"What?"

"Is your room nearby?" pressed the head of Insecurity. "Or your newspaper office?"

"What . . ." Poe repeated without an interrogative rise. He lifted the flask again, stared at it, and began to cry.

"There," said Hermann, pointing to a series of grimy windows on the second floor, built slightly out over the street. The jeep's headlight was sufficient to pick out the letters, one to each pane, in flaked coppery gold leaf: LÀ-BAS; and centered in smaller letters: *A Division of Time-Life*.

"Yes, come along," Reinhard said. He dropped the hammer of his pistol and stuffed it into the breast of his uniform jacket rather than attempt to holster the weapon one-handed.

Poe managed a step forward, still clinging to the shattered remnants of his bottle. A thighbone, as yet solid, rolled under foot and he looked down. The tangle of spears and crumbling bones unexpectedly sobered him. He dropped the flask and shook himself clear of Reinhard's support. "Sir," the journalist said, squaring his narrow shoulders beneath his cloak as he faced Hermann, "you have saved the life of a poet, a *great* poet. There can be no more noble act, and no act more nobly requited by its very performance."

"What about the jeep?" Hermann said, gesturing with a nod of his cap as he shucked a round into the chamber and reached for a sixth all-brass cartridge from his bandolier to fill the magazine tube.

Reinhard followed his companion's glance. The turbine was purring happily, even at idle comfortably handling the load of the headlight which illuminated the street as sunlight never did. The jeep was not blocking the traveled way, slewed as it was to intercept Poe as he started to run.

"We'll leave it," said the taller German. "Usually it doesn't want to start in this district." He put a hand on Poe's shoulder. "Sir, to your office where you can evidence the talents that made your life invaluable."

The journalist took three steps, his steadiness and sense of direction deteriorating every time his heel touched the ground. Reinhard, who had used the interval to holster his pistol properly, was ready to swing the little drunk's left arm over his own shoulders and proceed up the stairs to the second-floor newspaper offices with Poe in a fireman's carry. Hermann, sneering, followed with frequent glances behind him at the street where the liches were dissolving against the slush.

The glass-paneled door at the stairhead was locked. "Do you have a key?" Reinhard asked his charge. Hermann reached past both of them and thrust the buttplate of his shotgun through the glass. The Cheruscan stroked up, across, down, and back, following the sash like a dressmaker cutting a pattern. Then he withdrew the shotgun and stood aloof, waiting for one of the others to put an arm within the jagged edges and release the bolt.

Reinhard did so, thinking that something needed to be done very shortly to teach Hermann his place.

The offices of *Là-Bas* stank of ink and less identifiable organic substances. The odor worsened when Reinhard struck a sulfur match and turned up the wick of a lamp which certainly had not been filled with whale oil, even if the whale had been dead for months before being rendered. The long room was filled with rolltop desks, wooden filing cabinets, straight chairs whose varnish had blackened and cracked into miniature file teeth, and scruffy-looking computer terminals.

"How do they get them to work here, do you think?" said Hermann, his bayonet probing at the nearest terminal with the delicacy of a scalpel being readied to lance a boil.

"How does anyone get a computer to work?" Reinhard retorted as he rummaged through the bottom drawer of the desk at which he had seated

Poe. "Badly, of course. But what we need won't be in the mainframe, we know that."

The desk wasn't Poe's own—a plate half buried under the litter of papers bore the name Hildy Johnson—but there was the expected quart of whiskey at the back of the drawer.

"Tell us about the story they spiked, Edgar," Reinhard purred, tilting the bottle to catch the light just beyond Poe's reach. "The one about Hadrian, the secret place they're hiding him."

The journalist tried to raise himself to shuddering alertness. "Sir," he said and coughed, burying his face momentarily in the collar of his cloak, fouled with street grime and dried vomit. "Sir," he repeated, with an aura of dignity that suddenly shook itself over him like the cloak, "whom do I have the honor of addressing?"

Reinhard bowed and clicked his heels. "SS Obergruppenführer Reinhard Heydrich," he said, "and Hermann, son of Sigimer, King of the Cherusci—at your service."

Poe attempted to rise. "Sirs, in saving me from—" He began, and the string of his honor broke again and spilled him back in the chair. "Oh, sirs, they do not appreciate what they have in me, here," he blubbered into his palms. "A poet, sirs, and a *gentleman*—and they rip my art from the very bowels of the presses . . ."

"The story about Hadrian, then?" Reinhard coaxed gently. "The Supreme Commander?"

"Was that it?" the journalist said in puzzlement that replaced the bathos. He leaned forward stealthily, focusing his eyes on Hermann as his fingers quested for the bottle which Reinhard whisked behind his own torso for the moment. "The secret? Well, perhaps . . ."

"I'll shake him—" Hermann began, leaning his weapon against the wall to free both hands in preparation.

Reinhard, bent forward to put his face on a level with Poe's, shifted his body quickly in order to block the Cheruscan and wheedled, "We're your *friends*, Edgar, we've saved you. And we'll respect you so much more when you've told us about the secret."

Reinhard thought he felt Hermann's glowering presence recede for the moment, but he did not dare to look around and break eye contact with his subject.

The journalist straightened again and pressed his fingertips against his temples. "The secret place I had of Sir John Mandeville, yes . . ." he said. Again he attempted to rise, this time successfully. He raised his index finger and, looking sidelong at the fair-haired German, went on, "A man who is a fraud, gentlemen, even to his name; but *I* have nosed him out."

Poe walked to a file cabinet. He was more unsteady than he had been while trying to escape in the street; so unsteady, in fact, that the SS general at first thought that his subject was falling and reached out to help him. The journalist tugged his cloak disdainfully from the would-be support, though the motion almost toppled him onto the close-spaced desk adjoining. Reinhard backed away, feeling like a father watching his infant's first steps: unwilling to intervene, but fearful of a damaging fall.

The journalist braced himself on the pull of a file drawer. Instead of opening it, he turned to the Germans with a flourish which would have unbalanced him had he lost his handhold.

"A fraud, gentlemen," Poe declaimed, "but in this matter truthful. I have an infallible sense, a preternatural acuity of perception which permits me to detect impostures."

"And what," Reinhard pressed gently, "was the *nature* of the secret which your intellect permitted you to draw from Mandeville, Edgar?"

"A place," said Poe. He drew open the drawer beside him, gaining poise and steadiness from the attention he was receiving. "The most secret place in Hell, gentlemen."

He reached into the drawer with the aplomb of a sober man and withdrew from it a manila folder. "*This* secret."

Reinhard stepped forward to take the document, but Hermann was even swifter and far less concerned with appearances. His shoulder bludgeoned aside his taller companion, and while his left hand snatched the folder, his right angled the bayonet at Poe's throat as much in threat as by accident. He flapped the file open.

"There's nothing here!" the big Cheruscan said in a voice whose anger rose with each syllable.

Reinhard stepped between the other men, facing Hermann and forcing the shotgun aside with his own torso. "Well, let's see what there is," he said mildly, reaching for the folder and aware that at any moment the Cheruscan might vent his fury with the butt or blade of his weapon. In a killing rage, Hermann tended to ignore firearms . . . not that it mattered.

This time Hermann backed away pouting. Reinhard had set the whiskey bottle down on the desk when he followed Poe. The Cheruscan took it now, pulled the cork with his teeth, and began to drink.

That could be a problem very shortly, but for the moment Reinhard's attention was on the folder—which indeed was empty. On the locator tab, in a neat copperplate hand, was written, "The Place for Which All Search in Vain"; and below it, a signature that sprawled down the side of the folder: E. A. Poe.

"Edgar, my *friend*," the head of Insecurity said as he turned back to the journalist. "Has there been a mistake here, or . . . ?" and as gentle as the words were, no one who knew Reinhard Heydrich could have had the least question of how he would react to learning that he had been hoaxed.

Poe slumped, gripping the cabinet and file drawer to keep from collapsing entirely. He began to cry.

Reinhard took a step toward the journalist, and for an instant no one in the room—Reinhard least of all—knew exactly what his right hand was about to do: slap or soothe or draw the pistol from its holster. Poe, speaking toward the drawer over which he sagged, said distinctly, "That *driveler*, that cowardly purveyor of imagined degradations, that *Huysmans* . . . He had the gall, gentlemen, the poisonous gall to write in vermilion across the face of my story: 'Below the literary standards of this journal.' "

He lifted himself upright, chin high, his moustache splashed with gutter filth, quivering with

indignation. "So of course I destroyed it, gentlemen. I could scarcely permit *my* words to be pol-
luted by the hand of a mere editor, could I?"

In a changed voice, one charged with despera-
tion, Poe added, "I wonder, my good sir, the bottle
you hold—"

The Germans thought the pause was for effect
until Poe's knees buckled and he toppled backward. The crack of his head striking the hardwood
floor was too loud for the collapse to be faked in
order to avoid what the journalist must have realized would be the next stage of the proceedings.

Hermann walked over and poked at the fallen
man's rib cage with the bayonet.

"Try the whiskey," Reinhard suggested. The
Cheruscan poured a gurgling slug of the fluid—
water, methanol, cayenne, and gunpowder—that
splashed over Poe's face and mouth. It washed
away some of the muck without affecting the journalist's stertorous breathing or the way only the
whites of his eyes showed in the lamplight.

Reinhard kicked Poe as hard as he could, using
the heel rather than the toe of his high leather
boots. The crackle of the journalist's ribs was like
a handful of twigs breaking and provided the head
of Insecurity with the only satisfaction he could
draw from the entire interview.

"Let's go," he said, turning and walking into a
desk in the blindness of his rage.

"Huysmans?" asked the Cheruscan as he measured Poe for a lethal thrust and decided not to
bother.

"Mandeville," Reinhard snapped as he exited

the room. "No point in going to a thirdhand source when better's available."

"If he is better," Hermann noted, less concerned than his companion about the success or failure of their mission. The Cheruscan had never been able to regard work that served others as being of real significance.

"If that *bastard* De Bourgogne has kept this from me," Reinhard muttered, "when he's been on the payroll from the *beginning*, then he'll wish . . ."

One sign that they were nearing the harbor was the salvo of 21-centimeter shells shrieking to nearby impact. Bits of tile and roof beams flew up against the glaucous sliminess that passed for a night sky here in Hell. The bursting charges did not flash, and though rubble cascaded there were no explosions.

"Duds," said Reinhard with grim satisfaction. Far out to sea, there was a tremble of light to warn that another salvo was on its way.

"Somebody ought to do something about them," muttered Hermann, thrown near to funking by the howl of the shells which resembled the screams of the damned—only louder. The impacts themselves had not particularly distressed him, though a 130-kilogram projectile did not need to explode to do damage.

"The *Blücher?*" Reinhard asked as he swerved the air cushion jeep around a cart laden with marble facings and driven by a cowering man who looked a good deal like Nero.

The harbor came in sight again momentarily, past the upper stories of crazily leaning buildings.

Reinhard nodded in the general direction of the armored cruiser, whose war service had been limited to bombarding undefended ports. "It has," he said, "at least twice. There was an RAF flight fresh from bombing Dresden ... and more recently an Israeli combined-arms team put together over a period of years, *very* expert, aircraft and torpedo boats who'd been machine-gunning American lifeboats during the attack on the *Liberty*."

"Well?" Hermann demanded, gripping his Model 97 very fiercely to distract himself from the ragged salvo shrieking overhead.

"It causes a great deal of difficulty for the Undertaker, I gather," said Reinhard as their headlight caught the tavern sign for which he was looking, SAILORS' GREEN—a gob in bell-bottoms, vomiting over a ship's railing. "It's not the *Blücher*'s crew that was damned, you see."

The latest shells were duds also. The distant rumble of heavy guns sounded like a man cursing in frustration.

Sailors' Green had its own wharf, stretching out into the harbor, and it must have been from there or by foot that most of the customers thronging the common room came. The street outside was wide and covered with broad stone pavers, not cobbles, ancient enough to have been notched by use though they remained serviceable. The city's newest thoroughfares were cantilevered structures of boron composite, sweeping nobly from nexus to nexus—and collapsing with distressing frequency. It appeared that the Hughes engineers had underestimated the erosion caused by traffic at the same time they were overestimating the composite's resistance to torsional stresses.

The problems were undergoing study. They would be cured realsoonnow.

But the only conveyances parked at the tavern's landward side were the pair of horses with a hammock slung between them instead of being saddled, and something with tracks, a small turret and slab sides: an amphibious landing vehicle, Reinhard supposed.

No one liked change, no one but a madman, and in Hell, the Devil you knew really was preferable to the Devil you didn't. That was why they had to retrieve the Supreme Commander and get matters back on course. . . .

The common room was two steps down from street level, and the lintel would have brained a shorter man than Reinhard had he not ducked as he stepped down. The clash and curse from Hermann behind him indicated that the Cheruscan had miscalculated, at least by the length of his bayonet.

Within, Sailors' Green was furnished with ship's beams—false ones, plaster moldings; ship's lanterns—of plastic, some of them melted into outré shapes where they had touched the incandescent bulbs inside; and whores, who would offer any kind of release that did not threaten to stain their sheets or their underwear. In short, it was closely modeled on dockside taverns of the late-20th-century "upper world."

Men in the nautical costumes of more ages and regions than Reinhard could identify sat and drank; stood and drank; argued and drank; and vomited on the floor with racking passion so that they could drink more. The bartender served them all with a speed and deftness that suggested he had more limbs than anyone ever saw at the same time. By common report, though without solid evidence, he was the Old Man of the Sea—human or not human, depending on the informant.

The head of Insecurity, looking around the roomful of dingy drunken souls, suspected that the monster which clung inextricably to the backs of these folk was something less humanoid than the bartender with his silent grin.

There was a loud *bang* punctuating the ballistic roar of the *Blücher*'s shells. The lights blinked, dust and stench were shaken from the floor, and somebody began to shout that his mother was an angel, a very saint, and he'd fight any liar who claimed to have shared a crib with her. One of the big shells had finally detonated; but, short-fuzed, it had burst harmlessly a hundred meters in the air.

With Reinhard in the lead, the pair of Unsicherheit Dienst operatives elbowed their way through the crowd. The tavern was laid out in a sprawling tangle of connected rooms, all of which seemed to be served by the same bar; though the geometry which would permit that was doubtful and griped Reinhard's orderly soul.

As they passed between the tables, one of the vacant-eyed men battened upon by vacant-minded women lurched to his feet and clutched the arm of the fair-haired German. "Reinhard," he blurted. "I'm so *glad* to see you. I've been meaning—"

"Not now, Onesikratos," said the head of Insecurity, attempting to pry loose the other's hand.

The Greek clung fiercely to Reinhard's arm and Hermann, behind them, tried to raise his shotgun for a stroke with its butt. The bayonet caught in the ceiling.

"Listen," Onesikratos babbled, "everything in my account of India was true. I mean, all right, I may have, have gilded my own part in the invasion a little, and all right, that bastard Nearchos may have really have had command of the fleet—"

"Onesikratos, if you don't—"

"—but that's no reason to ignore *every*thing that I say, I mean, it's a *brilliant* account, and it's all—"

Unable to clear his shoulder weapon in the press, Hermann backed a step and kicked Alexander's pilot in the groin. The Cheruscan's footgear was supple, but the callused feet beneath the boots were hard as horn. Onesikratos swallowed his words and his tongue in an anguished gasp. He toppled away from them as Reinhard strode toward the alcove where he expected to find his subject: Jean de Bourgogne—Sir John Mandeville to most of those who had not read his confidential file.

Mandeville sat on a semicircular bench in a wall niche. Before him was a round table holding gin bottles and four-ounce jacks of leather waterproofed with tar, and to either side sat a man telling a story. The stories appeared to be the same, though one version was in Arabic and the other in Greek and both storytellers were using the first person. Mandeville listened greedily, combing tangles from his full, yellow-white beard with one hand while the other held the jack of raw gin from which he sipped.

Reinhard drew his pistol and stepped to the side of the Arabic speaker, distinctly the less formidable of the two storytellers. "Why don't you go have a drink at the bar, boys?" the head of Insecurity said, hooking his free hand under the speaker's armpit and lifting him bodily.

The Arab's head turned as he rose: his hand darted toward the wavy-bladed kris in his sash, but Reinhard's pistol was pointed at his left eye and close enough that the lashes would touch the muzzle if the Arab blinked. He froze instead of whatever his first instinct might have been, and then he began to obey the German's "suggestion" with care and no sudden moves, proving that he knew exactly how to take the threat in Reinhard's smile.

The Greek, a short man with the wrists and shoulders of a blacksmith, swept his glance across Reinhard and the gun and the big hand of Hermann reaching for his throat to chuck him out of the alcove. The storyteller's equipment belt clanked with a heavy revolver and a brace of fragmentation grenades, but instead of reaching down he raised both hands to block Hermann in what seemed a gesture of supplication.

"Noble sir, let me offer you this seat that I was honored to hold for you," he murmured, rising of his own accord and offering the bit of bench to Hermann with a flourish.

The fact that the Cheruscan's hand stopped in the air was a tribute to the Greek's strength rather than his persuasion, however. "*Watch* that one and don't turn your back," snapped Reinhard as the Greek danced out of sight in the swirl of customers. Hermann, who had met his own share of ruthless killers in life and afterward, was already trying to follow the fellow's exit, well aware that a grenade might sail out of the crowd at any moment.

Reinhard sat down firmly, trusting the Cheruscan to cover them at the same time his body prevented Mandeville from bolting. "It seems I need to talk to you, John," said the head of Insecurity, who had deliberately not holstered his weapon. "Since you tell other people things you don't tell me."

"You told Poe about where they took Hadrian," rumbled Hermann unexpectedly—and if Reinhard had expected that, he would have specifically warned the moronic Cheruscan to keep his mouth shut during this interrogation. The last thing you wanted a source like Mandeville to learn was the answer you hoped you'd obtain.

Mandeville was an old man, with a flush and plump features that others thought looked jolly. His eyebrows were as bushy and white as his hair and beard, so that altogether it was possible to ignore the fact that his eyes were too close set, *Schweinaugen*, and that they held substrata of creeping nastiness.

"The"—he began as he focused those eyes on Hermann, and then the momentary question went out of his voice—"Jews have captured him, you see, to carry him back to the upper world in order to frustrate the plans of honest Christian men like ourselves."

Hermann blinked and Reinhard poised watchfully, but Mandeville continued without hesitation,

"Just as it is well known that they, having murdered Christ, sought in Java a venom wherewith to poison all Christendom."

The Jews? thought Reinhard, and it was just possible since he'd given them reason enough for hate, Hadrian had, when his engineers turned Jerusalem into Aelianopolis and his legions depopulated Israel so thoroughly that it became Philistia, Palestine, for almost two millennia thereafter. The immediate question, however, was not "Who?" but—

"And where is it that they've taken him, Sir John?" asked the head of Insecurity in a voice as supple as the kidskin gloves he wore while his finger toyed within the trigger guard of the pistol laid on the table but pointed, still pointed.

"A place no one but I have seen," said Mandeville, portentous even now as he lied to a man who of all those in Hell was as bad choice for it as any. "A path not up but *down*, as befits the evil contrariness of their Christ-denying natures."

"*Where*, Bearded John?" said Reinhard very softly as his free hand wrapped spittle-stained curls of beard round the stark black leather of his glove. "If I have to ask you again . . ."

"The sewers," said the man who chose to be called Mandeville, even here. "Their secret path to the upper world is through the sewers, whence they return to bring further evil upon the Christians they hold prisoned here in despite of the Almighty."

"The sewers?" said Hermann, wrinkling his nose at the thought. "They're like the tracks of maggots in meat, here, no pattern, and no end. We can't follow—"

Mandeville held up a hand in prohibition, an arrogance which Hermann chose to take in good part as more of the *Blücher*'s shells thrummed past and made the bottles shiver. "Even so, my good sir," intoned the fraud who, nonetheless, *heard* things and was correct far more often than he was truthful, "even so. For this reason, the Jews have left markings along their pathway—"

He paused for breath and effect. Reinhard's left hand closed with the grim determination of an Iron Maiden, tensing to jerk the fat face into the pistol's rising muzzle.

"A painted spike like those they drove through the blessed hands and feet of our Saviour," Mandeville blurted, barely forestalling the violence that Reinhard prepared as much for release as to speed the story. "A line of spikes in the ceiling of the sewers, glowing in lantern light to guide them on their vile business."

"And why do you say they took Hadrian this way?" Reinhard asked, forcing his muscles to relax as he made the best of the situation into which Hermann's clumsy technique had propelled them.

"I saw them, did I not?" said the fat old man haughtily.

Almost certainly not, thought Reinhard, his mind as cold as his face. But—almost. And the true source of the story, which might not be the story quite that Mandeville retailed, would be hidden so deep in the fraud's psyche that there might be no way to retrieve it, even with unlimited time and ruthlessness.

Only time was limited, but that was enough.

"They took him through the entrance beneath

this very building, and that is the truth, by the Almighty," said Mandeville. Then, in an attempt at cleverness, he added, "And the truth as you had it from Master Edgar, was it not, though he betrayed me?"

"Why *did* you tell this story to Poe," asked Reinhard as his left fingertips smoothed the kidskin over the back of his right hand, "and not tell *me*, John, as your duty directed?" The head of Insecurity had not raised his voice during the whole of the questioning, but a mamba is no less deadly for the fact that it strikes without warning.

As Mandeville knew. Even though his interrogator had released his beard, it was now that the sweat sprang out on the fat man's forehead, plastering wisps of hair to the skin. "Lord Reinhard," he said, with his eyes turned toward the German but focused on the white infinity of torture that he knew might follow his words, "he told me that he would print my name in his journal. But he lied to me, he betrayed me: the story never appeared at all."

His voice rose, and the old man got to his feet, rocking the table, as he continued, "My stories never see print! It's the Jews who do it, you must understand, they follow me everywhere to torture—"

Mandeville jerked back, banging the plank wall behind him, but he did not fall because the spear that had slammed through the base of his throat pinned him upright as effectively as ever the nails had Christ.

Hermann jumped up, flinging the table and its contents against Reinhard as the head of Insecurity also tried to rise. The Old Man of the Sea continued to grin behind the bar, but from the trapdoor beside him that served the cellars were trooping liches with their own expressions of wry amusement. The foremost, which wore a tapster's apron like the bartender, had thrown its spear with unerring accuracy and the strength of a catapult.

The apparitions were ignored by some of the tavern's clientele, perhaps as being too similar to things their minds had showed them regularly even in life. Others bawled in rage or terror, and Reinhard's shot was not the first though he held his pistol ready in his hand.

Plaster dust and splinters flew. Several of the liches stepping onto the bar in bony deliberation toppled back, while a number of the patrons went down like tenpins in the wild shooting. The bartender waited with his hands spread on the zinc bar top, ignoring the chaos and ignored by the liches whose entry had caused it.

"Why do they keep following us!" Hermann bellowed, in fury rather than question. "Why must we—" and drowned the rest of his sentence in the red-mawed roar of his trench gun, ripping a buckshot trail through liches, furniture, and anything human that chanced to be in the line of fire.

Reinhard heard something louder even than the cacophony of cries and gunshots. "Get down!" he shouted to Hermann.

The Cheruscan had started to thrust his way toward the door by which they had entered the tavern. Despite his strength, it was a task as pointless as trying to compress a volume of water: the shouting bodies were packed too tightly to make way.

Hermann paused and shifted his grip on the shotgun he had emptied, preparing to use its steel-capped butt as a sledge on the nearest of those trying to force their way through the door. The first wave of liches had been smashed down by the buckshot and the hail of fire from other weapons, but more were beginning to climb into sight through the bullet-shattered bar.

Reinhard yanked on his companion's shoulder and kicked the inside knee joints with a booted foot. The unexpected shock threw Hermann over backward, his own massive chest and arms toppling him when Reinhard tipped them past his center of balance. The two Germans crashed to the floor together, Hermann squawking in rage, so that they were sheltered by the tabletop and bench when the shells hit.

The red flash was momentary but so intense that the staring faces of those caught by it, man and liche alike, were reproduced as chartreuse afterimages on Reinhard's retinas. The enveloping blackness that followed, momentary also, was partly the smoky residue of the picric acid bursting charge, partly unconsciousness from the shock wave despite the protection afforded by the heavy oak furniture.

Everyone—and -thing—in the direct path of the blast was shredded. The *Blücher* had finally managed a salvo of live shells.

Hermann rose into a shambling crouch, holding the trench gun by its balance. He was blinking and disoriented by the explosion, stumbling on bodies which lay in windrows where fragments from the air burst had flung them. "Reinhard?" he called in a voice that cracked because the swirling combustion products dried and bleached his throat. The blast had opened the ceiling of the common room to the lowering night sky.

"Quickly, the jeep," said Reinhard, laying a hand on his companion's shoulder as much to steady himself as to guide the Cheruscan. His head rang in synchrony with his pulse rate, and that pain mixed with the nauseating stench of this abattoir made his stomach and bowels surge. "Quickly," he repeated, "if it's still—"

Behind them, the Old Man of the Sea was mopping the bar where it was not completely buried by rubble. He grinned and whistled a chantey as he worked, the one that goes, "Yo ho, blow the man down . . ."

The jeep was as nearly untouched by the salvo as the Germans themselves were, though a second shell had struck within a few meters of the vehicle and on bursting had collapsed a hundred meters of pavement. The tracked amphibian had slipped sideways in the linear crater, but its bulk had protected the jeep from the blast and flying stone. Providential again.

A liche, crumbling as the Germans watched, was half-covered by a paver the size of a garage door.

Reinhard still held his pistol, but his precisian's mind recalled that his companion's shotgun was empty. There were no other liches present, however, dead or alive—if those terms had any meaning in the context.

As the head of Insecurity leaped into the driver's seat of the jeep, Hermann paused beside the vehicle and shook himself. Bits of plaster cascaded from him as he began to load the magazine tube of his shotgun.

The turbine lit with a thump, and the vehicle's headlight carved a blue-white track through the night. "Get in!" shouted Reinhard.

"Look," said the Cheruscan, pointing with the bayonet as he pumped a round of buckshot under the hammer.

A vaulted sewer had underlain the street. It was there that the 21-centimeter shell had detonated to collapse the paving. One of the blocks which had been flung upward by the blast, however, lay in the direct beam of the headlight. The symbol that blazed on what had been its undersurface— the roof of the sewer—was a tau cross with a short bar . . . or the spike that Mandeville claimed would lead to where Hadrian was being held by his kidnappers.

"Get in," Reinhard repeated in a change of voice. He blipped the throttle and the tiller to swing the air cushion jeep, bringing the passenger seat closer to his companion and angling the headlight along the portion of the tunnel which had been opened by the blast. The vault had been enormous, three or four meters high and comparably wide. The considerable quantity of rubble which had fallen into it when the street collapsed was not sufficient to fill or even choke the cavity.

The jeep rocked, then stabilized, as Hermann swung aboard and the automatic levelers compensated for the difference between the Cheruscan's mass and that of the fair-haired driver. "Why aren't we going to follow the trail?" Hermann asked, shrugging to settle himself in a seat made for smaller men.

"We are," responded the head of Insecurity, "but we aren't going to walk unless we have to."

He dialed on power again, and the jeep slid down the slope of debris into the long crater. There was plenty of room to enter the undamaged portion of the sewer, leading away from the sea as directed by the spikes which glowed in the tunnel arch when the halogen beam touched them.

When their headlight picked up the first of the liches, Hermann cursed terribly and tried to aim the shotgun, jostling Reinhard's tiller arm in the process. The jeep's skirt rasped and sang on the stonework as the driver swore in turn.

The sewer was an open channel two meters in width, flanked to either side by a narrow raised walkway. Down the central channel flowed a sludgy fluid that was more water than not, foul as everything in Hell was foul. It was of uncertain depth, but that did not matter to the Germans whose ground-effect jeep skimmed the surface, spraying liquid high against the masonry of the tunnel.

The liche strode stolidly along the righthand walkway, its back to the oncoming vehicle. It carried a spear sloped over its left shoulder and dragged behind it the nude body of a woman. Reinhard had been proceeding at 70 percent throttle along the unobstructed course of the sewer. Now he wicked up the power, lifting the jeep briefly in a redoubled slapping of liquid before the vehicle was able to convert the thrust into greater forward speed.

The liche, hunching against its burden, ignored the jeep even though the wake struck and stag-

gered it as the Germans roared by. Hermann tried
to track the creature, but he was too awkward and
the target was on the wrong side for a right-handed
shotgunner anyway.

"What do you—" the Cheruscan began trying to
shout over wind noise and the echoing thunder of
their passage. They rocked past a tributary arch-
way, lower and narrower than the main up which
they sped, and in the sidescatter of their light saw
a file of liches tramping toward them down the
branching line. The jeep's wash, reflected from the
masonry opposite the opening, tugged the vehicle
with it to brush the stone again in a duet of sparks
and fear.

Reinhard was holding himself under rigid control, but his lips moved in a prayer and the twist-
throttle was rotating toward full in his grip. The
headlight quivered as speed exaggerated every
touch of the liquid surface over which their skirt
danced. Spikes painted at ten-meter intervals
merged into a glowing line whenever the halogen
beam touched the vault in the far distance.

The walkways were lined with liches slouching
forward with the mindless determination of ant
columns. Each carried or dragged a human body.
Every time another tunnel joined the main, it added
not only to the sewage but also to the number of
liches plodding along the walls.

"T—" the Cheruscan said. Then, bellowing to
overcome ambient noise and the constriction in
his throat, he continued, "Turn *around*, damn you
for a fool, we'll find *another* path!"

The jeep's speed was over 60 kph, limited not by
the need for control which Reinhard had entrusted

to Providence but rather by the fact that the vehicle was large enough to be compressing the column of air ahead of it in the tunnel. Their course was that of a loose-fitting bullet in a musket barrel and, like that bullet, they brushed first one side and then the other of the straight tube. The steel-reinforced rubber sides of the plenum chamber sang and groaned.

"There isn't room to turn around," Reinhard said in a shrill icy voice devoid of all certain emotion. "None of the side tunnels are large enough for us, and besides . . ."

There was no need to complete the thought. Every tributary carried a line of liches trudging knee-deep in the doubtful fluid and, as they reached the main sewer, clambering up the steps to the walkway with their weapons and their human burdens. The corpses were rigid or flaccid, depending on the stage of death which held them.

But the liches seemed to notice the jeep as little as they did the stone arches above them. Even when the vehicle's skirt knocked backward one of the creatures as it stepped from a branching sewer, the liche made no attempt to hurl the spear or its shoulder.

"I don't really understand," said Reinhard in a tone of mild curiosity, as if he were commenting on the heatless red glow which had begun to permeate the stonework or the way that sounds were softening as if the Germans were entering a vast plain which gave back no echoes.

But nothing really had changed. They were surrounded by vaulted masonry, eyeless, grinning liches, and the painted markers like a line of square-headed coffin nails beneath which they swept.

Hermann was rigid and popeyed. He gripped his shotgun as if it were the beam supporting him over an abyss. The option of berserk rage which had always before been available to him was not in this case, because there was no enemy save an amorphous fear.

He remembered the causeway through the swampy Teutoburg Forest along which Varus's legions stumbled in darkness and terror while German warriors stabbed at them from the surrounding rushes. All the Romans had reached their destination that night, the goal at which all men arrive, death. . . .

The jeep plunged forward as if driven by something more powerful than the turbine and fans which no longer made its fabric tremble.

The stonework became a lambent orange which silhouetted the liches and the cadavers they bore. The tunnel did not broaden, but it became more and more nearly transparent. Their headlight faded, or else its quartz-hard beam was washed away by the fiery intensity of their surroundings.

There was something black ahead of them, looming against the inferno.

"Why don't we hear anything?" Hermann said. Then, shouting, he repeated, *"Why don't we hear?"*

But that wasn't true, because his voice rang clear in Reinhard's ears, and there was besides a moaning, a soughing, that had nothing to do with wind noise. Perhaps it came from the bony throats of the liches past which the jeep tore at velocities for which it had never been designed.

Despite their speed, the black terminus grew before them with the deliberation of a mountain range lifting itself before a traveler on foot. It had a form, however, or began to shape itself into one as they approached: human where the liches were only humanoid even in silhouette, human in all but size.

The change in scale from sewer tunnel to a devouring and endless translucence had been gradual; when their surroundings shrank and slowed again, it was awesomely abrupt. The figure that had been man-shaped was man-sized as well, the air cushion jeep was at rest on a plain with the dull sparkle of magma, and the double line of liches moved with the staggering implacability of gear teeth to thrust the corpses that were their burdens into a low-roofed building with a door like that of a box trap.

The sides of the building blurred and disappeared as if the ambient glow were fog that shrouded with distance. It must have led somewhere, because each body the liches cast onto the suppurating tangle within made room for itself, even though the mouth of the shed seemed to be packed already.

The lines seemed endless. Even after months of starvation at Auschwitz, the faces of those stumbling toward the gas chambers had too much flesh on them to grin the way the liches did now.

As omnipresent as the orange glow was a whine that could have been agony or great blades spinning . . . or perhaps both.

"Step down," ordered the figure that waited for the Germans between the line of corpses that had been human borne by creatures that were not. Both of them recognized the voice, though the form was unfamiliar, a middle-aged man with a gray suit and sallow face through whose eyes the fiery lambency seemed to leak. Neither man moved.

The figure that spoke in the voice of Satan gestured with one finger and the jeep disappeared, spilling Hermann and Reinhard onto the ground. The shimmering surface burned where they touched it, but even now it did not radiate heat.

The liches disposed of their burdens and stepped away, grinning past the moving columns of their fellows toward the Germans.

"Lord Satan," said Reinhard through lips that were as dry as if he stood at the mouth of a furnace, "we are going to rescue the Supreme Commander, in accordance with our, with our duty to you."

The palms of his hands had been seared when he fell. He squeezed them together in front of him in an attitude which was only subconsciously one of prayer. "We'll go back now," he added in a voice that thinned to silence as the eyes that held his brightened.

"You've come," said Satan, the words a pressure without direction though the lips of the figure moved in concert with them, "as these others have come, because it is time for you to be here."

The head of Insecurity looked around wildly. He recognized some of the corpses being stuffed into the square-sided opening; most he did not. "Master!" he cried. "These others are here by chance, but *we* are doing your will!"

"Nothing here is by *my* will," Satan whispered in a voice like granite slipping. "And nothing is by chance, Reinhard Heydrich, least of all this."

The grooved wooden grips of Reinhard's pistol were cool and a balm to his throbbing hand. As he touched the weapon, Hermann stepped between the man in a black uniform and the angel in a gray suit to shout, "Why am I here? What *is* this place?"

Satan's eyes blazed. He said nothing, but the jaws of the liches trembled with clicking laughter.

Hermann roared wordlessly and raised the trench gun with both hands for a stroke that could have punched the bayonet through the side of a car. The muzzle of Reinhard's pistol was so close to the Cheruscan's head that when he fired, tufts of smoldering hair flew in all directions from behind Hermann's left ear. The bullet did not exit from the top of the skull, but Hermann's eyes bulged and pinkish brains leaked through his nostrils and right ear.

As his companion collapsed bonelessly, the fairhaired German threw down his pistol and, with palms raised and open, babbled, "You see, I've saved you, master, you mustn't let me—"

His voice choked off when liches stepped toward him from either side and took his arms. His flesh sizzled as if the bones of their fingers were branding irons.

"I'm *alive!*" Reinhard screamed, and because his arms were pinioned he tried to gesture toward Hermann with one booted foot. "Take *him*, not me!"

"The Undertaker will dispose of him in good time," said the figure with eyes of fire and a smile like a headsman's ax for the man being lifted past him. "He has no part with these the liches brought, or with you."

The hands of the creatures holding him raised the chief of Insecurity with the effortless strength of hydraulic jacks levering a missile into firing position. Reinhard's perspective changed again, and the corpse-choked doorway became a shaft that plunged vertically toward the keening that could not come from the twisted bodies slipping down it.

"What are you doing to me?" whimpered the German. "Where am I going?"

"To pain, Obergruppenführer," thundered the voice of Hell. "To pain beyond the imagination of even those you penned in Dachau."

And the liches flung him down, toward the bodies and the sound that was louder than his screams.

BASILEUS

C. J. Cherryh and Janet Morris

Alexander had styled himself "Basileus" (Great King) after Darius' death to subdue further resistance among the Persians, then swept triumphant across the Kush, only to bog down in Bactria for three years so that marrying the Sogdian witch Roxane became the only way out.

He'd trekked across the desert to the Oracle of Ammon at Siwah to be declared son of Zeus, only proper for a pharaoh; he'd painted a great city black and flouted the prophets, entering Babylon from the west. He'd died there at 33, no taller than he'd ever been, but a god who could buy salvation for his beloved Hephaestion with golden ships' prows in Babylon.

No one could take that away from him: no matter the cost, he'd found Hephaestion a place in heaven; his Patrocles had been spared this Hellish fate.

And now he had a new Patroclos, the Israelite Judah Maccabee, tall and dark with rebellion, just the man with whom to raise an army to scourge Hell from sea to sea and bring the very Devil to his knees.

For that they were intent upon doing: they had nothing but time. In life he had said, "You, Zeus, hold Olympus, but I set the earth beneath my sway." In death, he had sworn to see if Maccabee was right—if Heaven could be won by vengeance and force of arms.

This he did because his new companion craved it, and because Alexander was a hero and a man who had dwelt too long in Hell not to realize that goals, even unattainable ones, were priceless.

Madness, if it came upon him from hopelessness, would last forever. Raising an army to fight the minions of Hell was infinitely preferable to becoming like Che Guevara—a quivering wreck, a melange of snapped threads, a fallen hero.

No one knew better than Alexander that heroic temperaments such as his own were subject to excesses: as he was excessively brave and extravagantly generous, he was excessively vengeful and extravagantly passionate when thwarted.

It was, Maccabee was fond of saying, this heroic soul of his which had killed him, wearing out his flesh.

"If ever you'd known to spare yourself, perhaps the fever that killed you might have spared you as well," Maccabee had said one night when intimacy was upon them.

That night, like this one, had been long and full of both their ghosts.

Tonight, Maccabee had another thing than intimacy in mind; Alexander could see it in his narrow eyes as he brought the newcomer, no taller than Alexander but dark with a curly mop of hair, to see the Macedonian in his tent.

"This is Zaki, Alksandr—from a time beyond ours."

The little Semite nodded his hooked nose in Alexander's direction and folded gracefully into a squat on one of the strewn cushions around the carefully banked cookfire over which wine was warming.

Maccabee was always bringing him Jews, and Jews believed only in their nameless god. They never bowed to him, never showed the proper respect. But Maccabee loved them, and Alexander loved Maccabee, although what kinship the tall, Homeric Israelite felt with these mongrel descendants of his, Alexander couldn't understand.

Now he said, as Maccabee came to sit beside him and both of them watched the hairy little fellow across the fire, "What news have you, Zaki, which Judah wants me to hear?"

"News?" The little Jew scratched his ear. "I don't know about news—I haven't been here long enough to hook in: we had a nuclear war in my time; I'm still adjusting . . ." The man's face tensed and calmed as memories flashed across it. Then he said: "I heard of Maccabee, came out to volunteer my services. I am, was . . . a modern Israeli; it is God's will, is it not, that we do not forget the Nazi murderers, even here? That we chase them down and plague them with their just punishments? . . . So I have heard, anyway, that you intend to do."

Judah Maccabee, shifting toward Alexander, said under his breath, "Basileus, be patient." Then, louder: "What our new friend means is that our plan to find the Germans who have found a way out of Hell, and wrest from them their secrets, is one in which cause he'll gladly labor. And he is— was—a spy. We are in need of spies."

"You're in need of the Roman empire," said the 20th-century man, "and Machiavelli, and that whole crew that orbits Caesar like well-trained satellites."

Maccabee's face grew dark: he hated Romans.

But certain Germans were reputed to know of tunnels leading out of Hell.

"Germans, Romans—it matters not to me, as long as what we do hurts the Satanic empire and brings us closer to heaven," Alexander proclaimed. "Gods—you do know I am one, Zaki—do not belong in Hell for longer than it takes to mete out special punishment to the especially deserving. But we're helpless without cavalry, and horses are scarce, not to mention—"

"With Caesar, you'll have cavalry and more; troops whose skills you know not of, here in the wilderness," said the small, rat-faced Jew. "We've reason to hate the Romans, ourselves." He bared his teeth. "But war makes new rules. If you want to go against Satan himself, you'll need me—my diplomatic skills, my modern knowledge—and you'll need Caesar and those who follow him."

"Who follow him?" Alexander repeated slowly,

a bad taste in his mouth. "As a ruler? As emperor? As—"

Maccabee shook his head and rubbed a big hand along his jaw. "As a god, I've been told, Basileus. A god like yourself. But don't let that bother you, he—"

"A living god?" Alexander drew himself up straight, wrath beginning to stiffen his spine. He faced Maccabee squarely: "Are you suggesting that we need the help of some pretender to godhead? That another leader is necess—"

"No, no, Alex," Maccabee demurred. "*He* needs *us*. As a matter of fact, Zaki says he loves you— loves your memory, reveres you, perhaps even tries to emulate you. You preceded him, you know. A good hero gives his worshipers a chance to worship, does he not?"

Alexander knew that Maccabee wasn't telling the whole truth, but he'd let Hephaestion manipulate him in the old days—it was one of the perquisites he bestowed on those he loved.

So he only nodded and said, "Fine. Set up a meeting with this Caesar person, Zaki: the specifics must only meet Judah's approval."

The little Semite grinned from ear to ear and rose to make his way out, but Alexander stopped him: "Wait. I want to know about this 'nuclear' war. Have a drink, sit back down. We have all night."

And Maccabee might have mumbled, "We have a thousand and one all-nights," although, when Alexander turned to face his friend, all he saw was the soft, suffused glow of happiness that was the single reward, the only pleasure, Alexander cared about anymore.

If Maccabee had wanted Alexander to treat with the Devil himself, the Madedonian would have attempted it. But since all Judah wanted was that Alexander meet with a fellow potentate, a self-proclaimed god, and (if Judah was right), a man who revered Alexander, it was much easier to acquiesce. The only difficulty would be in this Caesar's willingness to subordinate himself to Alexander.

For the Great King never, ever settled for second place or second best. It just wasn't Homeric.

On the trail to New Hell Alexander's party consisted of forty horses, ten wagons, nearly a hundred dray beasts, and twice as many camp followers, but the entire convoy was halted in its tracks when, during a nightlong stopover by a wooded stream, Alexander the Great came upon a lone sojourner washing in the stream.

The man was made like a god and came up out of the water in twilight looking as if his skin were molten.

Maccabee, who had been with Alexander, had gone back to camp for body oils and a blanket; the Basileus was alone when the vision came to him.

And the vision was, too.

In the lengthy dusk they stared at one another and Alexander felt a quickening of his heart as their glances met: this man had the look of eagles, the heroic brow, the fine features of Herakles. A Phidias might have sculpted him.

Alexander thought, *It's an omen—a specter, a sign that this plan is sanctified by Zeus*, and thus was not afraid. In fact, to prove it so, he slid down the bank and put his feet in the very water in which the vision was standing.

As he did so, the naked man came toward him, wading out of the water, and Alexander noticed a sword and shield of antiquity in the cattails by the stream.

And these were of fabulous construction: the shield was fully five feet high, as tall as Alexander himself; the sword was bronze and scarred, but as noble as it was heavy. In that light, on that night, it was as if Homer himself had dreamed this dream; not Alexander, condemned to Hell and making do.

Overcome with the power of the vision, wondering what he could make of these omens when he retold his tale, the Macedonian sat on the bank, ankles in the water, elbows on his knees and chin propped on fists.

But the apparition didn't disappear—it kept coming. And the spray its massive legs churned from the mirror of the stream spattered Alexander as if in anointment.

And it spoke: "Greetings, boy," holding out its hand in an ancient, welcoming gesture. "I am Diomedes. Have you lost your way? Where are your parents?"

Alexander was too shocked by the name given to bristle at the mistake the apparition had made: he was boyish in appearance and the light was bad; others had made that error and died of it. Without anger, suffused with wonder, the Macedonian blurted: "Surely not *that* Diomedes?" But he knew in his heart that it was.

"Which?" said the big man, who seemed about Alexander's age, as he came abreast of the Basileus and sat on the bank. "I'm the one who fought the Luwians—the Trojans, if you like. Or if you don't."

" 'Diomedes of the wise counsel'? *Homer's* Diomedes?" Alexander was so near tears the words came out choked and shaky.

"Homer? Sometime later, that was—him and his poem, I mean. We didn't know him. As for the wisdom of my counsel, ask Agamemnon, or Odysseus, about that." He smiled and offered his hand again. "And whom have I the pleasure of addressing?"

Alexander began then to explain himself. But it would not be until much later that he managed to explain just how much it meant to have Diomedes appear to him—to guide him, to sanctify his enterprise with his presence, to join Alexander in his quest.

When a hero meets one of his heroes, it's always a little awkward at first.

The room was his again, the sawdust and the broken glass swept away, the marginal signs of damage only a mended break on the bureau leg and a carefully reassembled curule chair which had gone in a dozen splintered, burnished and precious pieces when a Cong shell took the window out. Niccolo Machiavelli inhaled the fresh paint and lacquer smell, trusted his slight, black-clad frame very gingerly to the chair (if he were to be subjected to indignities, it was certain the door was closed and the others were *not* observing).

It held. He edged back with a sigh, adjusted it to face the fragile little desk, and with a careful knife cut the ribbon on the bundle of papers he had brought back to their proper place. His. His sanctum, like himself, spare and elegant, cream plaster walls, scant but expensive furnishings, each piece carefully chosen. Dante, for instance, surrounded himself with clutter: his room was a warren, a labyrinth, disordered as the man's mind, all stacks and clutter that drove sycophants mad in their attempts to arrange it.

Here there was nothing a sycophant could do, the bed invariably immaculate beneath its brocaded spread. The bolster exactly as he would have it. The sycophants kept the floor gleaming, the sills dustless, the spare curtains just so, and woe betide the sycophant who moved the single potted geranium one finger's breadth from its proper place, who disturbed the comb from its precise angle beside the brush on the bureau, the chair from its equally precise position by the window, or who disturbed the *prie-dieu** (about which one did not ask) with its Bible angled just so in the corner.

For one thing, it made the sycophants extremely nervous in this place, and dissuaded them from impertinences, which was all to the good.

They never, for instance, dared the desk drawer, the lock to which he had changed himself (one of Louis's intricate toys, suitably modified) and to which he kept the only key constantly on his person.

---

*A small, low reading desk for kneeling at prayer.

Into this drawer went the papers, one by one, as he sorted them into order.

Tap-rattle against his second-story window glass.

He startled, jostling a sheet of paper which sailed gracefully to the floor. And followed it, staying low until he had reached the wall. Then he ventured a cautious look, out past the shutters.

A man stood down among the replanted rose-bushes, next the ornamental hedge. A dark and smallish fellow. Niccolo gnawed his lip and took the chance, putting himself into the window, watching the hands for unseemly moves, the whole of the landscape for movement of any kind, his eyes wide-focused while centered on the stranger.

Two things were certain: it was not the Administration, who had their ways of requiring attention; and it was not anyone who dared give his business to a sycophant.

That left one outstanding possibility, and his nerves twitched. Dying was not attractive even when his death was assuredly a day's affair: connections assured that. It *hurt*, and he had never, applied to himself, liked pain. Or untidiness. Or indignity, of which he had had quite enough to suffice in his life and his death.

But he served several causes, most of which were best served by going down the stairs and into that garden.

The stranger was a wiry, unkept little man in 20th-century casuals, with curling hair and that profile that howled Eastern, and he stood wringing an already shapeless olive-drab hat to obliv-

ion, as if he distrusted what his hands might give
away. He talked with punctuations from one shoulder and the other, a nod of his head, little shifts of
his feet.

He might be playing a part. Niccolo thought
not. It was too thorough, too preposterous.

"You don't say." Niccolo discovered a brown
leaf on a transplanted rose, took out his knife, and
carefully pruned it against his thumb. "You want
Caesar. Do you realize you're poison here? Utter
poison. This house is very orthodox. The most
orthodox."

The little man gave another punctuation. Left
shoulder. "But you, but you, we know—aren't."

It was English they spoke. With an accent, a
different one in either case. So a good many people who had no wish to speak the language of their
factions—took to English nowadays. Particularly
those who walked a zigzag path. Or crawled one.

"What do you imagine would induce him?"

"Ah." The little man held up a hand, the one
with the ruined hat, reached ever so carefully into
his left shirt pocket with two fingers of his other
hand. Held up a gold ring. A massive one. "My
man sends this."

Seal ring. Niccolo took it very carefully, kept his
eyes on the man and held it up where he could use
part of his vision on it. It was gold and it was
heavy. In some cases you could take it with you.

"Old one, is he?"

"One of the old ones."

"And you won't give his name."

"Just say it's an old friend of Caesar's."

"The dagger-bearing sort?"

"Just take it to him. You want to set the place, that's all right. Just not public. My man doesn't—"

"—go out much in public. Of course. I'm sure he doesn't." Niccolo closed his hand on the ring. "I'll meet you tomorrow at noon. With particulars. Don't you realize half the house is watching us?"

"That doesn't matter. It's only ambush we fear. Not discovery. My man is willing to come here. He had rather, in fact, come here."

"Ummmm." Niccolo discovered another brown leaf, no longer worrying about the position of the man's hands, no longer worrying about watchers. Of a sudden it added up differently, and disinterest, not wariness, was the game. "High-placed old one."

"Very."

"I'll tell you what. You have your man come to the armory tomorrow night. And you take your chances whether he'll meet with you."

"This isn't enough."

Niccolo smiled. Tossed the ring and pocketed it. "*Ecco*, when you come begging, *signore*, you must want a thing very badly. When you want it very badly, you take risks to have it. Therefore, you must take the risk. The armory garage. I'm sure you can find it. I'm sure you know it will have adequate protection. And Caesar may or may not come."

"He will come," the little man said assuredly, and straightened the hat out and walked away.

That was one who walked the edges too. Niccolo pursed his lips and went to trimming roses, a few more brown leaves, until he had seen the little man walk along the hedge and around it and down the street that led along the park, a safer walk for the moment than it had been. Toward the city.

Eccolo. The professional spy. A man to make a man nervous unless one was very sure that this one was only a go-between at the moment, doing a set task. He was not dangerous today. Niccolo fixed the face in his mind, the mannerisms, down to the finest details of the man's walk. He would know this one again, in any distance, in any different dress. There was a thing about hair and untidiness. When one cleared it away one could look so different.

But the way the bones fit together, the way a man walked, the little mannerisms, it took a great actor to alter those things.

He would know this man.

He took out the ring and looked at it. And drew in a very quiet breath.

Now, *perdio*, for a very little he would drop this ring, and tread it into the soft earth of the freshly spaded rose garden, and say nothing at all. Let a very great and very angry king go begging in vain, Caesar none the wiser.

For not very much, also, he would take a walk himself, and manage to use a telephone, and secure a meeting. Or two.

But they were—he had not lied in this—watching from the windows. Certainly one could rely on Hatshepsut, who never let anything rest. And even that nuisance Dante, whose gratitude since the Rescue had thus far amounted to an embarrassing classical poem and a recitation at dinner, than which he had rather have died. Repeatedly. He wished desperately to offend the wretch, and he could not, dared not. It was not professional. If one had uncompromised and loyal connections, of whatever quality, one did not throw them away. Ever.

There was, for instance, the infamous computer. And the wretch was indisputably talented.

"Do me a favor, *Dantille*, dear friend. I'd like to find a certain record."

"Prego, countryman, I want to find a man, do you think if I gave you an account number, you could do a little investigation?"

He pocketed the ring again and went off around the back of the house where the Ferrari was garaged. A terrible scratch on it. Antonius' driving. It was forgiving too much to say that Antonius had been under considerable pressure at the time.

He sent a sycophant for the keys and, receiving them, backed carefully out of the drive and headed down the parkside drive.

In the other direction.

Julius Caesar turned the ring over in his hand, and looked up sharply at the Italian. "Meet him where?"

A shrug, elegant and delicate. The turn of a wrist. Machiavelli leaned against the door of the Ferrari, there in the armory parking lot, and Julius, khaki-clad and mud-spattered, stood by his waiting jeep. The call from the armory had not come at a particularly convenient moment. Emergency, the radio message had said. It was emergency out there, too. Mouse sat with the motor running, and kept it so until Julius made a sudden and decisive motion of his hand: Mouse reached and cut it off.

Two disparate vehicles, aslant in a parking lot mostly vacant and otherwise harbor to a pair of Volkswagens, a Hudson, and an Edsel, besides a small cluster of camouflage-painted motorcycles and a slatsided khaki-colored truck with a large shellhole in the driver's door.

One of Attila's lads had taken the Trip. Impressed the hell out of the new recruits.

"I set it up for here, tomorrow night," Machiavelli said. "After all—" He passed a gesture about them, by implication at the countryside beyond the armory perimeters. "You meet with worse, with fewer precautions."

"Nothing more dangerous, I assure you."

"I agree to that, *signore*. Fervently. On the other hand—you can always fail the appointment, with no disgrace, signore. I gave them to understand I had done this completely on my own initiative. Or you can equally well set ambush. This man's pride will drive him into it."

"Do you know him?"

"Only so much as you, *signore*. Which is certainly enough to caution me."

Julius slid the ring onto his finger. It was too small. He pulled it off with difficulty and settled it loosely onto his fourth. And looked up at the saturnine Italian. "You aren't playing any other game, currently, are you, little Niko?"

A quick denial, a theatrical denial flashed instantly to hands and shoulders. But Machiavelli's face sobered then. His dark, beautiful eyes got that look they had when they reckoned his own chances of life and death, and who he dared lie to. There was more truth between them than Machiavelli gave to most, and few illusions. "Not in this, Caesar, no, I swear."

"Then you don't need to know what I'll do."

There was little crueler than to leave this man in the dark. To take half his plan and shove him out. There was a little hurt on the handsome face.

But Machiavelli also had dignity. *"Cesare,"* Machiavelli said, knowing himself dismissed; and straightened himself from his easy stance against the car door, straightened the hem of his doublet, and walked around and got in.

"My friend," Julius said then, before he could start the motor. "I trust you will be here, tomorrow night. Discreetly."

"Can one be discreet with a legion, Caesar?"

"We assume he wants this very badly."

"I didn't have any assurance his party would accept this. I'm guessing. But the less time wasted in preliminaries—"

"Yes, the less time other sides have to arrange things. My own philosophy."

"Your student, *signore.*" A flourish. Machiavelli's face achieved pleasure, rare sight. Except over fine wines and the discomfiture of a rival. He flashed a grin, white, perfect teeth. And started the engine and drove off, with a little wave of his hand.

"The serpent," Mouse muttered at Julius's back.

"Oh, yes," Julius said. And came round and got in the other side. Mouse started up and geared the jeep into noisy motion. They spun past the truck with the shellhole. Out on the drillfield, a motley group of recruits was standing inspection. Recent arrivals. They came *in* shell-shocked, some of them, and took a while to adjust.

"Meet who?" Mouse asked.

"Alexander."

"Of *Macedon?*" Little got to Mouse. Julius looked askance at him, saw distress. And shrugged.

"He's with the dissidents," Mouse said.

Julius shrugged, and felt of the ring. The very, very old ring. And stared at the dirt road ahead, the way that led through secure perimeters to what was not secure.

He was afraid. Afraid not even in the way that a 17-year-old kid had been able to get to him, arriving to make himself a part of the household. Brutus he could adjust to, even a Brutus who loved and worshiped him. This Hell business was punishment for the likes of Machiavelli, but it was only afterlife, and not even a bad one, for one of the Old Dead like himself: he had figured out that much of the system. He was comfortable, mostly. Except for the fools and the bureaucrats who annoyed him beyond the grave. He had none of the ailments of the New Dead. None of their disabilities, for which he thanked the dubious gods his ancestors. Everyone in the house was immune. Everyone in the district. He spent his death doing what he did in life and with a certain lack of haste about it too, a wisdom painfully acquired.

But this. This insanity, so close after Brutus. Of a sudden he suspected malign and ill-disposed agencies, a turn in the Luck which was his only sincere deism. His own Luck. The Luck that had made Caesar synonymous with god.

Brutus idolized him. And followed Mouse with similar worship. That was one liability which worried him. He distrusted extremes of passion. Even devotion from a bastard son.

Second and greater liability: his own son Caesarion the fool had gone off with the rebels. Not enough that the young lunatic had lodged with Antonius over at Tiberius the Butcher's villa, rejecting any filial gratitude, but of course Caesarion had to commit the most injurious treason he could think of. Lunacy was not from his side of the family. He had forgotten, when he got a son with Kleopatra, just who her father was. The Fluteplayer. The idiot.

Then, annoyance and liability, Administration lost its precious boy-molesting Supreme Commander and replaced him with Rameses—Rameses, who lost the battle of Kadesh when the enemy ignored the appointment and the proper battle-field and ambushed him on his lunch break, a flagrant breach of then-existing rules. (And damned smart of the other side, Julius reflected.) But Rameses, surviving the debacle, straightway marched home, proclaimed the war a victory, and had it engraved that way on his monuments—first and present master of the Big Lie. His promotion to Supreme Commander evidenced that. Somehow he had convinced Administration he had succeeded in Doing Something About the Situation, even if Hadrian was mincemeat and the war department a shambles and the war department computers a disaster area. The crisis was over. Rameses stroked Administration and prevaricated with such a straight face no one would be so ill-mannered as to doubt him.

But Alexander? *Hó basileus*. Great King. *Hó wanax*. High King.

Could a king of such reputation, indeed, lie? Have feet of clay?

Well, there *was* always the King of Bithynia.

Indeed. But this man. This god.

Julius looked at the ring, the gold seal reflecting back the Hell-light of the sky, while the jeep bucked and bounced back down the dirt track that led to their current area of operations, a little matter of Cong spillover. Last mop-up, hoping the computer in Assignments did not *twice* blunder and drop the Cong *back* into Decentral Park.

He did not believe it would *not* happen. In fact, he rather expected it, as he expected most things, except such turns as this.

Mouse asked him no further questions. It was not a thing even Mouse was close enough to him or contemporary enough to understand of him, nor would he explain. Klea might understand. He winced at the thought of Klea. Of the look in her eyes.

He tried the ring on the index finger again, stubbornly. But the flesh and bone would not accept it, would not be that shape. To get the damned thing stuck would be humiliation upon humiliation.

The Established Order had sent him Brutus, his own son and murderer.

Now it sent him Alexander, who was (intelligence reported and Mouse faithfully reminded him) consorting with the enemy at best, very possibly one of them and high in their councils. That in itself was enough to set the fine hairs rising. Julius walked a fine enough line with Administration, and kept his own hands pure, and meant to keep them that way. He had a profound wariness of plots, a prudence learned in a reckless youth and a subtler old age. He had died old, had Julius. Wiser than his murderers, and too tired to be what he had only in that year learned to be, what he might have been if he had had his life to do over again, with the insight of the week of his death, combined with the vigor of his thirties.

Here, he had it. Had it all. He had forever, to do things the wise and the prudent way. Augustus knew it, and feared him, Augustus having reigned long and having died much the same death, of a weary disbelief in the energy and the persistence of his killer. Augustus and he were very well suited to each other. And from his side, he kept a certain truce: they were too wary and too wise to raise certain specters. So, even, was Kleopatra, who in her middle years had mothered Antonius along with all his quarreling brood (and fool Caesarion). They were all too canny to be young fools all over again.

Only this ring, this man—

He had *been* this man. He had been Alexander of Macedon, three centuries before he was born a Julian. He had been Achilles. Then Alexander. He always feared he had been others too, in his worst nightmares. But a man only had three souls. He had accounted for all of them.

Kleopatra called herself Alexander's great-great-granddaughter. And had reckoned herself once his new incarnation in his female principle, his *anima*. "No," Julius had said to her, when they stood hand in hand before Alexander's glass sarcophagus, there in Alexandria, this shrine, this only *place* Kleopatra had ever venerated—"No," he had insisted again, in bed, on a calmer night, there in the garden house near the Tiber, with his death only days away, and himself well knowing it. "The gods only send a soul back three times." Tapping himself on the chest. Head on pillows, musk in his nostrils. "Here. It's here. In this old man, Klea. I never lived to be old before. But I have. Third time, Klea."

"Who said that? Is that Roman?" Kleopatra's voice in the dark. Kleopatra's smooth skin. Young then as she was forever. And as beautiful. "Three times."

"Once for each of your souls. A human being has three souls." He counted them off on his fingers. "The ancestor-soul. That's the *manes*, the Good Spirit. The guardian that stays in a house with the *lares* and protects it from the bad ones. Then there's the Shade, the ghost that we pray to in February. Hangs around the tombs as long as people remember to visit it."

"The *ka*, the old Egyptians said. And the *ba* that comes and finds you if you fail the rites."

"See, they knew. And finally the *anima*, that gets reborn again and again and brings them all back together. But three, three, Klea. A human has three souls. And I think—myself, only myself, I think mine was special. Split three ways, never finished. I'm the third. Here, tonight. Alexander thought he was Achilles. I *know* I was Alexander. So I was both. I know that I was. And I never lived to get old before. Maybe somehow I'm complete.

Maybe I've finally got done what I was supposed to do."

"Don't talk like that!"

Laughter then. He knew. And she did not. Sad laughter. "You have to forgive me what I did, finally. You have to understand. I *was* there. I couldn't bear my own mortality. I refuse to accept it. Even yet." For a moment he did refuse. And was quite calm, knowing again it was inevitable and close. "You forgive me."

"What you did?"

"That. Yes."

A small shiver. "Alexander." She clenched her fists, arms stiff as she lay across him. "Alexander. Then we were fated. Don't you see? I'm your other half. The philosophers say that souls come divided into this world, always in search of what makes them whole. All of us have a natural other half. *Antonius* was never your Patrocles. *I* am."

He felt exposed in that small fiction. The partner. The partner he had supported in all his weaknesses. His alcoholism. His damaging extravagances. Antonius his personal and irretrievable flaw. "Not my Roxane." Mocking her fantasies. "Not my Briseis." The image of Klea in armor instead of silks was ludicrous.

"Patro-*klos. Kleo*-patra." Her small body was all atremble and tense. He shivered, himself, caught by the similarity.

"Hephaestion," he said. Pattern broken. Omen averted.

"That's why. *That* was why I always felt that way when I would go there. Into the mausoleum. That it was another part of me lying in that coffin.

My other half. The one I was waiting for. My god and my king."

Patroclus. Hephaestion. Kleopatra.

Tiber damp. Hell-sky.

Face of a dead god beneath Alexandrine glass, sere and golden.

Kleopatra: *You don't believe in gods.*

Himself: *I believe in my Luck. I believe in a god.*

And it was *me* in that casket. So I destroyed it. With my own hand.

The armory garage was great and cold, forbidding with the baleful light of Paradise, rufous and taunting, spilling over its rafters and the halogen brightness of modern illumination, evil and cold, glinting off the macadam of the parking lot and the chrome of the red Ferrari and the mudhole camouflage of the big tank sighing on its air cushion like nothing so much as a beached whale.

A *physeter*, perhaps, Diomedes thought, in the habit of making connections with his own acquaintance—a sperm whale changed by Athene, his patron, into a juggernaut of war.

But the tank, with its air intakes and its hatch and its long gun snout, was like the wooden horse they'd built once—a thing in which men could hide, in which mischief could be disguised.

The tank made the Achaean son of Tydeus nervous—no less when the little Jew Zaki went rapturous and danced about it, spouting gibberish:

"A hundred seventy tons or more," Zaki gloated, cavorting round it with upraised arms as his ancestors had over Torahs and lamps that burned too long, so that Maccabee shaded his eyes and turned away, on pretext of hunting hostiles in shadows (though the possibility of ambush was real enough, and clear enough to the man who'd raided the Trojan camps with Odysseus and, in the same company, murdered Palamedes).

Ambush, Diomedes thought, was the least part of their worries—traveling with Alexander of Macedon made Diomedes fully expect to turn around at any instant and see the little party transformed into birds.

But all that happened was that Zaki danced around the tank, singing his litany: "Twenty-centimeter main gun in turret; two-centimeter three-barrel Gatling cupola; antipersonnel charges around the skirts; air cushion; fusion-powered fans; iridium armor; steel plenum chamber skirts; and, thank God, the rotating tribarrel can be slaved!"

Startled at the concept of enslaved weapons, Maccabee turned his attention from the shadows (and Alexander, who was running his hands over the parked Ferrari) to the little Israeli.

"What's this?" said the ancient Israelite. "How is it that a noble juggernaut such as that can be a slave?"

Diomedes had been sent by his genius to guide this mismatched threesome he-knew-not-where, but he knew a trap when he smelled one.

His arms were pimpled with gooseflesh and his ears strained to hear the snorts and stamps of their horses, tethered beyond the parking lot where a chain-link fence enclosed the armory garage.

Had it been not a heroic impulse, but some vile, devilish one? Diomedes was no longer certain. The pretty, boyish king before him was no Odysseus.

In fact, he was addled: any man who thought Achilles the best of the Achaeans hadn't been paying attention even to the poets' versions of the War. Diomedes still thought of it as *the* war even though he'd been in others: he'd been part of the Epigoni excursion against Thebes; he'd restored his grandfather's honor and brought him back to the Peloponnesus, after his throne had been usurped, by killing all but two of the usurpers. But it was the birds who haunted him: brothers and comrades, bewitched and beating with raven wings off into the Italian sky. It could happen again.

And there was the tank, on the nearly empty lot under the awful lights men made and Paradise shed. The light had been awful in Troy that day—awful because the Luwians had lost their battle to the gods, not to men.

Athene had been on his right too many times for Diomedes not to know fated times when he was bound up in them.

The horses were too quiet; the tank smelled Hellish and made horrible noises like some dying thing in a land where everything was already dead.

And the Achaean was racked with memories of other wars and other tricks, even though his patron goddess couldn't find him here to make him sure. He didn't need surety—he needed only instinct.

But it had been a specter met on the road, a bird which turned into a man and told him: "Go find you Alexander the Macedonian. Promise him Achilles' acquaintance if he distinguishes himself."

Thus had the ghost spoken, and then disappeared. A ghost that looked like an old comrade but couldn't have been—Achilles had never become a bird.

Birds were evil and so were great breathing hulks of metal with killing snouts.

Just as Diomedes was about to stride forward and give good counsel, suggest leaving this awful, too quiet place and seeking other Romans, if Romans must be had to find Germans, or other feats of valor more likely of success than going up against the masters of metal, breathing beasts so vast, the machine before him gave a heartrending *squelch*, its top came up, and a head, then a second, peeked out.

Diomedes drew his sword in an automatic gesture, then, in a willful one, leaned upon his five-foot shield with as much nonchalance as he could muster: if the battle was joined here, he would fight it—the metal monster with the stentorian breath, its inhabitants, whomever, even should that snout point right at him and belch the Devil's own fire.

He didn't care enough about the others to intervene in their fates: it was a bird who had started all this, a bird who had used a Greek name to him: Alexander. Alexander had been Paris's war name as well. Diomedes had been attracted to the task because of the coincidence; in his time, such things had often meant more than they seemed, at first, to warrant.

And here among the Old Dead he'd never mingled, learned little, stayed to hills he could pretend were those of home—looking for Athene's shrine somewhere, to do penance, wrap the thigh of an ox in fat and say the words and make amends.

The Luwian Paris wasn't here; his crimes were no worse; but he'd long known Achilles would be.

So at the end of little Alexander's trek, should he complete it, was a meeting put off too long: among Achaeans, Diomedes had had the least use for the sulky prince of arms.

Like this child, Alexander, who walked with hands on hips, stiff-kneed, over to the giant metal dragon and spoke too boldly, Achilles hadn't an ass's ration of common sense.

But then, the two were, if the Macedonian could be believed, kindred souls.

And the situation was, in Diomedes' estimation, one which might end the Macedonian on the Undertaker's table—after which, he would be difficult to find among Hell's teeming damned.

So, having thought the matter through and found a personal stake in its outcome, the Achaean moved forward, as casually as he might with naked sword and shield in position, and met Maccabee, who was guarding Alexander's precious rear, in time to hear the Basileus say, "Is it really you, Caesar? Come down where I can see you."

A hand raised in desultory greeting; on its pinky a ring flickered. "It's me if this is yours, Basileus. Mount to meet me—do not fear. Use the intakes as a stepladder and set foot on Hell's finest throne—a battle tank."

The word "tank" reminded Diomedes of the little Israeli, Zaki. "Maccabee," he said under his breath, "where's the Jew?"

The Israelite shrugged, eyes roaming the distant shadows. "Gone, perhaps. But he'll be back. He's right enough—some one of us shouldn't be standing here, ripe for slaughter. Caesar is a snake with many heads."

Diomedes craned his neck, expecting, from the words, to see an actual snake slithering on the turret toward the Macedonian. He saw, instead, Caesar the Roman with outstretched hand helping the slightly built Alexander to climb up.

The second figure in the opening, revealed by Caesar's posture, was female and Diomedes caught his breath.

She was exotic beyond measure, wide of eye and gilded, with a black and beaded, square-cut wig and a neck like a swan.

"What—who is that?"

"Egyptian." The Israelite spat the word. "They all look alike to me. Probably Hatshepsut . . . or Kleopatra—both queens: one collected the penises of her enemies and strapped a stuffed member on when she led her troops to battle—against my people, among others; the other fucked her way to glory. Don't lie in with Egyptian bitches, if you want my company."

Diomedes heard the ancient prejudice, sharpened and honed deadly over millennia, and wondered how difficult this joint venture might prove to be, where hatreds he knew not of were involved.

Wars were won and lost over women, though— he'd slain his own wife when he'd found her in another's arms (no matter what the legends said); he'd seen too many die on beaches over wenches. Diomedes said only: "No women, of any blood, or I don't lend my hand to the Basileus's enterprise."

"Tell that to the Roman with the tank," snapped Maccabee.

Diomedes then looked full at the Israelite and saw such passion as had got the man here.

Hatred, blind and foul, with good reason behind it, but the sort that made a man unreasoning. And he wondered again if he knew enough of the motives of these men to be among them.

The answer was, he knew, that he did not. But a bird had, and that bird—some soul—had turned into a man and bid him hence. So hence he was, for want of better to do. The Achaean shifted his grip on his sword-hilt then, thinking in the way of his kind that there was no trouble here he couldn't handle, if push would just come to shove.

Mounting the tank had been exhilarating; descending into its maw was terrifying, even for Alexander the Great.

Being great, however, was more a matter of overcoming terror than never experiencing it: Alexander did as he was bid.

The man called Caesar, in his late thirties, was handsome—charismatic, well-spoken to a fault, and smart for an Italian.

The woman, however, was a problem: she spoke of souls and spoke in riddles: "By the egg of the Great Cackler, you are a little one; have you a dozen souls, or are you really part of mine—and his?"

Alexander knew what to do with women: one brought a blanket with their blood upon it back from the bower to display among the men; if not, share them out.

"Klea, mind your manners: she's my . . . friend," said the man who thought he was a god.

And there followed, then, a philosophical discussion about souls—their souls, his soul, Egyptian souls and Roman souls, which made the Macedonian realize that these two, though they commanded the fiercest war machines Alexander had ever seen, were mad.

But by then he'd determined to have these tanks, finer than elephants and even warm and smelly like horses. Since Bucephalus had not accompanied him to Hell, a part of him had pined for the steed's loss.

All he could think of, while the Roman and his Egyptian wench prattled on about being descendants of his and having portions of his soul, was acquiring this particular tank immediately and as many more as possible, as soon as possible.

And, of course, Diomedes' dropped-but-pointed hint that success here would lead to an assignation with Achilles.

"So, Basileus, you see, if you and your Israelite friend can put aside factionalism long enough to sneak into Che Guevara's camp and help free Hadrian, a prisoner there—or determine that he's not there—then my obligation would be to you ..." Caesar's eyes twinkled with humor at this infernal joke. "And the Administration would understand that I must honor it—grant you a wish, help you in a task ... whatever you desire...."

Even the little birdlike woman was silent now, and two pairs of eyes stared steadily at him in the dimness of the tank—close quarters for lying, for fighting, for anything but frank discussion.

Waiting for him to state his business, they were.

And since he'd come here to do just that, Alexander said, "I want to raise a levy of cavalry—and tanks—and, with your help, track down these Ger-

mans who are reputed to know a way out of Hell
through tunnels. Once I find them, you need not
concern yourself further. But Maccabee thinks I
need your help. He's a good friend and wise; thus I
came to—"

"Yes, yes," Caesar soothed like a seeress finally
having divined the fortune her client wants told,
"for your friend's sake—and not because you need
help, although tanks are hard to come by. Just
how large a levy would you want? We're fond of
New Weaponry . . . Klea especially . . . but we can
do without it. And when would you want it? Is
Maccabee your first lieutenant, then? And the other,
the Jew spy my people say is with you, what of
him?"

Once the questioning started, once they were
down to logistics and specifics, Alexander relaxed.
He felt a certain uneasiness among these mad Old
Dead, preoccupied with bits of souls and ancient
feuds, but he understood command and its neces-
sities: Caesar was willing, on receipt of Hadrian,
to give the Macedonian what support he needed.

Alexander had dealt with too many governments
and levied too many armies to doubt his ability to
get exactly what he wanted while giving little in
return. It was what had made him great.

And since the matter of godhead and qualities of
kingship hadn't yet come up, he didn't worry about
it. Years of campaigning had taught him that you
handled matters one at a time.

If Caesar needed Hadrian, Hadrian he would
get. If this painted whore must come along, and
other menials of the household, he'd deal with

that. With whatever he must, now that he had not only Maccabee, but Diomedes on his side and somewhere, beyond journey's end, lay a meeting with Achilles himself.

TO REIGN IN HELL

Janet Morris

To reign is worth ambition though in hell:
Better to reign in hell, than serve in heav'n.
                                                    —Milton

For Che Guevara, the new base camp was like
being back in the Oriente Province—before "Tania"
(Tamara Burke: whose agent was she? KGB's?
CIA's?) had seduced him and betrayed him in the
Bolivian Andes to Roberto Quintanilla, Bolivia's
security chief. Before Quintanilla had killed him
personally, putting a quick end to the rural warfare he'd so loved but which, in Bolivia, was dying
of hardship: he'd had only 50 Cubans, 15 Bolivians,
and 15 other assorted Latinos there . . . before his
death.

Before death. Before death and the anguish of
resurrection that followed: an elevator that went
neither down nor up, but elsewhere; a Welcome
Woman who was neither woman nor welcoming,

but had been right when she'd told him that his struggle was just beginning.

Here, in the mountains north of New Hell, he had learned that she was right. One night before the end of his life, unwinding from Tania's white-thighed embrace, he had had a premonition that his "long and terrible war" was about to come to an end. His anti-Soviet stance was making even Fidel nervous; and the woman Tania made him love life too much. So he had said, for the record, what needed to be said, though he had said it as he was soon to die—in obscurity in the Bolivian Andes: "We must above all keep our hatred strong and fan it to a paroxysm," he'd written that night he'd sensed death in the air; "hate as a factor of struggle, intransigent hate of the enemy, hate that can push a human being beyond his natural limits and make him a cold, violent, selective, and effective killing machine."

Thus he had written his own ticket to Hell even before he'd sent those words as his message to the Tricontinental Conference in Havana in 1966. A Red Brigade member who'd come to join him here in Hell's mountains had told him proudly that his words had been reprinted in the Brigades' house organ, *ControInformazione*, in '78, but by then he hadn't cared about what went on "above" anymore.

Hell was his adopted homeland now, and it was a land badly in need of liberation.

For a time—before he'd taken up once again the burden of the revolution—the past had been all he could think about: Tania, and Quintanilla, who had killed him. He waited long by the spot at which the elevator had deposited him in New Hell, which reminded him of Santiago, for his murderers to emerge.

Perhaps agents of the governments he'd so violently opposed were on the side of the angels had been his theory then, when Tania and Quintanilla didn't come; perhaps vengeance was forbidden the damned. But it made no sense: the superpowers were diametrically opposed. Not even God could be on the side of both.

Neither was his theory true—he'd learned that through experience. He had sent many enemies to the Undertaker's table, some of them agents of "foreign powers" who could not forget the old prejudices, some of them agents of the only power that mattered here—the Devil.

His greatest failure was that, no matter how he tried, how many newly damned he interviewed (of sympathetic or hostile persuasion), he had never determined the arrival or the location of his murderers. It was for this he waited: surely, if *he* had been condemned to Hell for "crimes" committed in the name of freedom, his executioners could expect no better. In the meantime, he had an insurgency to run.

His greatest triumph was that, so far in his sojourn among the damned, he himself had never been maimed or slain, never been driven to suicide, never ended up strapped to the Undertaker's foul table, a captive audience for racist remarks and offensive jokes and torture reputed to be the worst thing that could happen to you in Hell. Worse, his captive Hadrian kept telling him, than death itself.

But Che had never feared death in life, or pain or torture; he did not fear them here.

He had been Fidel's premier field commander—trainer *extraordinaire* of the *guerrilleros*—and in Hell he did the same, teaching recruits to make primitive hand grenades from metal fragments, gummed paper, black powder, and tin cans and how to construct homemade grenade launchers from shotguns (best for urban warfare from balconies, rooftops, terraces, and courtyards—practice for the day they brought the revolution to New Hell itself).

It was enough. He was whistling *"Guantanamara"* as he strode among the low tents pitched below a hillcrest, toward the tent in which Torquemada was interrogating Hadrian, foul commander of the Fallen Angels whose reign of terror kept Hell's *campesinos* in line.

The whistling dried in his throat as he passed the tent where wounded languished, the smell of gangrene so strong he nearly gagged. He had loved the art of healing, once; now destruction was the only cure he put his faith in. And faith, even here, was a problem among the ranks. The dissidents were more than motley; they sent him fighters from every age and moralists and "intellectuals" to boot.

He saw Confucious—still fat, though he got no more to eat than any other, just rice and beans and glory—arguing with Gandhi under a pine tree. Up in its branches, a bird he couldn't identify hopped from bow to bow, picking pine nuts from the cones.

If there was one darkness in his afterlife, it was that he had loved God's earth so well—all its beauty, all its bounty—and yet the struggle had drained the joy of it away.

Here, all things were barbed and tainted: the bird which sought only its due—to feed as Nature intended among the trees—was screeching now, caught by a darting snake who'd hidden on the branch.

He turned his head away as its beating wings began to slow their furious struggle, its head already gone into the snake's unhinged jaws.

It was a lesson he saw everywhere. Morale was a great problem, when the struggle must be an end, and not a means.

". . . beyond his natural limits . . . a cold, violent, selective, and effective killing machine." The greatest problem was that no one stayed dead in Hell. The Undertaker had a corps of assistants to handle the resurrections of the ranks.

He glossed over it with his troops—with the young Iranians and Iraqis, this was easy; with the more sophisticated Italians and Macedonians and Etruscans and Greeks, less so: neither intelligence nor perspicacity, he'd found, had aught to do with birth century.

Passing the mess tent, he heard a stanza of the camp song Homer had written for them; sung in common English, it hadn't the beauty of the original Greek:

> Heroes in Hell, all the big names,
> The best and the brightest
> Fanning the flames . . .

He walked on by, wishing once more that he could change the rules of Hell enough to decree

Spanish as the modern lingua franca. But Classical Greek and American English were the chosen tongues, and nothing he'd been able to do would change it. At least, nothing yet.

When he reigned here, Hell would be free, a different place. A man named Milton he'd met had told him a story, and in it had been the observation: "The mind is its own place, and in it self can make a Heaven of Hell, a Hell of Heaven."

The rest of the tale had been obscure, arch and ornate as only a Cambridge man from the 17th century could make it, but the one fragment of verse had hit home, rung true in Che's mind.

In front of the interrogation tent he stopped and turned his head—not at a noise, but at a sudden silence, a cessation of sound in which the groans coming from within the tent were suddenly loud and obscene in their loneliness.

Everywhere else, it was still. No moans came from the medical tent; no clatter of tin cutlery or stanza of song from the mess tent; no mule brayed or horse snorted or engine coughed up ahead in what was called, by the moderns, the "motor pool" even though diesel was scarce and gasoline near nonexistent; not even the laughter of men gaming in their tents or passing the camp women around could be heard.

Just utter silence: no birds, no wind in the lowering dusk which might last a moment or an hour or days on end.

Except for Hadrian's tortured sobs and grunts, it was wholly and eerily quiet.

It was as if no blade of grass or twig or insect or

man dared move; as if the whole of Hell had come to attention.

It spooked Che and he didn't like being spooked. He kicked a rock and the impact of his leather sole sent it skittering through the dirt, but its trip was soundless; the impact without report.

His hackles risen, he turned on his heel.

The regular guards outside the interrogation tent were absent this evening.

Discipline, in a camp like this, ought to be tighter, but the perimeter he'd just inspected was well-manned, and everyone knew who was inside the tent.

The interrogators didn't need protecting.

He pulled back the flap, stooped and ducked inside.

The torturer in red put aside the hot poker he'd been applying, in Iranian fashion, to Hadrian's exposed bottom.

"*Capitan*," smiled the seared and chasmed face of Torquemada, his long nose bobbling as he spoke. "We are making progress, slow but certain."

"Out, now," Che said. He still often pretended to broken English—a conceit that kept him vital in the eyes of his men, one of the people, and also kept explanations to a minimum.

He looked away from the body of Hadrian, bound to the tent's centerpole, and at the two others lounging on Persian carpets drinking officer's rations of watered wine—a pair of independent commanders Che was wooing, hoping to bring into his orbit and under his command.

One was Alexander of Macedon, young and brilliant, beautiful—tonight playing the good cop to

Torquemada's bad cop, his cold cruel smile belying the fiction. The Macedonian was the temptation continually offered Hadrian should he capitulate and give Che's army the secrets of the Tower of Injustice. Beside him was Judah Maccabee, the prototypical freedom fighter who had a personal score to settle with the entire Roman Empire and resembled a former love of Alexander's so much that the young conqueror sulked in his tent whenever Maccabee went out with a line unit.

But the pair's intricate relationship didn't bother Che—one used whatever was at hand. And with a pederast like Hadrian, these two vicious, handsome fighters would do more good than Torquemada.

Only, to prevent insult, he'd had to let the torturer have a go at the prisoner. Politics always intruded.

Alexander said, "Hiya, Che," with a winsome grin, and turned on his side so that his chiton rode up and Hadrian groaned, sagging against his post.

Che, relieved that, within the tent at least, sound had not been banned, squatted down and took a cover from one of the dishes between the two ancients. He always thought of the B.C.-types that way, even when their apparent ages, as in the case of Alexander, were near his own.

"It's kosher," Maccabee assured him with a sly grin. This killer was the ash from which the phoenix of the modern revolutionary had risen. Che respected him above all the others for reasons that could not be numbered, but sensed and seen in the deep brown eyes: a man who had fought to the death and led his men to suicide for a cause; one who would do it again, as many times as was needed.

Maccabee had stories about the Undertaker; Maccabee was sure God had simply made a mistake; Maccabee, who still loved his God and had a faith that overrode not only his condemnation here but the tales he'd heard from victims of Nazi atrocities, was sure there was a way out—that Hell was just a test of faith, that the valorous would find a way to heaven by force of arms, if nothing else availed.

Che disagreed, but Maccabee was valuable. And he could get women to do anything for him: the lamb was no doubt kosher; the chicken was roasted to a turn.

Eating was a transient pleasure; one paid a later price. Che didn't want to vomit or spend hours trying to take a shit. But he took a bite: "Good. Delicious."

It was a display for Hadrian's benefit.

Quasi-mortal bodies made demands.

"Water ... please, water," moaned the Roman who'd destroyed the Jews' Great Temple, through scabbed and cracked lips. Even swollen, his mouth was tight and mean. Blood ran down his legs, Che noticed.

And noticed that Torquemada had left without a sound, without complaint, just as Alexander mumbled around a mouthful washed with wine, "Old fart's going to kill this guy, and we'll lose him to the Undertaker. Then what use, all this trouble?"

"Water," Hadrian moaned again.

Alexander was a drunk—had been, was, and

would be. Sometimes he swelled up like a balloon
from all he drank.

"You should take it easy on the wine, Alksandr,"
Maccabee warned: they shared a tent, these two.

"Mind your own business, Yid. We've got the
dog to clean up the mess ... if we need him.
Anyway, a little wine won't kill me—would that it
could," giggled Alexander. And giggled more, and
rolled over on his back, holding his stomach in a
paroxysm of laughter at a joke only he found funny.

Che wasn't sure whether he meant the actual
hound which ate vomit, or Hadrian, tied to the
tentpole.

Maccabee watched with obvious concern: Alexander had been prone to fits in life—if he swallowed his tongue, they'd lose him to the Undertaker.
And the Macedonian knew too much. Any of Che's
officers or collaborators, if killed, instantly became
as great a danger as if he'd defected to the Other
Side by his own choice.

Damned difficult way to run a revolution. Che
had never had to be so conserving of life.

Maccabee said, "Shall we water the pig?" then,
without waiting for a word from Che, took a tin
pitcher and, standing before Hadrian, poured a
thin stream out in front of the bound captive—
right in front of his face, so that it broke on his
jutting, aristocratic nose and a few drops rolled
mouthward.

Hadria lunged forward in his bonds, dignity forgotten, tongue outstretched.

Che watched emotionlessly: interrogations took
time; they had all the time they needed.

Beyond the Israelite and the Roman bound to

the centerpole, the tent flaps rustled, then drew back.

Maccabee was intent on the suffering face of the Roman captive; he didn't look up.

Alexander was still chuckling drunkenly, muttering to himself, hugging one knee to his chest—he was a man of heroic humors, extravagant in bravery and debauch, generous to a fault with loved ones; likewise, his temper was legend, his crimes of passion spectacular. And his drinking bouts left him blind and stuporous.

So only Che saw, as the flaps drew back and the woman entered, that beyond her was not the grass and dirt and farther tents of the campsite, but only a featureless gray like deepest fog or storm clouds blowing in from the Pacific . . .

It took him only a moment to realize who she was.

Tania! Tamara Burke, the agent of his destruction.

Her eyes were large and soft, appealing. Her fatigues were of the tiger pattern, meant for jungle, designed by American hands.

"Che, my love, my heart," she said in Spanish.

It tore his soul. She had bandoliers slung in an *X* across her breasts; a Maadi AKM was on her shoulder; her hair was tucked up under a beret; and she was taking off gloves as black as the camouflage streaks on either cheek.

"*Madre,*" he muttered, then said in English, as Alexander stopped giggling and whistled slowly and Maccabee stopped pouring water on Hadrian's nose and even the Roman emperor turned his head to glimpse the owner of the sensuous voice: "What are you doing here, Tania?"

Or Tamara. The agent of his death, of his betrayal. Which was it, he wondered once again, KGB or CIA? Who had sent her, sicced her on him like a bloodhound, back when things like love and trust mattered and sex wasn't just an empty word and her thighs had been so soft, like velvet, so white, so . . . deadly?

"Someone named Andropov helped me find you." She unslung the AKM from her shoulder and he tensed. In his jeans waistband he had a pistol, a .45 Llama, a weapon from his own time, a talisman of his heritage. But he didn't pull it out. She was too real, too full of life.

He knew it was an illusion—it had to be. None of them were *alive* in the way the word was meant to be used.

But she was corporeal, physical and real. Her musk filled the tent and her animal magnetism made even Alexander sit up straight.

But then, as Maccabee was saying, "Aren't you going to introduce us, Che?" Tania replied to his question.

"Doing here?" she repeated as she fired from the hip, one-handed, spraying a three-shot burst at Hadrian's head, which exploded, spattering bits of brain and eye and skull casing over Maccabee as the Israelite threw himself flat, and over the tent walls, and over Alexander as he rolled out of her line of fire, his short cavalry sword snicking from its sheath.

It was too late to save Hadrian, Che knew even as he leaped toward Tania and the AKM's short barrel drew a bead on his gut; it was probably too late to save himself.

He didn't care. He just wanted to touch her, to squeeze the life from her himself after a time, but to save her from Alexander's sword ... at least until he got his questions answered.

He wanted one night with her, that was all.

But the Macedonian was quicker and she was distracted.

He saw the shortsword arc back and dived for Tania's knees even as she fired on him, hoping to take her down before Alexander followed through with his swing.

Bullets ripped into his thigh and then his shoulder and then he couldn't see anything but the grass and dirt and her jack-booted feet as she tumbled, the AKM discharging its whole clip skyward as her headless body convulsed.

When he rolled over, she was staring at him; Maccabee's strong and gentle fingers were probing at his jeans, cutting away the blood-soaked cloth.

She was staring at him.

It seemed that she was buried up to her neck in the ground. Her hair had always been beautiful. He'd loved the feel of it when they made love: Tania's silky hair against his naked buttocks.

Alexander and Maccabee were talking about someone who was wounded: "... shattered the bone. Going to need more than the bullets dug out. Get Madame Curie, Alex, and quickly."

But it didn't matter; Tania was watching him like she used to when they'd finished and there was just the night wind and their breathing and a flickering candle flame in the thin Bolivian air.

He reached out to touch her cheek and the head

rolled sideways, exposing the blood beneath and the severed neck.

Then Che began to scream.

But it didn't help the pain.

SPECIAL BONUS!

A sneak preview into the first
"HEROES IN HELL"
hardcover novel—

THE GATES OF HELL

by C. J. Cherryh and Janet Morris

Coming in April from Baen Books!

THE STEPS LED DOWN AND DOWN, a masonry track through living stone, where the air was cold. They were beyond the lightshafts now. Dim bulbs shone at wide intervals, and showed them an iron door in the shape of an embracing couple.

Chain rattled and the couple slid apart with a metallic thunder. Kleopatra never flinched, but walked through into the golden and orange light and the reek of incense and corruption, with Antonius beside her.

Smoke puffed and belched at her right. Fire shot out in a sudden blast and Antonius snatched her aside. "Damn this!" Kleopatra yelled to the surrounds. "Emperor, Egypt is here!"

"Careful—" Antonius said; as a second erotic gateway parted, on a dim room and a stark throne and a man in a black toga. There was a single brazier for light; the walls round about were painted with cabalistic signs.

It was a man at first glance in his fifties, hard-jawed and rawboned. He sat with his chin on his fist and his brows lowered. But the dryness of a mummy was about his skin, and his eyes when he looked at them burned with furtive and furious anger. "Well," he said, "well, I own Egypt. Do I own you, pretty pet, do I, pet?"

"I'm before your time, Emperor. I—"

"You've corrupted Antonius, have you? Turned him against me. They all turn on me. Do you think I'm a fool? Do you?"

"Would the pharaoh of Egypt call another emperor a fool? Absolutely not. We have our unique interests."

"You have Antonius." A dark and lascivious chuckle. "Damned, useless Antonius. Augustus killed him, you know. Your dear housemate killed him. Do you have unique interests with Augustus, mmmmn? That butcher. Married our mother, you know. Unique interests there too. He made her send that doctor. Augustus did. What's he like in bed? You do those things he likes?"

"Sir," Antonius said.

"Shut up. I'm talking to Egypt. What are you like, Egypt, what *do* you like?"

"What I'd like, since you ask—"

"Killed my brother. I walked. Wanted no part of horses. Hundreds of miles back from Gaul. He stank by then. I walked that funeral procession all the way back to that bastard Octavianus Augustus. *That bastard and my mother, do you know that, do they still visit?*"

"Never. Majesty—"

"*I am a god.*" He slammed his fist on the arm of the throne. Spittle flew. "*I am a god.*"

"Well, so, dammit to Set, am I!" It flew out. Careful with him, Antonius had said. Humor his fancies. She gulped a mouthful of air, felt Antonius' hand touch her back as she set her feet. "I'm Zeus-Ammon like my predecessor, I'm Osiris under the earth!"

His eyes flew open, burning bright and mad. "God of the dead. God of the dead." He gripped the arms of his throne and looked at her from one wildly-focussed eye, as if he were braced against some terrible wind. "Get away from me!"

"I want your damn Germans!"

The rigid body relaxed, limb by limb, the brac-

ing arm first, quite as if that impalpable wind had
quit blowing. "You want my guard? You want the
poor bastard Germans?"

There was no reasoning with this man, no nego-
tiating. A chill sweat was on her limbs. Her heart
was slamming against her ribs. "Yes," she said.
"Give them to me and I'll leave."

"Treason, *treason!*"

"Klea—" Antonius took her by the arm and pulled
her backward. "Get out of here, come on, Klea—"

"Treason!"

It *was* time to go. She edged farther back, hating
to turn her back on this lunatic. Then she whisked
about and matched strides with Antonius in haste
to leave this place.

"Osiris," the voice rang at her back. "Osiris!"

It was summons. She kept walking a pace and
another, and heard the rising note of petulance,
dangerous at her back. She glanced over her shoulder, just to see if there was a weapon there.

"Osiris. You want my Germans?"

It seemed a fool's act to stop. But the German
Guard was what she had come for, and it was a
coward's part to run skittering out the door with
this madman perhaps about to send assassins after them, which made it not at all foolish to stop
again and face this lunatic.

"Osiris is a woman," Tiberius said, and laughed,
giggled, this huge wreck of a grim old soldier. The
eyes went quickly grim, the right more focused
than its mate. The mouth grinned. "The lord of the
dead comes to visit me. Wants my Germans. What
will the god pay me? Come sit on my lap, pretty
god?"

"Klea." Antonius slipped his hand inside her elbow. "Klea, for the gods' sake get out of here."

It seemed like a good idea. She started to turn away.

"Osiris. My brother's dead."

She walked for the door, carefully, the doorway which was worse on the obverse than on its facing image. Her heart beat and fluttered like something trapped. The very air seemed strangling.

"You want my Germans, Egypt, find my brother!"

She stopped, resisting Antonius' hand. Turned and faced him again.

"Give me my brother," Tiberius said plaintively. His jaw knotted and his chin quivered. "God of the dead, give him back and you can have anything, I'll give you anything if you give him back."

The tears ran down the mummified skin. The lineaments of the face were suddenly, in the dim light, that of the stern old soldier who had lost the gentler part of him. Drusus had died of a fall off a horse. Not even a heroic death. Dead of a fall and nothing more.

And she drove right into the wound. "We might learn something. We might learn where he is. Give us the Guard and we might find him."

"Wonderful, isn't she pretty? Find my brother." Tiberius wiped at his eyes and put his fingers to his lips and gave a piercing and startling whistle, that echoed off the walls.

There was a rattle behind them. Kleopatra whirled about as Antonius did, and froze. A German stood in that disgraceful doorway, blond giant in leather and furs, with braided hair and beard and frosty eyes; and an M-16 in his arms dead-leveled at them.

A rustle from behind them again. "Heh. Doesn't speak anything civilized. It's Perfidy, isn't it? Yes, it's Perfidy." Tiberius' voice was closer, the rustle of his garments and the whisper of his steps on the pavings betraying his movements. "His twin is Murder. Heh. I give you Perfidy and Murder and all their band. Perfidy has a few words of Latin, don't you? Pretty fellow. Cut your throat, wouldn't he? Perfidy!" And a guttural and rapid discourse after, to which the blond giant's eyes flickered, and his face, no less grim, looked as if it had some life in it and some thinking going on behind it.

"Huh," the German said, and lifted up his rifle as Tiberius strolled into their vision, at the side.

"Loyal," Tiberius said. "Die with their chief. All of them do. Get out. *Get out*, go find my brother. Find Drusus. Find Drusus. I want him—"

She delayed for nothing. She darted out the door with never a backward look until:

"I give you Cowardice too!" the Emperor screamed after them. "I give you Antonius! Take him too, damned traitor, damned, damned damned *impotent* traitor, let death into my house, find my brother, find him, find him!"

Sobs attended them. And Perfidy's steps, quick as their own.

"Gods," Kleopatra said when that first door had closed itself, when they reached the hallway. She was shaking. She turned and grasped Antonius by the arms. And saw a dreadful look on his face.

"Let's get out of here," Antonius said.

"Don't—don't let—"

But there was no arguing with Antonius. She had been married to him long enough to know that look, that terrible, driven look.

All the while Perfidy stood there staring at them with his rifle in his hands, lost in his own uncomprehending world. As the erotic doors opened on the upward stairs.

Due east of New Hell, where the mountains guarded by the Erinys sloped to a pass through which an army could thunder—that was where Alexander had wanted to meet Caesar's forces. Not here, in New Hell by the sea, so far from the country and so completely out of Alexander's element.

But here they were—Maccabee, Diomedes, and he—to meet the man called Julius and his Egyptian whore and his armies of the night: the great physeters which were battle tanks (so much more impressive than Alexander's forty horse), the blond and smelly German guards and the retinue of an entire household (including countless flitting sycophants and a woman in a pink jumpsuit like a second skin who rode upon a litter that put Alexander in mind of Darius and his bathtubs and his familial baggage).

"This is not what I wanted," Alexander said, hating the slap of the parking lot's tarmac against his sandals and wishing that he had a horse under him, to put him eye-to-eye with his taller companions.

"Not?" said Maccabee, who had accompanied him into Che Guevara's camp to see to the liberation of Hadrian. (And "see" was all they'd done about it—the Devil had sent an emissary, a woman—fittingly enough—who'd killed the Supreme Commander to get him out of the clutches of the rebels and back to the Undertaker's table.)

"Not," Alexander snapped, with the fumes of hot tank in his nostrils and the hellish halogen light hurting his eyes.

Diomedes had come with them to the rebel camp's edge, but no farther. Without explanation, the hero had simply leaned upon his Alexander-sized shield, saying, "I'll wait here."

And he had done that, been right there. But it had ruined the whole adventure for Alexander. The Basileus wanted his new Friend with him, not waiting in the bushes to guard his back or do whatever Achaeans did. Alexander still thought it might have had something to do with Homer's presence in Che's base camp.

But now was no time to ask. Diomedes was in possession of the "Litton field phone," which the little modern Jew, Zaki, had bestowed on his betters. Into this, Diomedes would sometimes speak, as if to an oracle, asking questions.

And, like an oracle, the box gave answers—cryptic answers, bossy answers, ultimata. Alexander the Great didn't like taking orders from a box, no matter what Sibyl spoke through it.

But it was the will of the oracle named Litton that had brought them here, to meet with Caesar's army in the parking lot of the armory.

Like the Oracle at Siwah, it was not to be denied. Like the Sibyl at Cumae, it spoke in riddles. Like the Pythia, it was treacherous. And it needed no water to drink or bay to chew or leaves to write upon. Nor did it sit upon a tripod over a smoking chasm of the gods. It merely belched or farted out its orders, and even the best of the Acheaens obeyed without question.

Even now, walking toward the glare of light in which men and arms and weapons of death and mighty chariots with rearing horses (who knew as well as the Macedonian that those tanks were frightful beyond flesh's ability to bide), Diomedes spoke into the Litton as if to a lover: his lips to its talisman, its scepter, his fingers stroking its nipples sensuously.

The jealousy which Alexander was beginning to feel toward the Litton oracle was of proportions which presaged violence: either Diomedes must be persuaded to renounce the Oracle, despite the seductiveness of its wisdom, or Alexander would destroy it. Where was Bucephalus when the Macedonian needed a trusty war horse with iron hooves to rend and pound?

At that thought, the Basileus shook off his black mood—Bucephalus had not come to hell. The very recollection of the steed was one he shied from; he'd not wish it here, but he missed it more than any man. Sometimes he missed it more than life.

"Not," he said again to Maccabee, while with his other ear he listened as Diomedes whispered Zaki's name to the Oracle of Litton and the box hissed back like a brazier. "How is it that we can raise an army in New Hell without raising alarms? If there was no triumphant procession for us— returning heroes from Che's camp—how is it that this Julius can command the very streets of the Devil's lair?"

"You suspect a trap?" The tall Israelite swiped backhanded at his chin, though it wasn't hot enough this ruddy night in New Hell for sweating. Eyes which had withstood a desert and the Roman empire turned to him and held, with gentleness there for a spirit who'd not lived long enough to fail and thus had never learned the lessons which had brought such as Maccabee—and Caesar—here.

"There'll be no trap, Alksandr," the handsome ancient promised. "Not of the sort you mean, at any rate. Holes out of Hell you want, holes we'll find. We've got Germans as auguries. We can split one and read his liver, if you don't believe me. Or ask Diomedes, who's been in touch with Zaki this whole time."

The implication was, of course, that no Jew would ever let Maccabee down, that Jews didn't make the sort of error Alexander half expected. Maccabee, when on the subject of his Jews, was tiresome.

But Maccabee was like an extension of Alexander, like an arm or any other member of his body, as necessary as moonlit nights or wine . . . Then Basileus remembered there was no moonlight here, just the glare of New Hell in the night sky and Paradise glowering down in its phases.

So, to cover his discomfiture, he asked Diomedes, as they came up to the chicken-wire fence and two German hulks crossed spears to bar their way, "And what does Litton say, Achaean? Are the omens good? The prognostications pleasing? Where's our little spy?"

"Spying. As your army is arming and your camp followers following and your horses snorting at the wind back at the pass where the trek begins."

"In other words, all things are in their place in heaven and earth—and hell?" The voice that interjected itself into a private conversation was female.

Alexander looked right and left, before and behind. To the right was the baggage train's refuse, to the left an open street, deserted but for parked chariots-with-no-horses—cars, as Zaki said. Before were still the pair of Germans barring the gate with festooned, long-handled spears or axes. Behind was only the night and the way they'd come.

Yet the woman's voice came again, tinkling with laughter: "Basileus, are you there? Is it really you? And your army—is this the whole of it?"

Then the Oracle of Litton farted and Diomedes snatched its appurtanence from its cradle with a heavenward rolling of eyes. "Who speaks to us? Name yourself, and say why we should hear you."

The box hissed like a cat with its tail underfoot. Diomedes shook the thing he held, and swore in Zaki's name, and at the same time, Maccabee's iron grip came down on Alexander's arm, to slow and caution him, with its promise of protection welcome in the city's night.

The Macedonian had stayed away from this hellish haven of the Old Dead who were his juniors, of the New Dead and their weird ways, for many reasons: he sought a new empire to make him its Great King in the hills; he sought elephants and chariots; he thought to placate Zeus and come here, some day, triumphant and a conqueror, entering a city on its knees in a parade of blood and blossoms.

He'd sought none of this—oracles trapped in boxes, women's voices from the air, the New Dead

with their madness which Zaki said had destroyed
the living world above—until Maccabee had come
into his life and made him think there was a way
out from here. He'd been, metaphorically, sulking
in his tent until Reality came to its senses and
petitioned him to come out and lead it to glory
once again. Maccabee had convinced him that, in
the Devil's world, human nature could not repent,
foolishness was rampant, and a man—even a
Basileus—must take the initiative and revenge all
slights, eye for eye, tooth for tooth.

Yet he mistrusted his decision to rejoin the struggling masses at that moment, while Diomedes quieted the oracle of Litton and slung it over his
shoulder, pointing with his spear to a form for
which all chaos parted, even the giant German
guards.

"Ite! 'Agite!" the oncoming woman swore like a
general, and the huge Germans backed away. *"Perdi,*
Great King, you must forgive these . . . creatures:
Perfidy and Murder, this pair, the twins. We've
just got them, and they don't have much of any
language."

Behind Kleopatra, the Germans closed, crossing
their war implements with a *thunk* as final as
burial.

Over her shoulder was slung a second Oracle of
Litton; around her throat was an intricate piece of
Egyptian jewelry which had a serpent that curled
up toward her mouth but didn't touch it. She
strode right up to Alexander, without more than a
bob of head as obeisance, and put her hand on her
hip: "I asked, is this the whole of your army? If so,

there's the matter of command. If you're not bringing an equal share? . . .''

"You!" Klea, as Julius called this creature of wiles, this woman who thought like a man and thought she was in possession of a piece of Alexander's soul, had spoken through the Litton oracle. Oracles, Alexander well knew, could be corrupted into tools of political manipulation. At Siwah, he'd been greeted as a Son of Zeus and the rest of what was said hadn't mattered . . . much. Inside, where the doomsayers had spoken evil, he'd closen not to believe them. Now, in public, a more forceful statement was necessary. He held out his hand to Diomedes, without his eyes ever leaving the beautiful, pouting face full of challenge before him. The woman would have to learn her place.

"The box," he demanded.

Diomedes gave it into his hand, and its weight was a surprise. It took all the stubbornness which had made Alexander great to keep his arm from dropping with the weight of the Oracle of Litton he now held. He felt muscles burn, and knew that later his arm would be sore to the elbow; but with grace and very slowly, in a very kingly fashion, he raised the box high, still eye-locked with this slut whom, Zaki had told them, slept with not only Julius but also with an underling of his called Antonius.

Then he opened his left hand and the Oracle of Litton crashed to the macadam while, with his right, Alexander drew his sword.

The action caused Diomedes' long and weighty sword to leave its sheath also, and the Achaean's eyes to sweep the shadows for unseen threats. Into

Maccabee's big hands came not a sword, but a magical and thunderous slingshot called an Uzi, a souvenir from their trip to Che's camp.

Both companions had misconstrued, however: it wasn't the woman, Kleopatra, or any stalkers-from-shadows that Alexander sought to rend, but the Oracle of Litton.

Three times he drove down, from a full overhead swing, into the heart of the oracle with his ivory-hilted sword.

Light came from the box, sparkling shards that hissed and magic that ran up his sword and bit his fingers the first time. But Alexander was full of rage, the pain a thing to be dealt with later. On the second swing, worms of many colors were revealed within the broken casing; on the third, the Oracle was halved and shattered.

But there was no blood. There was, in fact, nothing inside of flesh and blood—no tiny person, as he'd suspected, sitting in a tiny chair over a tiny brazier, no tiny skull mashed to pulp. Just worms of many colors and shattered Roman glass and enameled bosses like pieces of an Egyptian collar.

The woman had given back a pace, but not knelt as had both of Alexander's companions. More disrespect: her head was higher than his. And behind her, all the others were still standing.

Maccabee saw the direction of Alexander's glance and touched his arm: "Ignorance, my lord Basileus. And strange customs, from different lands. Tolerance."

It was a watchword of kingship, one that had helped make him great.

And in that interval, the woman had knelt down,

also. She was close enough that, despite her khakis and her New weapons, he realized for the first time what attribute had made her the single confidant of Caesar on their first meeting: she had magnetism which was like tides in the distant sea.

Alexander felt it, and so did both men, on his right and left. With Diomedes' muttered curse, she cocked her head: "Think of me not as a whore, then, but as a brother." She offered a gamine smile. "I am a king, a great king. I am Egypt. Respect the office, hero, and we'll do well enough." As she spoke, her fingers stirred the wreckage. They were long and shapely fingers, gilded on the nails.

Maccabee reached out to imprison her wrist, and stopped his hand at the sound she made. But he said, "Our forces are at a safe place; we'll meet with them soon. Where's your . . . friend, the Roman?"

Her laughter tinkled again, but this time it was as deadly as the shards of sharp glass that were all which remained of the Oracle of Litton. "Which Roman? Meus Iulius? Or Antonius? He's coming along, did you know? Caesar didn't, and he's not pleased. Decius Mus, perhaps? Or Musius Scaevola? All these Romans have found this little outing to be of interest. As have Machiavelli, and (though let's not tell the others just yet) Hatshepsut. So, are you going to tell me? Or must I guess?"

"Caesar, woman. It's him with whom I treated, king to king."

"It's him and me with whom you treated, king to king to king," she said, did the frail creature, running her fingers through the worms of Litton, her eyes now on Maccabee's Uzi. "Tell your Jew to put his weapon by."

Alexander nodded and Maccabee did, backing a step in a crablike fashion and excusing himself to "go find Zaki. If she's witched him, or the Romans have, this goes no further."

"And does he speak for you?" said the woman who was beginning to seem like a Pythia, the more because Alexander couldn't seem to stop watching her hand fondling the shards of the oracle.

"Sometimes," Diomedes interjected before Alexander could think of an answer due a woman who thought she was Egypt that would dismiss her—he couldn't be seen chatting with women—without too obvious a slight.

"Then," said Egypt, "perhaps you'll tell me, hero, the answer to my question: will you tell me, or must I guess, why you destroyed the field phone? They're shielded, I'm told. Your own man Zaki gave this one his blessing."

"If we want oracles, we'll get them at New Cumae," Alexander said without waiting for Diomedes, and without forethought. "As a matter of fact, we'll stop there when we've met up with my forces. The Sybil will speak of holes with less artifice than your Oracle of Litton."

Kleopatra blinked and it seemed that she ordered her face very carefully before she rose up saying, "I see. Well, Great King, if an oracle is what you want, we can definitely do better than the . . . ah . . . Oracle of Litton, you're correct in that."

Diomedes was rising as Alexander did, his gaze

beyond, where Maccabee was on one side of the German guards and Zaki on the other.

When Alexander reached the impasse of Jews and Germans, the two blond giants made some sort of primitive obeisance in his direction, their eyes eloquent where their mouths could not be.

And the man who had formed the Companion cavalry saw, in the big Germans named Perfidy and Murder, loyalty aching to be bestowed on someone worthy, honor covered with grime and starving to be redeemed, and much else of lost time so poignant that Alexander's eyes filled with tears.

Then he gave the two Germans, each nearly twice his size, a look which had won him more hearts and minds and sword arms than any soul in hell, and they melted before him like water, to fall in behind, their previous gate duties forgotten or given over to others.

Alexander didn't ask, and didn't have enough Latin to tell whether Kleopatra had directed them to follow him, or complained when they did.

With the two Germans on his heels, and Diomedes, Maccabee, and Zaki at his side, he strode straight up to a commotion of horseless chariots and dray beasts—if he wanted to confront the Roman Caesar, he had to do it around, not through, Kleopatra.

And he must: as a Great King, he had spoken a decree before witnesses that he would visit the oracle at New Cumae. And visit it the party would, or the venture would end here and now, before it had even begun.

Caesar might be breath and life to his family, every tendril of it like a spider's web, but Alexander had wanted only his tanks, and Germans.

Even though these Germans, if they knew a way out of Hell, could not have told him, they were Germans. And Alexander had long ago learned that fate was no respecter of hell: like Diomedes, who had come to him unsolicited and would stay until his word was good, the journey done, and Achilles met on the other side of it, the Germans were fated to be his.

He could just feel it. You didn't become king of the known world without paying more heed to your instinct than to all the "wise counsel" of your advisors, even if one of them was Diomedes who'd fought on the beach at Ilion.

So when he found Caesar in the midst of a chaos of logistics, sitting on what he referred to as a "jeep" with two men he introduced as "Aziru, late prince of Amurru, who'll be coming with us as my driver, and Sargon, Great King of Akkad, who won't," Alexander made his wishes known clearly and concisely.

"Caesar, we need to leave immediately. This party is too big as it is, but we'll manage. I'll cut down on the size of my own retinue to accomodate you."

Caesar ducked his chin magnanimously, his eyes never leaving Alexander's, eyes that were full of fire and briliance and made Alexander remember that rumor said how Caesar loved him; eyes that drew more words from Alexander's lips than those meant to hide the fact that this army was more than thrice what Alexander the Great could field.

"If, that is, you'll accommodate me, Caesar."

"In any reasonable request, Basileus, you have the power of Rome behind you." The voice was cultured beyond measure, promissory of more than accommodation.

Alexander said, feeling a hot flush creep up his neck, "I want to stop at New Cumae and ask the Sibyl about the . . . journey ahead. Unless you've unearthed a German with a map?"

"No map, Basileus, and only what Germans you see here—those of the guard. But I agree, we should stop at Cumae. I haven't had an oracle I could stomach in years."

"It's agreed, then? We start within the hour, Caesar?" Behind Alexander, the two Germans who had followed him from the gatepost still stood, at a respectful distance, their eyes on him and the eyes of Maccabee, Zaki, and Diomedes on them for any twitch of betrayal or havoc in the making.

"Within the hour, but only because we are both 'Living' Gods," said the Roman with wry humor, surveying the chaotic comings and goings of well-wishers and sycophants, and spying Machiavelli threading his way through the crowd. "But only on one condition, Basileus."

Alexander stiffened to his full height. "And that is?"

"Call me Julius. All my friends do . . . Alexander."

Here is an excerpt from Fred Saberhagen's newest novel, coming in February 1986 from Baen Books:

FRED SABERHAGEN
THE FRANKENSTEIN PAPERS

Chapter 1

May? 1782?

I bite the bear.

I bit the bear.

I have bitten the white bear, and the taste of its blood has given me strength. Not physical strength—that I have never lacked—but the confidence to manage my own destiny, insofar as I am able.

With this confidence, my life begins anew. That I may think anew, and act anew, from this time on I will write in English, here on this English ship. For it seems, now that I try to use that language, that my command of it is more than adequate. Though how that ever came to be, God alone can know.

How *I* have come to be, God perhaps does not know. It may be that that knowledge is, or was, reserved to one other, who has—or had—more right than God to be called my Creator.

My first object in beginning this journal is to cling to the fierce sense of purpose that has been reborn in me. My second is to try to keep myself sane. Or to restore myself to sanity, if, as sometimes seems to me likely, madness is indeed the true explanation of the situation, or condition, in which I find myself—in which I believe myself to be.

But I verge on babbling. If I am to write at all—and I must write—let me do so coherently.

I have bitten the white bear, and the blood of the bear has given me life. True enough. But if anyone who reads is to understand then I must write of other matters first.

Yes, if I am to assume this task—or therapy—of journal-keeping, then let me at least be methodical about it. A good way to make a beginning, I must believe, would be to give an objective, calm description of myself, my condition, and my surroundings. All else, I believe—I must hope—can be built from that.

As for my surroundings, I am writing this aboard a ship, using what were undoubtedly once the captain's notebook and his pencils. The captain was wise not to trust that ink would remain unfrozen.

I am quite alone, and on such a voyage as I am sure was never contemplated by the captain, or the owners, or the builders of this stout vessel, *Mary Goode*. (The bows are crusted a foot thick with ice, an accumulation perhaps of decades; but the name is plain on many of the papers in this cabin.)

A fire burns in the captain's little stove, warms my fingers as I write, but I see by a small sullen glow of sunlight emanating from the south—a direction that here encompasses most of the horizon. Little enough of that sunlight finds its way in through the cabin windows, though one of the windows is now free of glass, sealed only with a thin panel of clear ice.

In every direction lie fields of ice, a world of white unmarked by any work of man except this frozen hulk. What fate may have befallen the particular man on the floor of whose cabin I now sleep—the berth is hopelessly small—or the rest of the crew of the *Mary Goode*, I can only guess. There is no clue, or if a clue exists I am too concerned with my own condition and my own fate to look for it or think about it. I can imagine them all bound in by ice aboard this ship, until they chose, over the certainty of starvation, the desperate alternative of committing themselves to the ice.

Patience. Write calmly.

I have lost count of how many timeless days I have been aboard this otherwise forsaken hulk. There is, of course, almost no night here at present. And there are times when my memory is confused. I have written above that it is May, because the daylight is still waxing steadily—and perhaps because I am afraid it is already June, with the beginning of the months of darkness soon to come.

I have triumphed over the white bear. What, then, do I need to fear?

Only the discovery of the truth, perhaps?

I said that I should begin with a description of myself, but now I see that so far I have avoided that unpleasant task. Forward, then. There is a small mirror in this cabin, frost-glued to the wall, but I have not crouched before it. No matter. I know quite well what I should see. A shape manlike but gigantic, an integument unlike that of any other being, animal or human, that I can remember seeing. Neither Asiatic, African, nor European, mine is a yellow skin that, though thick and tough, seems to lack its proper base, revealing in outline the networked veins and nerves and muscles underneath. White teeth, that in another face would be thought beautiful, in mine surrounded by thin blackish lips, are hideous in the sight of men. Hair, straight, black, and luxuriant; a scanty beard.

My physical proportions are in general those of the race of men. My size, alas, is not. Victor Frankenstein, half proud and half horrified at the work of his own hands, has more than once told me that I am eight feet tall. Not that I have ever measured. Certainly this cabin's overhead is much too low for me to stand erect. Nor, I think, has my weight ever been accurately determined—not since I rose from my creator's work table—but it must approximate that of two ordinary men. No human's clothing that I have ever tried has been big enough, nor has any human's chair or bed. Fortunately I still have my own boots, handmade for me at my creator's—I had almost said my master's—order, and I have such furs and wraps, gathered here and there across Europe, as can be wrapped and tied around my body to protect me from the cold.

Sometimes, naked here in the heated cabin, washing myself and my wrappings as best I can in melted snow, I take a closer inventory. What I see forces me to respect my maker's handiwork; his skill, however hideous its product, left no scars, no visible joinings anywhere.

February 1986 • 65550-7 • 320 pp. • $3.50